Ellen erupted from beneath the covers, swinging her feet over the edge of the high bed. "She did not see you!"

"Probably could not," answered Lord Wulfric.

"Nor did she hear you."

"Apparently that is true as well."

"So only I can see and hear you? I think I hit my head too hard, and this is all my imagination."

He picked up the book from the stand where Marian had left it and carried it toward the shelves. As he passed the dressing table mirror, only the book was reflected, floating as if by some dark magic.

When Ellen gasped, he glanced at the mirror.

"If you are a . . ."

"Go ahead and say it. A ghost." He chuckled. "You don't believe in ghosts? You are a pragmatic Scot after all, I fear."

Ellen narrowed her eyes and said, "We Scots believe in all kinds of things that rumble about in the night."

His gaze captured her, pinning her in place as surely as if his hands had pressed her into the pillows. Her heart beat so loudly, she was sure he could hear its pounding. The dark patch covering his eye only added to his roguish demeanor. Mischief sparkled in the other eye, warning her that Corey Wolfe, the late, yet unmourned Lord Wulfric, intended to be a spirit unlike any she had ever heard of.

"Lord Wulfric, there is no need for you to remain here. You have lived your life. You should go on to your reward."

He leaned on the post. "Well, Miss Dunbar, I owe you a debt."

* * *

Also by Jo Ann Ferguson from Zebra Regency:

THE FORTUNE HUNTER
THE SMITHFIELD BARGAIN
"Lord Chartley's Lesson" in A MOTHER'S JOY
AN UNDOMESTICATED WIFE
THE WOLFE WAGER
"Game of Harts" in VALENTINE LOVE
MISS CHARITY'S CASE

Writing as Rebecca North:
"Chloë's Elopement" in A JUNE BETROTHAL

A PHANTOM AFFAIR

Jo Ann Ferguson

Zebra Books
Kensington Publishing Corp.

ZEBRA BOOKS are published by

Kensington Publishing Corp.
850 Third Avenue
New York, NY 10022

First Printing: October, 1996
10 9 8 7 6 5 4 3 2 1

Printed in the United States of America

With gratitude, this book is dedicated to my students.
Your talent and enthusiasm consistently inspire me.
Thanks for teaching me as well.

One

"He is more than a bit mad, you know."

Corey Wolfe chuckled as he drew on his boot, bending to polish the tip of the toe. His hope that Lorenzo would fail to hear his amusement faded when he straightened and saw the disapproving expression on his cousin's long face. Yet Lorenzo's face was perpetually lengthened with some concern or another. Corey wondered how his cousin had managed to oversee Wolfe Abbey for those months he had been gone.

Standing, he frowned as well when he realized his left heel had not settled into his boot. Blast these boots! He was not usually such a slave to the vagaries of fashion, but he wanted to look his best tonight when he was throwing open the doors of the Abbey for the first time since his father's death more than four years ago, only a few months after Corey had purchased his commission and was sent to fight the French. He stamped his foot on the thick rug, but the stubborn leather refused to yield.

"Take care," cautioned Lorenzo.

"The stone floors of the Abbey have been battered far worse over the centuries." He tried again with no more success. "By the by, who is mad?"

"The boots are too tight," Lorenzo continued, adding to Corey's vexation. Why was his cousin so obsessed with these blasted boots when he should explain his comment?

Gripping the top, he gave a tug. He tried wiggling his toes to reach the very tip of the boot. Nothing worked. He pounded the heel against his bedroom floor once more.

"They shall cut off your circulation," Lorenzo continued.

"The goal of all clothing one would wear in good twig, I collect."

Lorenzo's frown threaded lines into his forehead and marred his jaw's firm line, which was as much a part of their family as their name. "Your clothing need not be uncomfortable, Corey. Why, if you are dissatisfied with your rig-out, I can suggest an excellent snip who can make you up a set that will be *à la modality.*"

"You misunderstand me," he said, chuckling as he sat on a wooden chair beside the oak tester bed. "Although I cannot guess how you might be baffled when my Aunt Carolyn is forever after me to select a wife who can give this grand old place an heir."

"I still do not understand."

Each word was punctuated with a shove of his foot into the boot. "Proper clothing is geared at catching the eye of the proper miss, who shall in turn garner my attention and my heart. Soon *I* would be out of circulation."

Lorenzo shook his head. "With such comments, I can understand why you remain unwed."

"I do not see you leg-shackling yourself to a buxom lass, cousin."

"I am not the Marquess of Wulfric. You have a duty to this family and this estate."

Corey rocked the boot on the end of his foot and silently cursed the arbiter of fashion who had decreed that a man's riding boots should be so tightly fit. "You had the duty once, cousin. It could be yours again."

"Nonsense." He shuddered and brushed his hands against his dark green coat. "You are home now. Are you going to go to the fête like that, or will you see sense and send Armstead for another pair?"

Corey glanced across his bedroom to where his man was trying to keep a somber face. Armstead and he had shared too many adventures for too many years for his valet to hide anything.

The short man, who was as round as Lorenzo was thin, asked,

"Would you wish me to fetch you another pair of boots, my lord?"

"That would be a needless task, when they all are of a size." With a satisfied smile, he jammed his foot into the boot and stood. "There. All set."

"Then mayhap," said Lorenzo, "you will listen to what I came in here to say. That ancient cabbage-head in the stables is unquestionably dicked in the nob."

Corey took his black wool coat from Armstead and shrugged it on. Adjusting the high collar beneath his dark hair, he asked, "Do you mean Fenton?"

"You know exactly whom I mean."

Again he resisted laughing aloud. He did know exactly what his cousin meant, and as well, he knew why he was complaining. Fenton had been one of the few at Wolfe Abbey who had resisted Lorenzo's wardship during the war. How many times had Corey heard the aged man say that no one but the old marquess's lad should look after the Abbey? Apparently Lorenzo had heard it, too.

"What has he said now?" Corey asked.

"That you should cancel the fireworks tonight."

"Did he say why?"

"Said they were sure to cause trouble, shedding light where there should not be any but heaven's."

"Even to celebrate the end of this blasted war?" Reaching for the tall beaver that Armstead held out to him, Corey patted his cousin on the shoulder. "Lorenzo, when you start heeding the words of an old man who is more set in his ways than this house on its foundation, you deserve to be bothered."

"He should be retired."

"Retired?" This time he allowed himself the luxury of laughing aloud. "Fenton has been here since long before you or I was born. I suspect he may be here long after we hop off the perch and leave this earth."

Lorenzo did not relent. "You may speak the truth for yourself, Corey, but that crazy old man could cause all kinds of trouble in the midst of his delusion. I had thought your sojourn on the continent, when you nearly lost your life at the hands of the French army, would put an end to your reckless ways. Mayhap you should listen to Fenton."

"I thought you disagreed with him."

"I am concerned he might do something to create trouble. Fireworks are dangerous. You know I think only of your best interests."

"My best interests are in entertaining my guests tonight as I promised."

Lorenzo sighed. "I had hoped you would listen. However, my words seem to have had no effect."

"No effect?" This was the most laughable thing Lorenzo had said all day, but Corey had no yearning to laugh.

He turned away, catching a glance of himself in the mirror. Damn! He usually avoided mirrors . . . or he had since he had returned from France. Not that he was vain, for it was not bruised vanity that unsettled him when he saw the patch covering his right eye. It was the gut-wrenching reminder of the days, weeks, and months lost to the war.

But self-pity had had its day. Tonight the Abbey would be ablaze with fireworks to celebrate the glorious conclusion of that conflict. No doomsayer, neither his cousin nor an old man in the stables, would ruin this night that he had feared might never come.

"I thought three would be your lucky number, Ellen."

Ellen Dunbar was glad for the twilight oozing through the open windows of the carriage. It hid her smile as she heard her bosom-bow, Lady Marian Herrold, sigh deeply. Dear Marian fretted herself far too much about Ellen ending up on the shelf for the rest of her days. Marian had been her friend since the first time they met at an assembly hosted by the Duke of Westhampton to announce the arrival of his first great-grandchild. Marian had rescued Ellen from a conversation with the duke and her husband,

Lord Herrold, about the merits of various breeds of hunting dogs. Marian shared Ellen's disinterest in the hunt, and soon they discovered they both had been raised in the country. Although Marian had been raised in genteel grandeur along the coast here and Ellen in a far simpler house north of the Scottish border, they could laugh over many similar adventures they had enjoyed as children.

From that moment until now, Marian had been unceasing in her efforts to find Ellen a husband, so she might be settled happily as she was in childhood. Through the next two Seasons Ellen had spent in London, Marian had had her hopes dashed many times.

"Apparently not," she replied. "Mayhap four will be fortunate for me."

"How can you jest about such an important matter?"

Tapping her fingers on the edge of the window, Ellen peered past the tulle brim of her green satin bonnet and watched as they came closer to the lights of the grand house on the water's edge. She had lost count of the number of times she had listened to Marian lament about how Ellen had gone through yet another Season without a betrothal.

"I shall find a match eventually," she said quietly.

"Will you?" Marian gave a most unladylike snort, astounding Ellen, for her manners usually offered no source of complaint. "How can you when you are waiting for a combination of your blessed St. Andrew and some hero out of a Scott novel?"

"We Scots are uncommonly romantic at heart."

"Then how can it be that you have found no one to fall in love with?"

She toyed with the gold fringe on her French silk shawl. "Oh, I have fallen in love a dozen times."

"But—"

"I fall right back out. I have discovered that falling in love is the simplest thing to do. Staying in love is more difficult."

Marian sighed. "Will you cease your funning? This is a most serious matter."

"On that we agree. That is why I will not give my heart to a man who will not cherish it as I shall cherish his." She leaned her elbow on the open window and stared across the shadowed fields. Birds darted through the navy velvet sky, enjoying a feast of insects and welcoming the stars. "Marian, you have no idea how much I wish I could fall in love to stay."

"You need only open your eyes. You have many admirers. Surely one of them will touch your heart." A sly smile brightened her face. "I understand our host Lord Wulfric remains unwed."

Ellen did not answer. There was no answer other than the one she had already given Marian. She had seen what happened when two hearts found each other despite impossible odds, and she wanted that splendid joy for herself. She was sure that, once she found it, the waiting would be worth that happiness.

The carriage followed the curving road along the side of the cliff edging the sea. Seeing Marian tense and look away from the view of the ocean, Ellen remained silent. She had noted how her friend avoided any windows at Herrold Hall that offered a glance of the sea beyond the fields. Curiosity had taunted her, but she had said nothing. If Marian wished her to know what unsettled her, she would speak of it.

When the carriage slowed, Ellen stared out at the meandering building that must be Wolfe Abbey. The house seemed to be a part of the cliff, a flower that had blossomed from a rocky garden. The house's wings unfolded like a trio of petals, flowing along the precipice. Dozens of windows were candle-lit against the night.

Music caressed Ellen's ears as she stepped from the carriage. Not the sound of a bow upon the strings of a violin, but a more primitive song. It drew her to the waist-high wall edging the road. Looking down, she saw starlight splattering the froth-beaten boulders at the base of the cliff. The sea retreated, only to fling itself back upon the rocks in a never-ending, ever-changing quadrille.

"Do come back from there," Marian said with a shudder. "You must be careful."

"I'm in no danger." She leaned forward to look at the very base of the stone wall. " 'Tis wonderful!"

" 'Tis frightening!" Marian hooked her arm through Ellen's and tugged her away from the wall. "I have always abhorred coming here unless it is dark. During the day, when I can see the base of the cliff so far below, I cannot help but envision the carriage careening over that crag to leave us broken on the shore."

"How horrible! Has such a thing happened?"

"No," Marian said with another shudder, "but it may one day."

"If folks are careful—"

"But folks don't always take caution." Closing her eyes, she whispered, "I have not trusted these cliffs since the day, as a child, when I took a misstep and tumbled down one that was not as viciously steep as this one."

"Oh, Marian, were you hurt?"

"Just enough to convince me to put as much distance as possible between me and the seawall when I must travel along this road. In the dark, I can pretend the cliff is not there."

Putting her hand over Marian's, she smiled. She would have guessed a ride through the night along the seawall to be much more terrifying, for any curve could betray the driver into making the wrong turn. To speak of that would only unnerve her friend more.

The darkness thickened around them as they walked through the front garden, settling on their shoulders like a favorite cloak. Dew sparkled in the glow of candles set along the garden path. The flowers had tucked themselves away for the night, but their perfume remained on the air, a seductive invitation to excitement.

Ellen resisted reaching out to run her fingers along the leaves. How she loved the country! Although nothing could match the whirl of life in Town, she longed too often for this simple world, which she had enjoyed in Scotland.

It seemed impossible to believe that three years ago, she had not imagined she would see any more of the world than the small village where she had been raised. Although her stepfather had served the king and then the Regent for many years in the English army, she and her mother had lived all her life in the same cottage near Coldstream.

A snowstorm had swept the Duke of Westhampton's granddaughter into the cottage to find shelter that winter. When Romayne had returned to England, she had invited Ellen to join her for the glorious Season in London. With such a sponsor and a generous dowry offered by the duke in gratitude for helping his granddaughter, Ellen was welcomed wholeheartedly among the *ton*.

That first Season and the ones that followed had been as wondrous as she had created in her fantasies. Yet in spite of the attentions of many gentlemen, she had not found a single one who touched her heart and set it dancing. Romayne had taught her never to compromise her dreams. It was a lesson she had learned well, and one she would not forget, for to settle for less than her heart's desire was certain to end up breaking it.

She had no time for memory, because the prattle of cheerful voices emerged from the shadows to draw them toward a crowd of the marquess's guests. Looking at the score of people gathered in the center of the front garden, she wondered which one was Lord Wulfric. Marian had been oddly reticent about their host, save for her comment that he was unmarried.

With a silent sigh, she knew that her friend had no intention of letting her die like Jenkin's hen. She almost chuckled. How long had it been since she had last thought in the Scottish phrases she once had considered commonplace? Mayhap it was time to go home.

Again Marian's words intruded, giving Ellen no time for introspection as she was kept busy greeting the other guests.

An older woman, whose silk gown was such a bright blue that the color was visible even in the deepening darkness, eyed Ellen up and down candidly. "So you are Marian's young friend who has spent the past three Seasons in London?"

"Yes, I am." She refused to take insult. *She* was the one who had decided not to accept any of the marriage proposals which had come her way.

"I was telling my dear son Kenneth just the other day that it was time we had a gathering at our home," the older woman said.

Ellen resisted rolling her eyes in dismay when she heard Marian answer with excitement. Would there be no end to her friend's matchmaking? Somehow she must persuade Marian to listen to good sense. Ellen would not settle for less than her heart's desire. If the man of her dreams did not exist, then so be it.

When the first round of fireworks exploded above the Abbey, Ellen was glad. Not only were they wondrously lovely, the blues, reds, and yellows brighter than the stars, but the gabble-grinding ceased. A crack of thunder followed the next rockets skyward.

"How beautiful!" she said.

"As beautiful as the company I would venture," came an answer in a voice much deeper than Marian's.

Ellen looked over her shoulder and found herself staring at the shadowed front of a man's coat. As her gaze rose over a firm chin and a smile, she swallowed her gasp. If the darkness was not betraying her—and she suspected it was not—the man wore a patch over one eye. It looked out of place with his easy smile.

She was saved from having to reply as another burst scattered fireworks across the sky. Beside her, Marian was applauding in delight.

Marian crowed, "That is the best one yet." Not even pausing to take a breath, she said, "There is Mrs. Richards. I must speak with her about—"

Another crash in the sky swallowed Marian's words as she scurried away. Ellen considered following, but she did not want to appear rude to the gentleman who still stood behind her.

"Are you enjoying the fireworks?" she asked as the glitter faded into pale smoke that disfigured the stars' glow.

"Unquestionably. And you, Miss—"

"Dunbar. Ellen Dunbar." She smiled. "I, too, am enjoying them very much. I saw some in Hyde Park last month, but I believe these are even more glorious."

"I thank you." Her eyes widened when he gave a slight bow

in her direction and said, "Allow me to present myself. Corey Wolfe, Miss Dunbar."

"Lord Wulfric?"

"One and the same now."

She thought she heard a tinge of sorrow and scoured her memory to remember when the previous Lord Wulfric had died. She could not recall, which suggested that the previous marquess had passed away before she had first come to London.

"Having fireworks like this was an inspired idea," she said before the silence between them could grow as heavy as the dew on the grass. "The moonless night is perfect for them."

"Save that the trees close to the Abbey obscure some of the lower ones. Would you like to watch them from where they look even lovelier?"

"Lady Herrold will be distressed if she discovers I am gone."

He chuckled. "Think how much more distressed that fine lady shall be if she learns that I have failed to play the good host to you." He swept his arm out. "I shall take you no farther than your voice can carry. Therefore, if I am the least indecorous to you, you need only give a cry for help."

"That sounds as if you have had cause to check the distance, my lord."

"Only when I was young enough to be certain that my governess was out of earshot."

Ellen could not help laughing. Lord Wulfric was charming, and to own the truth, Marian would be pleased to see Ellen talking to their host. After all, Marian had been sure to tell her that the marquess was still without a marchioness.

As they walked along the gravel path back toward where the carriage had stopped, Lord Wulfric said, "I saw you speaking with Marian and Mrs. Pratt, and I thought you might appreciate a chance to escape."

"That was very perceptive of you."

"Not very. I have seen them scheming together for many years. Their hearts are well meaning, but I assume they have already arranged for you to welcome Mrs. Pratt's inimitable son at Herrold Hall."

Again she laughed. "Not quite, but only because the fireworks began."

"No wonder you looked so pleased." He motioned toward the seawall. "If you stand here, Miss Dunbar, I think you shall see . . ."

Ellen pressed her hand to her breast as the next round of fireworks ignited. Their lights reflected in the water as the sea came alive with all the colors painting the sky.

"How magnificent!" she whispered, for speaking more loudly seemed somehow irreverent.

"You aren't scared to stand so close to the edge of the cliff?"

She shook her head. "Only if one is foolhardy does one need to worry."

"And you are never foolhardy, Miss Dunbar?"

"Almost never."

His laugh was low and rumbled deep within her as powerfully as the explosions overhead. "Honesty. That is always refreshing."

"And much easier in the long run."

Leaning one hand on the wall, he faced her. "You sound as if you are very much the pragmatic Scot, Miss Dunbar."

"I can only be what I am, my lord." She was not surprised that he had guessed her birthplace, for its accent filled every word she spoke. "Although I must own my mother has said more than once that I would misplace my head if it were not firmly connected to my shoulders."

"You are—if I may be so bold—a delight. Are you visiting Herrold Hall for long?"

A trill of happiness burst within her as more fireworks sparkled above them and in the sea. "Marian has asked me to stay with her and Lord Herrold until the end of the summer."

"As the summer is only half over, it seems you shall be here for a while."

"Yes."

He took her gloved hand between his broad ones. "Then may

I be so presumptuous as to ask if I might give you and Marian a look-in before this week comes to a close?" He grinned. "That is, if you are not receiving Mrs. Pratt's dear son at the same time."

Even through her kid gloves, she could sense the warmth of his touch. She raised her eyes to meet his gaze, which was even warmer. As a smile eased across his lips, heat drifted through her like a slow, lingering caress. She knew she should say something—anything—but all words had melted in this sweet fire sweeping over her.

In the back of her mind, a persistent, annoying voice reminded her that other men had held her hand and set her heart to beating too swiftly. Those men had seemed as charming as Lord Wulfric in the midst of a dance or while standing on a balcony, with a garden waking to the glory of summer's blossoms. Later, when they had called, she had discovered the magic had belonged to the night, not to them.

A faithless heart was what Marian called it. A sensible heart was her stepfather's opinion from Scotland. A lonely heart was her own belief.

"You hesitate, Miss Dunbar," he said, releasing her hand. "I beg your forgiveness if I have overstepped myself."

"No!" she gasped.

When he chuckled, Ellen asked herself how she could sound like a girl still in the schoolroom. Had three Seasons in London made no impression on her?

"Does that mean you will not forgive me?" His dark brows arched. "Or can it be you have decided to grant Kenneth Pratt the favor of being the first to call upon you here in grassville?"

She relaxed as she heard amusement in his voice. There was nothing cruel in Lord Wulfric's sense of humor, for he was laughing as much at the silliness of this conversation as at her. "You have mistaken my hesitation to consider Marian's hectic schedule as something else." She soothed the pulse of guilt by reminding herself that those words were not totally false. Marian was her hostess, and her plans must take precedence.

Another volley of fireworks splashed across the sky, but she barely took note as Lord Wulfric folded her fingers between his again. He *was* bold as brass!

"So, may I call upon you at Herrold Hall, Miss Dunbar?"

She was delighted her voice remained much more serene than she felt as she said, "I believe Marian holds an at home on Wednesdays."

"Thursdays here in the country," he corrected with a grin, "if Marian has not changed her ways, which seems most unlikely."

"She is a creature of habit."

"Since I have known her." Not releasing her hand, he leaned back on the low wall. "I have no doubts that she shall soon regale you—if she has not already—with the pranks I played upon her during our younger days."

Ellen shook her head. "She has said nothing of that."

Again he chuckled. "Come then, Miss Dunbar. Let us find your good friend Marian, so she does not fret about your absence. If I have won her forgiveness for those long past crimes, I must endeavor to do nothing to forsake it again."

When he held out his arm, she put her fingers on it. He drew her hand within his arm as they strolled back toward the garden. Although he said nothing, the silence was not uncomfortable. She did not need to strain to find words which had little use save to fill the quiet.

A figure burst out of the darkness. Corey tightened his hold on Miss Dunbar's hand as the shadow ran toward them. He relaxed with a silent curse when he realized it was Fenton. The old fool must be all about in his head to race through the dark like this.

"Lord Wulfric!" he shouted like a sentry calling an alarm. When fireworks flashed in front of the stars once more, he crouched. "My lord, I asked ye to put a halt to this."

Corey took a deep breath and released it slowly. To Miss Dunbar, who was unfamiliar with Fenton's eccentricities, the old man must appear even more bizarre. "As you can see, nothing is amiss. I appreciate your concern, but—"

"Ain't done yet."

"We're within ambs ace of being done. If I calculate correctly, there should be only one or two more rounds waiting to be sent skyward." He patted the bent man on the shoulder.

Fenton shuffled away, muttering.

"I apologize, Miss Dunbar," Corey said.

"No need. It speaks well of this household that he is comfortable enough to come to you."

"That is, I believe, a kind way of telling me that you think he is as queer in the attic as Lorenzo deems him to be." When she glanced at him, confusion on her heart-shaped face, he smiled. He wondered if she was as pretty in the daylight as she was when the fireworks glittered in her eyes. The curls slipping along her shoulders must be red, and he could not help pondering if she had a temper as fiery. "I speak of my cousin, Lorenzo Wolfe."

"I have not had the chance to meet Mr. Wolfe."

"I speculate you shall within moments, for, if I am not mistaken, I can see him speaking with Marian at the moment. He— Watch out!"

Something sparked. Something eye-searingly bright. Ellen held up her hands as she heard Lord Wulfric shout. He grabbed her, twisting her back toward the road. The whole world erupted into chaos. Noise struck her like a blow, propelling her away from Lord Wulfric. She was thrown from her feet. Pain scored her arm. Her head struck the ground. The world ebbed into darkness, but she would not be swallowed by it.

Sitting, she moaned as she leaned on her right arm. Fire, as fierce as the flames consuming the bushes at the edge of the garden, seared her when she fell back to the earth. Shouts came from every direction, but no words made sense. She put her left hand to her forehead and resisted the temptation to fade into the senselessness. Anguish surrounded her in a cold aura, making every motion impossible. She struggled to breathe, to hold on to consciousness.

She thought she had lost the battle, then a groan came from her right. Turning cautiously, for her head threatened to disobey even the simplest order, she scanned the scorched grass.

"Lord Wulfric!" she cried.

He was lying on the ground, his arms flung out as if he had taken a facer. Blood flowed down his waistcoat. She put her fingers close to his lips. The uneven pulse of his breath brushed her palm.

"Help!" she called as she slipped her arm beneath him to keep his head out of the wet grass. "We need help! Lord Wulfric is hurt!"

Instantly she was surrounded. She was gently brought to her feet as a man knelt beside the marquess. An arm around her shoulders steadied her. She did not look to see who was helping her. Her gaze riveted on Lord Wulfric, who had not moved.

When the kneeling man tore aside the marquess's coat, she cried, "Be careful! He may be hurt badly!"

"He is a doctor, Ellen," said Marian softly. "Hush, and let him see what he can do for Lord Wulfric."

What he did was issue a series of quick orders that could not reach past the pounding in Ellen's head. She thought she heard him order both her and the marquess back to the house, but nothing made sense.

"How is he?" she whispered, reaching for the lanky doctor's arm. Her fingers closed inches from it.

He looked at her, his lips strained and puckered. "Young lady, Miss Dunbar, is it?"

"Yes."

"You must lie down. You need quiet to recover from this horrible event."

"But Lord Wulfric . . . How is he?"

For a moment, she feared he would not answer. He turned away to watch the marquess being placed on a litter which must have been brought from the house. A deep sigh raised and lowered his shoulders like bits of flotsam on the sea. "He took the brunt of the explosion."

"But how is he? Is he hurt?"

He faced her again. All emotion left his voice as he said, "Miss Dunbar, I'm sorry, but after examining Lord Wulfric's wounds, I doubt he will last the night."

Two

The sitting room was uncomfortably bright. Light glared off the polished marble fireplace and the mahogany furniture. In a corner, behind the gold settee and the chairs flanking it, a long case clock tolled the hour.

Only eleven o'clock.

Ellen shook her head as Marian asked her—yet again—if she would like to rest. To own the truth, she was not sure if she could stand to go into one of the bedchambers on this floor. She did not recall how she had gotten to this room, although she suspected it must have been with Marian and Mr. Wolfe's help in the wake of the last fireworks detonating on the ground.

Pain seared her arm at the thought. The debris had sprayed throughout the garden, but she and Lord Wulfric had been the only ones struck. Marian had called that fortunate. Ellen could not agree, for she could imagine little worse than sitting here and waiting for the doctor's latest word on the marquess's condition.

Mr. Wolfe, who was pacing in front of the door leading into his cousin's bedchamber, was nearly distraught with worry. A bare-bones man, he had a gaunt handsomeness that was enhanced by his hair. It was as dark as Lord Wulfric's. From the tip of his shining boots to the top of his mussed hair, he looked ready to ride to the hounds.

Until he turned to catch her eyes. Then she saw the horror in his face. It spoke, more than any words, of his anxiety for his cousin's well-being.

"Miss Dunbar, are you sure you don't wish to lie down?" he asked, his amiable voice adding to the ache in her skull.

"I would as lief wait to hear what the doctor has to say."

"It will not be good, I fear." He rubbed his hands together and forced a strained smile. "Marian, you, too, are kind to be with me at this grim hour."

"I fear we are burdening you more," Ellen said as Marian gulped back a sob.

"Nonsense." He cleared his throat. "I would not wish to be alone now."

She did not know what to say to the man whose long face was made even longer by his sorrow. His blue eyes, which were nearly so pale that they were colorless, were filled with tears. No words were necessary to show how fond he was of his cousin.

"Forgive me, Miss Dunbar," he said, dabbing at his eyes with a handkerchief. "This is most distressing. We thought we had lost Corey once before during the war. He was returned to us, but now I fear death will catch up with him."

"Forgive us," she answered. She wished Marian would stop hovering over her. Each breath was harder than the one before it, for a weight seemed centered on her chest. A throb ran along her arm, increasing in strength with every heartbeat. "You do not need unexpected guests now."

A hint of a smile returned to pull at his lips. "Corey would not want you to drive home near the nadir of the night." He hesitated, then added, "And, Miss Dunbar, if I may own to the truth, I would appreciate your company as well as Marian's."

"I understand," she answered, although she wondered where the other guests might be. Putting her fingers to her aching head, she sighed. Of course, the other guests had taken their leave in the wake of the accident in the garden. Only Marian and she remained. Another wave of pain washed over her as she imagined riding along that bumpy road back to Marian's house. Closing her eyes, she leaned back against the silk upholstery. The conversation flowed around her. The cushions shifted, and Marian's cool palm brushed her forehead. She nearly cried out in pain.

"I fear she is hurt worse than we had thought," Marian murmured.

Ellen did not hear the answer. A bolt of pain struck her as viciously as the fireworks detonating in the garden. She moaned, the sound resonating through her tender skull. Confused, frightened shouts crashed over her, and she wondered if all those who had stood in the garden had come into the Abbey. The pain stole her breath from her. She had never suffered its like. Darkness smothered every thought. She did not fight it, but drifted through the fathomless quiet.

When she opened her eyes again, she had come into another room. A bedroom, for she sat beside a bed whose gold curtains were closed on two sides. Beyond the oak bed, a chair was draped with a man's coat. The material was stained with dirt and what she suspected—with a cramp in her stomach—was blood.

Slowly she turned her gaze to the bed. Beneath the covers, Lord Wulfric was lying. Only the rise and fall of the blankets told her he was still alive. His skin was an odd shade of gray beneath its rich summer tan, which bespoke that his customary life reached far beyond the walls of this dusky room. Across his brow, his hair was matted. She shuddered as she wondered what hideous wound might be hidden beneath it.

She sat alone beside the bed. Her forehead ruffled in surprise. Her head must have been hit far worse than she had guessed. Again she could not remember how she had gotten to where she was.

She saw the doctor's case open by the bed and a folded paper with her name scratched across it. As badly as her head throbbed, she might have lost consciousness if the doctor had examined her. Mayhap he had wanted to do that examination here where he could keep an eye on Lord Wulfric. She searched her mind. It was befuddled with half-formed thoughts and memories she could not trust. Yes, she seemed to recall Mr. Wolfe's gentle concern as he helped Marian bring her to the doctor, who refused to be budged from Lord Wulfric's side. Remembering that short journey from the other room, she swayed on the chair and clutched the bottom before she could fall. Each step had sent more anguish reeling through her until she had surrendered to the near-oblivion of letting others control her motions.

The doctor had examined her . . . hadn't he? She could not remember. Everything was a bumble-bath in her head.

Then where was the doctor? Where were the others? When she heard the doctor's muffled voice by the door, she sighed. No doubt, he was giving Mr. Wolfe a report on his cousin's condition. Deteriorating condition, if Ellen was not mistaken. Lord Wulfric's breathing had become more shallow even while she sat here.

The voices swarmed over her, and she looked around to find that the others were lined up around the bed. She blinked, wondering why they had rushed into the room so quickly. Mayhap it had not been quickly. Each blink of her eyes seemed to leap her forward in time as she fought to hold onto her senses. She wondered how much time had vanished, unnoted, into the eddy of pain swirling in her head.

She tried to focus on Marian's face. She could not. Shifting her eyes to the man beside her bosom-bow nearly undid her. She tightened her grip on the chair as she stared at Mr. Wolfe. His face was nearly as gray as Lord Wulfric's. She wanted to ask him why.

Mr. Wolfe's words answered the question she did not ask. "I shall inform the rest of the family of his death. How ironic that he should risk death with the army across the Channel and die here in his own garden."

"Dead?" gasped Ellen. "Lord Wulfric is dead?"

Marian put her hands on Ellen's shoulders and helped her to her feet. "You must lie down, my dear. I have never seen you so drawn."

Tears fled down her face as she tried to shake her head. She subsided with a moan.

"The bedchamber next door has been prepared for Miss Dunbar," Mr. Wolfe said quietly.

"Thank you." Marian turned her toward the door. "Come

along, Ellen. You must lie down before you injure yourself more."

Ellen considered protesting, but had no strength. She let Marian steer her out the door and across the hall, stumbling on nearly every step.

The bedroom was smaller than the one they had just left, but decorated as grandly with art and a wall of books edging the fireplace. The one small part of her mind that was still working suggested these might have been the marchioness's private rooms. The soft grays and yellows were a shadow of the brilliance of the marquess's bedchamber, but more restful and feminine.

Marian's prattle bounced through Ellen's head as a maid held out a nightdress Ellen guessed had been retrieved from a storage trunk in the attics. The scent of herbs, which would ward off insects, billowed from it. Compliantly, as if she were no more than a babe, she let Marian help her get ready for bed.

The thick mattress surged upward to envelop her. As she rested against the pillows, she stared at the material shirred between the tester posts of the mahogany bed which was flushed with russet fire in the light from the hearth. Flowers rippled across it in a glorious copy of the garden.

"Here," Marian whispered, holding out a handkerchief. "You must stop crying. This household has suffered a horrible loss tonight. We must not encumber Lorenzo with our own grief."

Ellen wiped the back of her hand gracelessly against her wet cheeks. "You don't understand, Marian. Lord Wulfric was so wondrously amusing. I was ready to fall in love with him tonight."

"As you have with so many others."

"But I never had a chance to fall *out* of love with him."

"Hush." She pulled a chair from the dressing table closer to the bed.

The sound added to the cacophony in Ellen's head, but she said nothing as Marian spoke softly. When her friend vowed to stay by her side until she could sleep, Ellen closed her eyes and burrowed into the pillows. She winced as she tried to make her arm comfortable.

"Shall I read to you?" Marian asked.

"If you would get me a book, I shall read to myself."

"I would be glad to read to you."

Ellen wondered how anyone who was trying to be so nice could be so irritating. She struggled to smile, but was only able to grimace as she said, "No thank you. Find me something dull, so that I shall have no choice but to sleep."

Marian set herself onto her feet and bustled to the hearth. Pulling out a book, she brought it back to the bed. "This should bore you. It appears to be some sort of parish report."

Taking the book, Ellen nestled into the pillows again. She opened it and stared at the words. They threatened to blur together as she swallowed her tears. When she heard the door close behind Marian, she sighed. She did not like being false with her bosom-bow, but all she wanted was to be alone.

She set the book beside her and leaned back. Staring at the flowered material in the canopy, she let the tears slide across her face and onto the linen beneath her. She wondered if Lord Wulfric would have seemed as unappealing in the daylight as her other admirers. Now she never would know.

A low whistle lilted through Ellen's dreams. She sat, then groaned as she bumped her bandaged arm. When had it been bandaged? Her head was clearer now, and the gaps in her memory taunted her. Searching the darkness, she saw a wisp of a cool glow near the window beside the dressing table. Could it be dawn already? No, for the other drapes still swathed the other windows in starlight and shadows.

The whistle came again.

"Who is there?" she called. "Marian, is that you?"

Her eyes widened as she watched, unable to move or speak, as the glow by the window thickened and coalesced into a shape.

It was taller than the lyre-backed chair, taller than her stepfather, but not as tall as the spindly Mr. Wolfe.

A man!

What was a man doing in her room at this hour? Any of the servants would have knocked or, more likely, delayed their errand until she awoke. An intruder?

The glow edged closer. As it separated from the river of starlight flooding the carpet, it stepped between her and the mirror on the dressing table. Nothing reflected in it but the starlight.

"Forgive me for disturbing your slumbers, Miss Dunbar."

That voice . . . she knew that voice! She gasped in a strangled whisper, "Lord Wulfric! But you're dead!"

Corey could not keep from smiling as he saw the shock on Miss Dunbar's face. It was a face he would have enjoyed looking at under any circumstances, but with her ruddy hair loose around her shoulders and her sapphire eyes heavy with sleep, she was even prettier than he had guessed when he took note of her in the gardens. Her downy skin had been burnished pink by the linen cover on the pillow, and the splatter of freckles across her pert nose accented the curve of her cheeks.

And her other curves—

He chuckled as she grasped the blankets and pulled them to her chin, interrupting his pleasant perusal. "No need for such a maidenly reaction," he said, coming around the end of the bed, "when you have nothing to fear from me."

"But I heard them pronounce you dead!"

"True."

"Then this must be a dream."

"You did strike your head very hard on the ground." He reached toward her, but she pulled back. "I wished only to be sure that Mr. Bridges tended to your injuries. He is a good doctor, but I was concerned he would concentrate only on me and not turn his attention to you. I assume he bandaged your arm."

She did not want to own that she had no idea who had seen to her arm. "If you are but a dream, I can wake up." She squeezed her eyes closed. "When I open my eyes, all of this will be gone."

Corey leaned one shoulder against the upright of the tall bed and folded his arms across his chest. He hoped she would not persist with this. He had guessed her to be more fanciful than the other pragmatists who surrounded him. That was why he had chosen her to talk to in the garden. If he had come to his cousin now, Lorenzo would have dismissed him as nothing more than an impossibility. Tonight Corey needed someone who was willing to look beyond the obvious. He hoped Ellen Dunbar could.

When her eyes opened, he smiled into their warm depths. No, she was not beautiful, for her chin was a bit too assertive and her hair a bit too red. Yet . . .

She opened her mouth to scream. He held up his hand, and she cowered.

"Don't be frightened," he said. "You were not scared by the seawall. There is no reason to be scared now."

Ellen stared at it. She could not—even in her thoughts—call whatever this was Lord Wulfric. Her fingers slid along the bed. Gripping the book, she drew it from beneath the covers. She threw it as she shouted, "Get out of here! If . . ."

The book flew right through him. It struck the wall behind him. As he turned to look over his shoulder, he mused, "Very good shot, Miss Dunbar. You would have been an asset to our cricket team during my days at school."

"Oh, my," she whispered.

A knock sounded at the door. "Ellen!" called Marian. "Are you all right, my dear?"

Ellen continued to stare at . . . what was it?

"Go ahead and answer the door, if you wish," said the voice which sounded exactly like Lord Wulfric's. "I can wait." He chuckled. "It looks as if I have all eternity ahead of me."

She swung her feet over the side of the bed and groped for the borrowed wrapper. When it was tossed to her by the—by the whatever that glow was, she pulled it over her shoulders. She tensed, fearing it would be as clammy as death, but save for one cool spot, the silk was warm with the breeze fluttering through the window.

Rushing to the door, she jerked it open. Marian stood on the far side, her hand raised to knock again.

"What are you doing out of bed?" she chided. "The doctor ordered you to rest."

"Marian, I . . ." Ellen stepped back as Marian bustled into the room.

"Come back to bed and go to sleep." Marian smoothed the covers. "You need to settle your head."

Ellen glanced uneasily at . . . whatever. A broad smile added a rakish gleam to—she might as well call it Lord Wulfric, for lack of a better name—to Lord Wulfric's face. Swallowing roughly, she watched him as she asked, "Marian, will you look over by the hearth?"

"Did you see a mouse?"

"No."

"A rat?" She shivered and yawned. "Get back in bed while I check."

Ellen took one step, then paused as she watched Marian cross the room. Her friend walked right past Lord Wulfric, bent to look at the hearth before coming back to Ellen, carrying the book.

"There's nothing amiss here, and you would be wise to be cautious with such a valuable book," Marian said in her sternest voice. "Now to bed with you. Promise me you will stay in bed until noon."

"Marian?" Her voice quivered on the single word.

Her bosom-bow's frown softened. Guiding Ellen toward the bed, she said, "I know this has not been an easy night for you, but you must rest. If you would like, I shall sit with you until you are asleep. We can talk about plans for the rest of the summer. There are several young men I would like you to meet." Her lips curled into a predatory smile. "If all goes as I hope, you may be announcing your betrothal before your visit is over."

Despite the fact that she would as lief speak of anything but the parade of suitable suitors Marian had lined up in her head, Ellen almost said yes. Her answer faltered as her gaze was caught by Lord Wulfric's. A nonchalant shrug of his shoulders reminded her of his words. He was prepared to wait for as long as necessary until he told her what he wished. Would he then leave?

"I shall be fine, Marian," she said faintly while Marian tucked the covers around her.

"Of course you will."

She flinched when she realized Lord Wulfric had answered.

Marian did not seem to notice Ellen's reaction as she echoed, "Of course you will. Just rest, and you shall be well in no time." She bent to kiss Ellen's cheek. "Good night, my dear."

"Good night," she replied automatically, but she stared past her friend to where Lord Wulfric was walking to the hearth.

Marian closed the door quietly behind her.

Ellen erupted from beneath the covers, swinging her feet over the edge of the high bed. She ignored her aching head and arm. "She did not see you!"

"Probably could not."

"Nor did she hear you."

"Apparently that is true as well."

"So only I can see and hear you?"

"What do you think?"

"I think I hit my head too hard, and this is all my imagination."

He picked up the book from the stand where Marian had left it and carried it toward the shelves. As he passed the dressing table mirror, only the book was reflected, floating as if by some dark magic.

When Ellen gasped, he glanced at the mirror. The sardonic arch of his eyebrows could not hide the surprise in his voice. "By all that's blue, I did not suspect that would happen."

"If you are a . . ."

"Go ahead and say it. A ghost." He chuckled. "It is not a word that is uncomely on the lips of a lady." When she said nothing, he added, "I noticed that you did not tell Marian there was no rat in your room."

"What are you?" Ellen watched him put the book back on the shelf. Except for the odd radiance around him—and the lack of a reflection—nothing seemed amiss. *And the book flying straight through him,* came the taunting reminder.

"You don't believe in ghosts? You *are* a pragmatic Scot after all, I fear."

She narrowed her eyes and said, "We Scots believe in all kinds of things that rumble about in the night."

"I have been a very quiet and considerate ghost."

"You woke me with a whistle."

"You would have preferred I woke you with a kiss?"

Heat across her cheeks warned Ellen she might be blushing. Hastily she asked, "Why are you here?"

"I live here." Again he chuckled. "Or I should more properly say I *lived* here."

"But Marian didn't see you."

"Neither hide nor hair nor rat's tail."

"This is no time for silliness, Lord Wulfric."

"Really?" He walked toward the window. The incandescence surrounding him did not dim as he waded through the swath of starlight flowing into the room. "You should call me Corey now. It would be more appropriate."

"Excuse me?" She had not thought she could be more baffled, but every word he spoke added to her confusion.

"I'm not really Lord Wulfric any longer." He gave a shrug as he sat on the windowsill. "To be honest, 'tis just as well. The title never fit me comfortably. Lorenzo was a good sport to surrender it when I came back from France, and now it is truly his. That seems only fair." Glancing around the room, he mused, "And the Abbey will belong to Nessa and her family."

"Nessa?"

"My sister Vanessa."

Ellen recalled meeting Lady Vanessa Wolfe at an assembly in London a Season or two ago. The young woman had been the talk of the *ton* because she had failed to find a match. Apparently, she had made a choice if she now had a husband and child. Marian would know. Marian was attentive to all those details of London life.

Again he laughed. "Too bad Nessa's first was a girl. Lorenzo would have happily stood by to let the title go to her son. Now he has it again."

"How can you be here?"

"That I don't have an answer for, but I know why I am here."

"Why?"

He stood and gave her a rakish grin. When he walked toward her, she tried to make herself small against the grand headboard. She slid toward the opposite side of the bed, but his hand settled on the coverlet. The odd glow surrounded it. She recoiled, not wanting to guess what might happen if she touched that light.

When he spoke her name, she found his face too disturbingly close to hers. His gaze captured her, pinning her in place as surely as if his hands pressed her into the pillows. Her heart beat so loudly she was sure he could hear its pounding. The dark patch covering his eye only added to his roguish demeanor. Mischief sparkled in his other eye, warning her that Corey Wolfe, the late, yet unmourned Lord Wulfric, intended to be a spirit unlike any she had ever heard of.

His hand rose to cup her cheek, then drew back. She did not speak. She did not dare to voice any of the thoughts careening through her head as she remembered the sweet fire of his touch by the wall. But now . . . would there be warmth or no sign of life? When he sighed and turned away, she suspected he was as unwilling to discover that as she was.

"Lord Wulfric?" She hastily corrected herself when he glared back at her. Worse than being haunted by a ghost that set her heart to racing would be being plagued by a furious phantom. "Corey, there is no need for you to remain here. You have lived your life. You should go on to your reward."

His sharp laugh startled her. "After so many people have wished me to go to perdition throughout my life, including your dear friend Lady Marian Herrold on more than one occasion, I think it is the better part of good sense to remain here." Again he leaned on the bed post. "And besides, Miss Dunbar, I owe you a debt."

"A debt?"

"For what you did in the garden."

"You owe me nothing. I did nothing."

"You tried to save me. You sat beside me when no one else did."

She frowned. "How could you know that? You were bereft of your senses."

"Not all of them." Chuckling again, he sat on the edge of the bed.

She watched the brilliance spread over the counterpane like oil across water. It inched nearer to her, but stopped before the light could brush her. She drew her legs back, not wanting them to be touched by that iridescence, which might be as fiercely hot as the flames on the hearth or utterly lifeless. Fear thickened in the depths of her heart.

"I saw you," Corey continued, bringing her eyes back to his suddenly somber face, "sitting beside my deathbed when you should have been lying here, letting the household worry over you. Are you always so stubborn?"

"Always."

"Then it is just as well that I never had a chance to call on you, for I have been told I have less sense than a pair of obstinate oxen myself. No doubt, we would have been in the midst of a brangle within minutes."

"No doubt." She bit her lip to keep it from trembling.

He grinned. "Don't look so dolorous. I enjoyed living, and I intend to enjoy this experience by repaying you the duty I owe you."

"But, my lord—I mean, Corey, I told you that there is no debt between us."

He stabbed a finger against his chest. She half-expected it to fly through as the book had, but his finger stopped as if it had impacted on living flesh. "I feel there is a debt to be paid." His eye closed slowly. "Blast, 'tis impossible to wink at a pretty girl while I wear this patch."

"Do you still need it?" she asked hesitantly.

"I assume so." Folding his arms in front of him, he grinned

again as he said, "You are changing the subject, Miss Dunbar. I will repay you. Don't forget. I warned you that I am as stubborn as a Scot."

Ellen could not keep from smiling. "That is, indeed, stubborn."

"At last, you have seen the sense of not arguing. So what shall it be, Miss Dunbar? What can I do for you?"

"I have no idea."

"Come now. There must be something you want that I can help you obtain."

"No." She prayed her face would not betray her, for she could not speak the truth. She wished Corey were alive, so she might learn if this fluttering of her heart each time he smiled at her was something more than calf-love.

"If you don't know what I can do for you, then I shall have to come up with something on my own." He rose and strode back and forth between the bed and the hearth. Suddenly he snapped his fingers. "I have just the dandy! If I cannot repay you, I shall do something nice for your dear friend Marian."

"That would be nice, although," she added uneasily, "wouldn't she need to see you?"

"She would faint away deader than me." His rumble of laughter sounded like distant thunder. "So I shall accede to her dubious wisdom and help her get what she wishes for you."

Her eyes widened in horror. "No! You cannot be serious!"

"Of course I am." His satisfied chuckle did not lessen the gravity of his words. "I shall do as your dear friend wishes and help you find the perfect husband before the blooming of the chrysanthemums signals that the summer is over."

Three

"How does she fare?"

Marian smiled and gave Lorenzo Wolfe's skinny arm a maternal pat. "Ellen remains agitated, and I fear she did not sleep well last night, for she is as gray as a ghost. However, the doctor assures me she will heal like winking. Her injuries are not grave."

He shuddered. "Watch what you say."

"What?"

"Ghost. Grave. There are stories this old Abbey is still haunted by the spirits of the brothers who were turned out when King Henry dissolved the monasteries."

"Lorenzo, that was centuries ago."

"I know." He walked with her along the hallway toward the stairs leading down to the first floor. "Forgive me. It is simply I am discomposed by having to mourn my cousin a second time. Before we clung, albeit feebly, to the hope Corey was alive. We have no such hope this time."

"I shall be glad to assist with the funeral in any way I can."

"Would you?"

Marian smiled again. "My dear Lorenzo, we have been friends for so many years. I consider you as dear as a brother. Do you think I would turn my back on you now?" She gathered up her wrapper as she hurried down the stairs. Over her shoulder, she threw, "And Mr. Bridges insisted Ellen remain in bed for the next two days, so we shall remain your guests."

"Shall I have word sent to Reggie?"

"I have already informed my husband that I shall be delayed returning home. He will join us as soon as he can, I am sure."

Ellen strained but she could hear nothing more as Marian and Mr. Wolfe—no, Lord Wulfric—continued down the stairs. With a sigh, she closed the bedroom door and leaned against it. Her hope that last night was nothing but a nightmare had disappeared when she woke to the pain in her shoulder and the confusion in her head.

The accident had been real, but the rest . . . Tears battered at her eyelids. She was unsure of anything past the moment when the fireworks had exploded too close to the ground. Marian's conversation with Lord Wulfric confirmed what she had hoped was nothing but the vagaries of a battered brain.

Corey Wolfe was dead. He had pulled her out of the way of the explosion, mayhap at the cost of his own life. She shivered. She owed him more than she could ever hope to repay, but she wished none of this were true. Yet she knew how futile it was to pretend everything was as it had been yesterday.

Denying the truth must have brought on last night's dream. What had she told Marian last night? That all Scots were romantics at heart? Mayhap her dream had been born of the myths filling the dales and braes, along with her yearning to get to know Lord Wulfric better.

How charming he had been! She had laughed with him as she had not laughed with anyone in a long time. His teasing had allowed her to be honest as lief hiding her feelings behind the polite words of the Polite World.

"Miss Dunbar?"

She whirled at the voice. Her pounding heart slowed when she stared at a startled woman. The woman's hair was as black as the soot on the hearth, and her dark eyes were ringed in red. Even as Ellen watched, another tear inched along the woman's cheek.

"Pardon me, miss," mumbled the woman. "I did not mean to startle you. And . . ." She wiped away the tear. " 'Tis right sad about the lord dying right in the middle of our celebration."

"You do not need to apologize." Taking a step toward the bed, she swayed.

Instantly the woman was at her side. Ellen was grateful to be able to lean on her as they went back toward the bed. Gently the woman helped Ellen sink to the bench padded in purple velvet.

"Thank you," Ellen said. With a sigh, she managed a feeble smile. "I had no idea I was so light-timbered."

"You need to expect some weakness in the wake of your accident. Mrs. Griffen—the housekeeper, you know—told me you were hurt right bad." The woman's eyes got wider. "Said she had heard the sense had gotten knocked clear out of you."

"I suspect she was right. If you have told me your name before, I must ask you to tell me again."

The woman clicked her tongue in pity. "Dear me, you have clean forgotten me helping Lady Herrold bandage your arm last night, haven't you? Do you remember anything about what occurred last night?"

"I must own I am not sure about anything at the moment." That was a decided simplification of the facts. Her head was reeling as if she had been spun about in the wildest quadrille. Memories of the most peculiar happenings filled her mind. Had her injuries unhinged her brain?

"My name is Sullivan, miss. Mr.—" She gulped back another sob. "His lordship asked me to help you."

"Thank you." Ellen touched the bandage on her arm. "I fear I will need assistance until this heals."

"La, you are a lucky lady, miss."

"Yes." She was tempted to add all her luck might be bad, but she did not want to add another tear to the collection dotting Sullivan's bodice.

"When she realized you would not be returning to Herrold Hall as you had planned, Lady Herrold sent for some of your things last night, and they arrived just before I came up. Would you like something simple to wear?" She hesitated, then said, "Lord Wulfric is sure to wish to give you a look-in to make himself easy in the head about your welfare. I doubt you wish to receive him in your nightdress."

"True."

"What do you wish to wear?" She smiled. "If you wish, I will pick out something appropriate from among your things that were in the box from Herrold Hall."

Ellen nodded. Letting someone else make decisions seemed to be the wisest course right now. She did not trust her own thoughts. The jar to her skull must have been harder than she had realized.

With Sullivan's kind and careful help, Ellen was able to change into a pale green gown. The vandyke sleeves brushed the top of the bandaging on her arm. She adjusted the wide white ruffle along the bodice so it would not brush her sore arm more.

Ellen was breathless as she sat again while Sullivan brushed the snarls from her hair. Bits of grass and earth fell onto Ellen's shoulders, warning her that she must have looked a frightful sight.

With a laugh, Sullivan swept the debris away.

Ellen smiled, because she did not wish to down-pin the kindly abigail with her own grim spirits. Spirits? She shivered, sending another wave of pain along her arm. It was day. She must let the nightmare go. Mr. Wolfe had said the house was haunted, but not by his cousin.

Sullivan offered to bring Ellen something to break her fast, and Ellen agreed. Not that she was hungry. The idea of food threatened her already unsettled stomach, but she did not have the strength to argue and disappoint Sullivan.

Ellen stretched out her legs on the chaise longue set in an alcove which gave her a view of the gardens below. She leaned her chin on her hand and watched the sea beyond them. The water disappeared into the gray horizon where a bank of clouds promised a storm before nightfall. Although she wished the tall window was raised so she could hear the sea throwing itself on the shore, she did not want to risk her arm.

Sounds came from the door leading to the dressing room. She smiled when she recognized both voices. Marian and Sullivan. She was not surprised Marian had waylaid the abigail to give Sullivan instructions on how to watch over Ellen. Marian was a dear soul.

"Marian?" she called, although she doubted if her bosom-bow could hear her through the thick oak door. With a tired laugh, she leaned back in the chair and said softly, "Patience, Ellen. One of them will come in soon and open the window."

Her eyes widened and her mouth gaped as the lower window slowly lifted to bring the sounds crashing upon her. How had that happened? The house was too solid and too old to shift and set the window ajar. If . . . She stared as a cloud of colors began to materialize as it had last night.

In her nightmare!

Gripping the arm of the chair, she whispered, "Go away!"

"Now that is a fine way to greet your erstwhile host."

Ellen scanned the room. The voice was definitely coming from near the window, but no one was in the room with her. She slid her feet off the chair and stood. Her knees wobbled, and she locked them in place. That did not help, because now she could not move a step. If she tried, she feared she would fall on her face.

"Who is it?"

"Corey."

She wanted to rush over to the window and look out. There must be a ledge beneath it. This must be someone's cruel idea of a joke.

Ellen stared as a form took shape by the window. The gold buttons on a waistcoat glowed like cat eyes before a broad chest appeared. Hands slowly drew arms to attach to muscular shoulders as legs reached down toward shiny boots. Last, the face emerged from the shadows—a smile, the stern line of a jaw, ebony brows . . . and a patch to match.

Corey Wolfe!

Holding onto the back of the chair, she whispered, "This is impossible."

A frown stole the merriment from Corey's face. "I had hoped we would not need go through all that silliness again." Slowly he turned around. "See?" he asked when he was facing her again. "One bona fide ghost."

"Impossible!"

"Ellen!" he fired back in the same tone. "I have as much of eternity as you wish to waste on revisiting this discussion, but you have a life to get on with. May I suggest you put the moonshine behind you now?"

" 'Tis simpler for you to say when you are not facing a ghost." Her heart slowed its frantic beat. At the very least, Corey's reappearance proved she was not deranged. Or mayhap it proved she was mad. This might be another mind storm brought on by her injuries.

"Not as easy for me to say as you might believe." He reached up to run his fingers along the cheval glass. Stepping in front of it, he shook his head. "I have no idea how long it will take me to become accustomed to *this!*"

"I did not know that ghosts could come out during the day. I thought you could only appear after dark."

He shrugged as he faced her. "I have yet to learn all the canons of ghostly society. Mayhap when I have mastered them, I shall disregard them as I did the canons of the *ton.*"

"Is that so?" She smiled coolly. "Your clothes would belie your words."

"True." His gaze slid along her with slow appreciation. "You look much better this morn, Ellen. Like a summer blossom."

"Thank you." She was unsure what else to say. This conversation was in so many ways so commonplace she could have had it a score of times, save that she was speaking with a ghost in her bedchamber.

"I thought you would want some privacy while you dressed."

Ellen stiffened. "How did you know I was dressing?"

He grinned. "Are you asking me if I was peeking at you while you were in *déshabillé?* Now there is a tempting thought."

"Were you?"

"Would you believe me if I told you no?"

"Yes, I believe most people are honest."

His brows arched. "You should be careful judging others by your own standards." Sitting on the chair by the hearth, he smiled. "I do, however, possess ethics to match yours. I shall never invade your rooms when you wish privacy."

"Corey." She took a faltering step toward him, then paused. "You should not be here."

"In your rooms? Actually they are my rooms, if you wish to own the truth." He grimaced. "Or to be most honest, they are Lorenzo's. Damn, this is going to take some getting used to."

"There is no need for cursing."

"I apologize if I have said something your ears have never endured."

Ellen smiled as she sat facing him. It was easier to sit when her knees threatened to betray how unsettled she was. "My stepfather is a military man. I assure you anything you might say I have already heard."

"We shall get along well while I find you a match."

"Not that again!"

He set his legs on the table beside her. When she started to remonstrate, he chuckled. "Now, Ellen, I cannot ruin the finish on the table when my boots are not really on the wood. This existence does have a few advantages, after all."

"Then go and enjoy them."

"I made a vow to help you, and help you I will." He counted on his fingers. "Now let me think. This shire is not without its eligible men. Kenneth Pratt is looking for a wife as are, I believe, Josiah Adams and Terence Marshton. Of course, there's my cousin Lorenzo. He could well use a humdrum to keep this house in order."

"I shall choose my own husband, thank you." She rose and went to the door to the dressing room. Listening, she was glad to hear Sullivan still in conversation with Marian. If they chanced to come into the room, they would think her half-mad to be talking to herself. She looked back at where Corey still sat. "As you left this life as unmarried as when you entered it, I doubt if you are much an expert on making a match."

"But I know the thoughts of a man far better than you." Setting himself on his feet, he strode toward her.

Ellen gasped when he put out an arm to block her from edging past him. She recoiled from the luminescence that might burn her or freeze her heart in midbeat. With his hands against the door behind her, he held her in a prison that did not exist.

Slowly she raised her gaze past his smile to see the truth. He made no attempt to conceal the longing she had seen there so briefly last night. Then she had thought of him holding her and kissing her. Now that was impossible. He should be beyond such thoughts. Shouldn't he? She had no idea.

His voice was as soft as a caress. "I know well the thoughts of any man who could look down into your luminous eyes and imagine losing himself in their sweet fires. A single glance at your lips is enough to urge a man to vow to fight a dragon to the death if he could win even a single kiss."

"Corey, you are being ridiculous."

"Am I?"

"Yes," she said, but her voice quivered as his mouth lowered toward hers. Her fingers tingled, and she fought to keep her uninjured arm from raising toward his shoulders.

"Is it ridiculous for a man to let his fingers discover the silken warmth of your skin, and to drown in the scent of your perfumed hair?"

"Corey, you should not . . ." She closed her eyes, overmastered by the images he was creating in her mind.

"Probably not, but others will."

Ellen stiffened at his easy chuckle. Staring up at him, she wondered how any man could be so seductive and vexing at the same time.

When he turned to walk back toward the hearth, she tried to think of something to say. Something to console him. He might irritate her past words, but every sight, every sound, every smell must remind him that—for him—life was over.

"Corey?"

"Do not feel sorry for me, Ellen."

Her forehead threaded with confusion. "Can you read my mind? The window, and now this."

"You wear your thoughts plainly on your not plain face, my dear Miss Dunbar." Dropping to sit on the stones of the hearth, he grinned again. "You are welcome to revile me, for I know I can be bothersome. You can snarl at me, or you can coo sweet court-promises at me. Just never, never pity me. No one can pick the life—or the afterlife—to be dealt to them."

"Why do you still wear the patch?" she asked, crossing the room to stand by the bed.

"Mayhap for the same reason I wear these blasted boots." He scowled at the sleek boots that clung to his legs. "This is what I was wearing when I kicked off this earth. If I had had fair warning, I would have chosen something more comfortable. However, they do make me look quite the dashing spirit, don't they?"

"I have never seen a ghost in such prime twig."

His chuckle swept away his frown. "Now I understand why you have failed to make a match. Pity the man who must suffer the sharp edge of your tongue for the rest of his days."

"I would not want to marry a man who failed to appreciate all of me. I—"

Corey leaped to his feet as she winced. "Ellen, what is wrong?"

" 'Tis nothing save my arm. It pains so at times."

He cursed his own selfishness. Because his pain had receded along with his attachment to his corporeal form, he had ignored hers. How could he forget the severity of what they both had suffered out in the garden? She might forgive his insensitivity—considering the circumstances—but he could not. For the first time, he noted the rose of her cheeks was frosted with pallor and her eyes were bright with anguish.

As he reached out to help her sit, he stared at the odd light blossoming off his skin. By the Lord Harry, this was the worst muddle he could imagine.

Corey swallowed his frustration and said, "Please sit down, Ellen, before you swoon. I do not know if there is a single vial of *sal volatile* in all of the Abbey."

"I make it a practice never to swoon." Her faint voice belied her assertion.

"Sit."

"I think you are right."

Again he swore under his breath. That she was so acquiescent warned him she might be hurt even worse than he had been led to believe when he listened to the doctor speak with Lorenzo. That old addle cove had delivered every babe born in Wolfe Abbey in the past forty years, but he knew little about tending anything more serious than indigestion.

"Wait here," he ordered.

"Where—?" Ellen bit her lip as she realized she was alone. *That* was something that must change posthaste. He could not go popping in and out of sight like the moon playing hide-and-seek with the clouds.

Was she all about in her head? None of this could continue. The wisest thing would be for her to leave Wolfe Abbey. She must collect Marian and leave without delay.

Ellen pushed herself to her feet. A single step almost undid her, but she forced herself to take another. Any sign of weakness would persuade Marian to follow the doctor's orders and remain here.

"Where are you off to?"

She spun and collapsed onto the bench by the low table. When Corey held out a glass of red wine, she watched her own hand raise to take it. She stared at him, then at the wine.

"Go ahead," he urged. " 'Tis no ghostly brew, just some good burgundy brought by an interloper from France. It may return some of the color to your cheeks."

"Where did you get this?" She looked at the dressing room door. "How did you get this in here without being seen?"

He smiled. "Don't forget. These have been my rooms since I came home from France. Even before . . ." He scowled, then rushed on, "I could slip through these rooms without anyone seeing me. It would be a shame if I could not skulk about them now."

Ellen took a slow sip of the wine in the delightfully chilled glass, then another. The sturdy flavor of the bracing wine flowed through her, cooling the trepidation burning in her heart. Lowering the glass, she said, "All right. What do we do now?"

"Rest."

At Marian's cheerful voice, Ellen glanced over her shoulder. Marian bustled into the room, looked around, and smiled as she gave Ellen a buss on the cheek. While Sullivan set out the dishes on the tray she had brought in, Marian flitted about the room, adjusting a book here and moving a figurine there. Ellen smiled her thanks to Sullivan, even though she doubted if she could swallow a single bite of the toast.

"Marian, you should be pleased to see that I am sitting quietly," Ellen said, wondering how she could convince Corey to leave so she might speak with her friend in private. If he vanished, that would be worse, for she could not guess if he were eavesdropping.

There was no worry about that. Corey settled himself on the chair by the fireplace, a grin warning her that he was enjoying the whole situation far more than he should.

"Go away!" Ellen mouthed.

"Did you say something, dear?" Marian asked. Her pale yellow wrapper flowed back to reveal her ankles, which she would never have bared if she had had any idea a man might see.

"Only that I wish to go home."

"Soon, my dear." She tapped her chin and frowned. "I need to send word to your family of this mishap."

"Mishap?" repeated Corey with a chuckle. "Marian has developed a rare talent for understatement, I see."

Ellen wanted to hush him. Her lips tightened when he folded his hands behind his head and grinned at her. Blast him! He was relishing every moment of her discomfort. What kind of gentleman was he? No kind, she reminded herself with a suppressed shudder. He was a phantasm.

Marian went to the window and lowered it. "The doctor said no drafts, Ellen. You must not sicken in addition to your injuries." She pointed to the chair by the hearth. "May I sit and keep you company during your breakfast?"

"No!" she cried. "Don't sit there!"

Marian paused, her back end only an inch from Corey's lap. "Whatever is wrong, Ellen?"

"Sit here." She grasped the back of another chair and pulled it closer. The squeak of its legs against the floor ached through her head, and she decided the truth would be the very best excuse. "My head hurts, and I do not wish to shout across this grand room."

"As you wish." Marian took the seat. With a frown, she said, "You seem uncommonly unsettled."

"It has been an uncommonly unsettling day."

Corey interjected, "No truer words have ever been uttered."

Ellen flashed him a scowl, but fixed a smile on her face for her friend. "You can see that I am resting as the doctor ordered."

"I am glad you have come to your senses." Marian toyed with the lace on the front of her wrapper. "I had feared you would stay in the dismals for days. You were barely consolable last night when you were told of Lord Wulfric's death."

"I have cried enough."

Corey grinned and rocked the chair back on two feet.

With a gasp, Ellen jumped up. She shoved his chair forward. Its feet crashed onto the floor.

Marian leaped to her feet. "Ellen, whatever are you doing? You shall break that chair."

"I thought it was tipping over."

"How could it tip over all by itself?"

Ellen had no answer for that. Certainly not one she could give Marian. Mumbling that her eyes must have been playing a trick on her, she let Marian settle her in bed. Honestly, she was delighted to rest against the mound of pillows that Marian arranged around her.

"You must be more sensible," Marian cautioned. "Poor

Lorenzo is quite beside himself to think of what you have suffered here."

"He is not to blame for what happened."

Corey stood and came to lean on the bedpost across from where Marian was tucking the counterpane around Ellen. He said wryly, "Lorenzo will exult in the chance to apologize for days to come. You shall find his endless attempts at atonement a trial, I can assure you."

"He could not," Ellen went on, "see into the future. No one can. Can they?"

"Not I," Corey replied with a grin. "Otherwise, I vow I would have listened more carefully to Fenton."

"Of course not," Marian said.

"Fenton?" Ellen asked. She looked at Marian. "Who is Fenton?"

"What are you talking about?" Her friend's face lengthened with bafflement. "My dear, mayhap I should have the doctor come back and examine you again. You seem unable to follow the course of a simple conversation."

Corey chuckled. " 'Tis because this is no simple conversation. Fenton is the old man who warned us about the fireworks, Ellen."

A knock on the door spared Ellen from having to answer either of them. She was surprised when she almost laughed as Corey stepped back and gave a deep bow as Marian rushed past him. Somehow, he made even these bizarre circumstances amusing. She never had met anyone quite like him, and she could not help wondering what he might have been like if he had remained alive. Was he always so whimsical?

Marian opened the door only wide enough so she could see out. Then, telling Ellen she would return straightaway and to eat, she slipped out into the hall.

"Lorenzo probably has some crisis," Corey said, sitting on the bottom of the bed. "Marian is right. You should eat. You are nearly as pale as a specter, and who should know that better than I?"

"Is this how it is going to be? Must I suffer your endless pranks?" She flung out her hands. "If I had a smidgen of good sense, I would go out there and denounce you before the whole household."

"And they would lock you away in Bedlam." He pointed to the plate on the tray Marian had set on the table beside the bed. "Please eat. There is enough sorrow around here without you causing more by cocking up your toes in the wake of my demise. You need to eat and get yourself back on two solid feet."

"And then?"

"What do you think? I shall find you a match made in heaven." He chuckled. "Or as close as Corey Wolfe can come to it."

Four

Ellen cautiously entered the stable. She still did not trust her knees to hold her up, but with every hour, her strength was returning.

Hay crunched beneath her high-lows, and she was glad she had chosen her boots instead of slippers. The aromas from the beasts and the recently cleaned leather brought back beloved memories of her simple life in Scotland. Then she had fantasized about living a grand whirl of parties and *soirées* in a splendid house like Wolfe Abbey. It was most peculiar now that she was staying in such a magnificent house, she found the most welcome within the stables.

Of course, she reminded herself sternly, when she had journeyed south into England, she never could have imagined her life would take this absurd turn.

Something shifted in the shadows. Not something, she realized, but someone.

A small man, not as tall as she, inched out of the darkest corner. He was bent like the trees clinging to the seashore cliffs. She could not guess how old he might be. His hair was lined with silver, but his face was one that would look as old at a score of years as at three times that number.

It was almost as if he had been waiting for her, as if he knew she would be coming. He put his fingers to the brim of the floppy felt cap.

"Are you Fenton?" she asked.

"Aye. Who be ye?"

"Ellen Dunbar."

His brows shot up. "So ye be she?" He walked around her, reminding her of a small songbird chirping and hopping about. "Ye were with the master the other night."

"Yes." Dampening her lips, she said, "I heard you warning him about the fireworks. Why?"

"Simple, 'tis. Just repeatin' what I'd told the master before. Warned him that the blind buzzard firin' off the rockets had no more sense than one of the sheep down on the lea."

"Why didn't he heed you?"

"Wanted those rockets powerfully bad. Been lookin' forward to celebratin' the end of Boney's war."

Ellen nodded. The old man's words confirmed what she had already learned about Corey. He apparently had been in the army during the war. At one point, his family must have given him up for dead if Mr. Wolfe had taken the title of Lord Wulfric for a time. It was all most confusing, but she would not ask Fenton about that when she had other questions for him. Later she would quiz Marian.

"But how did you know there would be an accident?" she asked.

He bent to rub his right knee. "Heard it in my bones."

"Heard it?"

"Creak like the roof of the stable in a storm when trouble be coming."

"Do you hear anything now?"

"No."

"I am glad." Ellen forced a smile. What had she expected him to say? That his bones were shrieking out a warning?

"But ye be disturbed."

More than you can guess, she was tempted to answer. "It is always disturbing to have someone die so young."

" 'Tain't right."

"I agree." She took a deep breath, then said, "I wish he had listened to you."

"Aye, so do I. Then this wouldn't be happenin'. 'Twould be easier on all of us, 'specially ye, Miss Dunbar."

Ellen was unsure how to answer. She appreciated his compassion, but she did not want it. To surrender now to the pain bubbling within her like a witch's cauldron would strip away every bit of her façade. She could not reveal the truth of her disquiet. Nobody spoke of what happened to those who lost their minds, but it would not be pleasant to be shut away for the rest of her life.

With difficulty, Ellen raised her parasol as she walked back out into the afternoon sunshine. The expanse of garden between her and the Abbey seemed wider than when she had crossed it only minutes ago. Maybe it was only her frustration that made it so. She had hoped for a simple answer, but only found more questions.

The soft sound of a bird in the bushes and the buzz of insects closer to the ground were nearly lost beneath the crunch of the seashells beneath her boots. The shells which had been spread out in a meandering path were as dry and white as fleshless bones.

She shuddered, trying to throw off her dreary thoughts. Tears pricked her eyes. Even that simple motion sent a pain down her arm. Pausing beneath the cool shade of an oak, she stared at the ocean past the house. Without a division between earth and sky, the grayness stretched endlessly.

"More confused?"

Ellen whirled around, then scowled when she saw Corey behind her. "Did you ever consider how many years you could take off a soul's life by sneaking around like that?"

"The shells on this path make it impossible for anybody to skulk about." He toyed with a few of them with the toe of his boot.

"Any*body*, yes, but not a ghost."

"Oh."

She laughed at the chagrin on his face. "I suppose you shall accustom yourself to that eventually."

"I suspect I must."

"I did not expect to see you out here."

Corey folded his arms over his chest and looked around. "All of this is my home." His gaze returned to her. "Odd that you seem to know more about what I should and should not do than I do."

"We Scots are fond of ghostly tales."

"You should tell me a few. Mayhap then I would know what the parameters of this new existence are for me."

"You are English!" She laughed as they continued along the path toward the house. "I doubt if our old stories would have any bearing on this."

"So what did Fenton tell you?"

Ellen stopped and faced him. "Are you spying upon me again?"

He held up his hands, laughing. "I told you I did not peek into your rooms. Nor did I sneak after you to eavesdrop on your conversation. 'Twas only a guess. You are coming from the direction of the stables, and I saw how you tensed when I mentioned Fenton's name earlier."

"He is an eccentric chap."

"But his idiosyncratic ways have proven to be worthwhile. I should have heeded his warnings." He took a step closer to her. "I fear my mind was on other matters at that moment. Matters of the scent of a sweet cologne that teased me and a slender hand upon my arm."

"Corey, please don't," she whispered.

"You would deny me the enjoyment of recalling those last memories of physical pleasure?"

"No, but to speak of them now . . ." She rushed along the path although she knew it was as impossible to escape from him as from the longings his words brought to life. She did not want to remember how strong his arm had been beneath her fingers and how she had imagined that arm drawing her into an embrace as his lips caressed hers.

No! She must never think of these things. Never!

She settled the parasol on her shoulder where it would hide her face from Corey. Then she wondered if she could conceal anything from a man who apparently could wander through walls at will.

"Ellen, if I said something to offend you—"

"Offend?" Her laugh was terse. "No, you did not offend me. It simply is too late to talk about what might have been."

"Now that is the sensible Scot speaking."

"You think this can be changed?"

"Who can tell?"

Ellen had no answer for him. Listening as he spoke of recent work on the garden as if no harsh words had been exchanged, she was glad he did not ask her any more questions. Her breath banged against her side when they reached the steps leading up to a side door. Only now was she discovering how she had been sapped by her injuries.

Blinking, as she waited for her eyes to adjust to the dusk within, Ellen closed her parasol and loosened the ribbons on her bonnet. The small entry was at the foot of a set of stairs leading to the hallway near her bedchamber, and she wanted nothing more, at the moment, than to kick off her boots and relax in her bed.

"You did too much," Corey said as he leaned his elbow on the black walnut banister. "You should have sent for Fenton to come here."

"On what pretext?"

"A good question to which I do not have a good answer."

Footfalls came toward them. Ellen waved Corey to silence, although it was unnecessary. No one could hear him save her.

A man, who was not much taller than Fenton, walked toward Ellen. He possessed an aura of serenity that contrasted with Corey's sudden gasp. Wanting to ask what was amiss, Ellen could only smile.

The man stopped. "Miss Dunbar?"

"Yes."

"I am Armstead. I was my lord's man."

"What can I do for you, Armstead?" Her voice was colder than she wanted, but she was too aware of Corey listening.

He struggled to smile and failed, his face gaining years as his wrinkles deepened with sorrow. "I heard you sat with him at his last breath, Miss Dunbar. They kept me out, but I am glad you were there."

"I recall so little of that." She touched her head. "My brain was muddled."

"I understand. I simply wished to tell you that I am glad my lord was not alone."

Corey said, "Tell him how much I have treasured his years of service."

"I am sure," she said to the distraught man, "Lord Wulfric treasured your attentive service over so many years."

"How kind of you to say that, Miss Dunbar."

"What Lord Wulfric would say himself if he were able."

Corey grinned and nodded. "You are doing a famous job with this, Ellen."

"Thank you, again." Armstead squared his shoulders and smiled sadly. "I wished to speak to you before I left."

"Leave?" Corey shouted, but only Ellen's ears rang. "Where are you going? Ellen, ask him where he's going!"

She flashed Corey a frown, but obeyed.

"Mr. Wolfe—excuse me, Lord Wulfric has granted me leave to visit my family in Manchester for a few weeks," the old man replied. "My sister has long wished for me to spend some time with her."

"Spare me another frown," Corey said, moving to stand beside Armstead so Ellen could not avoid looking at him. "He never mentioned that to me. I would have gladly allowed him some time to take a flying visit to see his sister. He even could have had longer, although I must own I was grateful for Armstead's help with more than my wardrobe. If Lorenzo had half a brain, he would glean every bit of advice Armstead can offer before he sends the man on his way."

Ellen twisted her fingers through the ribbons on her parasol.

"Have a good sojourn, Armstead. I know Lord Wulfric will be pleased to see you upon your return."

"Yes," he said, but his tone suggested he might stay in Manchester.

"Damn!" Corey's hands fisted at his sides. "Persuade him to come back, Ellen."

"I shall leave after the funeral services tomorrow, Miss Dunbar," the old man went on, "but I wanted to speak with you before I left. Good day."

Ellen ignored Corey, who continued to demand she tell Armstead to return to Wolfe Abbey, as she bid Armstead a good day. As soon as the valet was out of earshot, she whirled to face Corey and nearly fell. She gripped the banister to keep herself on her feet. "I am fine," she said, waving him aside.

"Why didn't you tell him what I told you?"

"How was I to explain how I know these things?"

His smile was cold. "You have been doing well making up bangers so far."

"You are beastly."

"Is that any way to speak of the dead?"

She stared at him. When a slow smile spread across his face, she could not help laughing. "You *are* beastly, you know."

"Who is beastly, dear?" Marian hurried into the foyer. "Is someone causing you trouble? You need only to speak to Lorenzo, and he will be certain it is dealt with in lickety-split time."

"No one." Ellen took a step up the stairs. "Just talking to myself."

"Calling yourself beastly?"

"Just this blasted bandage."

"Ellen, be careful of your language." Marian put her arm around Ellen's shoulders and guided her up the stairs. "Just imagine what Lorenzo would think if he heard such things at a time like this."

Ellen ignored Corey's laugh as she went with Marian. She did not look back to see if he was following. She doubted if he would leave her alone for long, and she was unsure if she looked forward to his next appearance or dreaded it.

The chapel at the back of Wolfe Abbey was small and dark and stank of age and winter damp. Dust motes swirled in a soundless waltz within the colored light flowing through the two arched windows facing each other across a pair of stone pews.

Ellen flinched when her fingers brushed the stone. It had been smoothed by countless hands before hers. Lowering herself gingerly to the hard seat, she looked around. Although nearly every pew was full, no more than two score mourners had gathered in the tiny chapel. She recognized several faces from the *soirée* on that tragic night, but either she could not recall the names to go with them or she had never been introduced. Much of that night was lost to the memory stolen from her by her injuries. Odd, that the parts with Corey remained seared so clearly into her mind.

She nodded to a gray-haired woman who looked somewhat familiar as she passed down the aisle to take a seat in a pew closer to the front. If Marian had been there, she could have told Ellen each person's name and relationship to Corey, but Marian had been delayed within the house by a servant with a question about the food to be served after the funeral for Lord Wulfric was over.

An involuntary smile tugged at her lips. Lord Wulfric. Not Corey Wolfe. Even to herself, the body in the closed casket could not be connected with the impish spirit that haunted her.

She touched the lighter bandage on her arm. Mr. Bridges had changed it that morning after she had dressed. He had reminded her again of how fortunate she was to be alive. As she raised her gaze to the simple casket, she blinked back sudden tears. Corey had taken the brunt of the explosion, saving her life. She had never thanked him.

"May I sit with you, Miss Dunbar?"

Smiling at the new Lord Wulfric, Ellen eased to the far side of the pew. Lorenzo Wolfe's spindly knees pointed toward the ceiling when he sat beside her. She never had seen such a bald-ribbed man.

"I am pleased you are here," he continued.

"Did you think I would stay away?"

"You met Corey but once." He scanned the nearly empty chapel. "Not long enough for him to vex you with his peculiar sense of humor. Too many of the people in the shire did not understand that his honed wit was meant only to jest."

"I can see how they might feel that way after what I have endured."

He faced her, bafflement on his face. "When?"

Ellen swallowed roughly. She must be careful. Unthinking words would betray her. "At the gathering before the fireworks, of course."

"It wasn't," Lord Wulfric said, looking again at the simple pulpit beneath the huge sounding board suspended from the rafters, "that he meant to be vexing. He was so much his father's son. The late Lord Wulfric—the late, late one—was ever a jester. Corey enjoyed teasing all of us."

"That is the way of many families."

"Yours?"

She was glad she could answer with the truth. "My family is far from here in Scotland, so I seldom have the pleasure of their company."

"Sad."

"Yes, very sad."

"Excuse me?" Lord Wulfric asked.

Only then did Ellen realize that the words of commiseration had been in a deeper voice. Swiveling slightly, she bit her lip to silence her gasp as she saw Corey sitting on the back of the pew, his boots nearly brushing her skirt. Except for the peculiar glow around him, he looked as solid of flesh as his cousin.

"What are you doing *here?*" she mouthed, unable to speak the words aloud, for Lord Wulfric would overhear.

"I cannot make out *your* soundless words, so you must forgive me if I fail to answer. However, you can hear me." Corey looked around the chapel. "Sorry showing, isn't it? I thought more folks would come to say good riddance to me."

As if he were privy to Corey's words, Lord Wulfric said, "I do not mean to suggest this small gathering is the result of Corey's pranks. Without his sister Vanessa and her family here, I thought we would have a simple funeral. Later, when they return from the continent, we shall have a memorial service which will be more suitable for the passing of a marquess."

"You always liked ceremony, Lorenzo," Corey grumbled.

Ellen glared at Corey, then gave Lord Wulfric a smile. "I think that is a wonderful idea. How soon do you think his sister and her husband can return?"

"Her husband is busy on the government's business. Last month, we received a letter telling us they were in Vienna, but I am not sure they are there now. The message of Corey's accident was sent to their address in Vienna as well as to several of the ministries in London which might know where they have been sent." He clasped his hands on his knees. "Ours is a most unusual family."

"Only to you." Corey copied his cousin's pose. "To the rest of us, you are the odd bird, Lorenzo."

Wanting to warn Corey to be silent, Ellen had no chance. The minister in his dark surplice paused by the pew. He shook Lord Wulfric's hand and murmured a few words of sympathy before looking at Ellen.

"Miss Ellen Dunbar," Lord Wulfric supplied quickly, "this is Reverend Stapleton. His parish includes Wolfe Abbey."

"Reverend," she said as the portly man dipped his head in her direction.

"Miss Dunbar was hurt in the same accident that took Corey from us," Lord Wulfric said with a sigh. "It is our good fortune that she is healing well."

"You were a friend of Lord Wulfric's?"

"We had only met."

"But," Corey interjected, "we are getting to know each other better all the time."

Ellen bit back the words that would not be fit for a clergy-man's ears. When she saw Corey's mischievousness grin, she was tempted to utter the truth.

She was saved from her own flummery by the door to the chapel crashing open. Marian rushed down the aisle to grasp the minister's hands.

"Late as usual," Corey said with a grin. "I doubt if she was on time to her own birth."

"Forgive me, Lorenzo," Marian gasped, sitting in the pew across the aisle. "I am so glad I could get here in time. So much to do. So much to do. Your servants need more guidance, Lorenzo. I know Corey never cared for such mundane matters. This household needs a competent hand to oversee it so the cook need not ask about every dish to be served after this cere-mony is over. I told her what should be done, so I believe all will be well. As for the footman at the front door . . ." She shook her head in dismay.

"I appreciate your help," Lord Wulfric said and patted her hand. Looking at the minister, he added, "We all are here, Rev-erend. May we begin?"

"Of course."

Ellen was pleased when Corey was respectfully silent during the prayers Reverend Stapleton spoke. Hearing Marian's sobs, she wished she could be honest with her friend. Corey might be dead, but he was not gone from Wolfe Abbey. Yet, to speak the truth would leave Marian thinking Ellen was out of her mind.

The minister began his service, his voice resounding off the sounding board as if he were exhorting the angels themselves to come into the small chapel. By the end of a half hour, how-ever, Ellen was wondering if he ever grew tired of listening to that echo.

"He always has had more tongue than teeth." Corey chuckled as she shifted on the uncomfortable stone pew.

"Shh!" she cautioned.

"Why? No one can hear me save you."

Ellen wished she could argue with that logic. "Then please be silent," she whispered, "so I may hear Mr. Stapleton."

"He never says much worth heeding."

Ignoring his laugh, she stared at the fubsy man at the simple pulpit. Again she had to concur. This eulogy could have been spoken for almost anyone. There was nothing uniquely Corey Wolfe in anything he said. She resisted the temptation to yawn as her eyes grew weighted.

"But Corey Wolfe, the Marquess of Wulfric," said the minister, drawing her attention back to him, "shares one thing with his ancestors who founded this prestigious house."

"He died," Corey said grimly.

A laugh burst from Ellen. She quickly disguised it as a sob as she held her hand over her face. Lord Wulfric stroked her uninjured shoulder gently, and she hoped he guessed its quivering came from sobs, not her efforts to keep from giggling.

"No Lord Wulfric ever shirked his duty to country and king," continued Reverend Stapleton, although he glanced in Ellen's direction. "Corey Wolfe followed their grand tradition."

She calmed herself and nodded her thanks to Lord Wulfric, who turned to comfort Marian. This was absurd!

"Corey Wolfe, like those before him, risked his life to safeguard his nation . . ."

At a low groan, she glanced over her shoulder at Corey. She had never thought a ghost could blush, but an unmistakable flush darkened his cheeks.

". . . and lost nearly a year of his short life while he was a captive of Napoleon's accursed empire."

"There is no reason to eulogize my stupidity," Corey growled.

"Being a hero is not stupid," she whispered.

He leaned his chin on his fist. "Not only is it jobbernowl to be a hero, but 'tis a damned burden. Once you do something others consider courageous, you have to spend the rest of your life with them watching to see if you will repeat your grand deed."

"You are free of that now."

"True." He flashed her a grin. "Maybe dying was not so bad."

Ellen looked away. No matter how he pretended, she could sense his frustration. He was caught somewhere between life and eternity, and he had no idea what he should do next. That must be horrible for a man like Corey Wolfe who, if the minster was not just being complimentary, had always known what new gamble he would take next.

Why was Corey still here? The minister's words left no doubt that Corey had been a man of honor, albeit a man of honor with a peculiar sense of humor. Nothing anyone had said suggested he had done anything during his life to deserve being shackled to earth as a ghost. She believed the praise she had heard lauding his bravery and kindness was honest, not just adding a stone to his cairn. Mayhap everyone who died lingered for a time close to the place they loved. That would explain the many tales she had heard, as a child, of haunted places among the rolling hills of the Scottish borders. None of those stories had explained how one became a ghost or for how long. Mayhap the only way she and Corey would learn the truth was to wait and see what happened to him.

The service drew to a quick close. When Lord Wulfric offered his arm to Ellen, she gratefully accepted his help in rising and walking toward the door at the back of the church. She looked back, but saw no sign of Corey as the coffin was lifted to be carried out to the wagon in front of the chapel.

The small cemetery overlooked the sea. Salt stained the stones which had been tilted beneath the onslaught of the sea winds. As the iron gate opened on hinges that had been recently oiled, for Ellen noted drips on the rust, she was sure there could be no better resting place for this family. If all of them loved the sea as Corey did, they were close to it forever.

A heaviness filled her eyes, but she refused to let the tears fall. He was not dead to her, so how could she mourn him? Every day, every conversation, he became more and more alive to her.

When the minister spoke the last words over the casket which had been lowered into the ground, Ellen was glad to turn her back on it. The gravediggers began to fill in the grave even as the mourners went through the gate.

Marian sat next to Ellen in the carriage that would take them back to Wolfe Abbey. Her hope they would return to Herrold Hall today had come to naught. Marian insisted she must help Lord Wulfric greet his callers while Ellen had another day of rest.

As Ellen gazed out at the rolling hills lifting themselves from the sea, Marian asked, "Who were you talking to in the chapel?"

She fought not to tense. "Lord Wulfric and—"

"No, during the service."

Ellen put her hand to her chest in mock dismay. "I would not think to intrude on a funeral service by talking."

"I heard you whispering."

"Mayhap it was someone's prayers you heard." She loathed being false, but how could she be honest?

"I thought 'twas you I heard. The voice was a woman's, I am sure."

She smiled. "Marian, it may have been me. I am so unsettled by all this that I might have been whispering what I thought was only in my head."

"Dear Ellen, I did not mean to accuse you." Her eyes were wide. "I only wish to be certain you are well."

"As well as can be expected."

"Mayhap we should go back to the house in Town. Putting some distance between us and this tragedy would be for the best." Marian tapped her chin. "Of course, we cannot leave before the village fair or the gathering which the Pratts are hosting or . . ."

Ellen let her bosom-bow prattle on about all the plans ahead of them during the next month. Marian did not pause until they had reached the house. Helping Ellen into the grand foyer with its huge chandelier hanging from the ceiling two stories above, Marian led Ellen up the stairs and into a small room beneath the next curve of stairs.

It was a simple room. The single window was covered with dark green drapes, but a lamp was lit on the table near the hearth.

Marian motioned for Ellen to sit on the chair beside it. Pulling up a stool, she drew off Ellen's slippers and set her feet on it.

"You need to rest," Marian said. "I shall close the door, and you can rest. You look as peaked as if this had been your own funeral."

Ellen shivered as her friend hurried out of the room, shutting the door. Surely Marian would speak differently if she thought before opening her mouth. But her words were unsettling.

The wing chair by the hearth welcomed her. As she relaxed into the thick cushions, quiet wrapped about her like a favorite shawl. This room was nothing like the grand chamber where she had been sleeping. It had a coziness that would not have been out of place in her parents' house, although the wood on their walls was not grand mahogany like this. The dozens of books lining the glass-fronted shelves were a luxury she had never known until she came to England.

Closing her eyes, she sighed. This was wondrous. She had not been able to relax since . . . Slowly she opened her eyes as she felt a gaze upon her. Corey stood by the hearth, his elbow upon the mantel as he smiled at her.

"I was not sure if you would return," she said.

"You thought I was buried along with the casket." He chuckled. "Or mayhap you hoped?"

"The thought of how simple things would be if you were not about did cross my mind."

"Honesty again. Much better. Then I shall be as honest with you and say I had no yearning to witness my own casket being put under the daisies." He paused by a pipe rack on the table. A wry grin tipped his lips. "I think I miss my pipe most of all."

"So what happens now?"

He picked up a pipe. "I have no idea. I have not had your good fortune to meet a ghost."

"Good?" She watched him turn the pipe over in his hands. "I swear Marian considers me half-mad after intruding on so many conversations since the accident."

"Mayhap you are."

Ellen frowned. "You think this is nothing but my imagination?"

"I no longer know what to think." His grin returned as he crossed the room to sit on the marble hearth. "I would as lief enjoy this extraordinary adventure and see where it leads. After all, I have made a vow to help you find the perfect husband, Edie."

"Edie? My name is—"

"Ellen Dunbar. E-D." His chuckle was as warm as the fire. "Pet names were a game we played in our family save for Lorenzo, who always has been as somber as an undertaker."

"Not you, too!" She leaped to her feet. "Must you speak of funerals and undertakers incessantly?"

"But 'tis true. Lorenzo is a most somber chap."

"Then say it that way! Don't speak of death and undertakers and all that!"

"Edie—"

"My name is Ellen." She clenched her fingers as she blinked to keep the tears in her eyes. "Blast you! Will you leave me alone?"

"I wished only to tease you."

"Please don't."

"You need to laugh."

"No!" She ran to the window and pointed out. "Begone."

"Edie—"

"My name is Ellen!" She gripped the thick drapes. How she wished she could cocoon herself in this smothering velvet! To shut out everything and everyone and to protect herself from the insanity around her. "Why don't you leave me alone?"

"Is that what you wish?"

She dropped onto the window seat. "I don't know. I am so confused."

"You need to smile, Edie."

"My—Blast it! Call me what you wish!"

He frowned. "I did not intend to send you flying up to the boughs. Only to tease you."

"Don't you understand? I do not want to laugh. Then I might

feel something. I do not want to feel anything." She bent her head. "I wish I never had to feel anything ever again."

Corey knelt beside her. "Do not wish that. That is as good as being dead."

She raised her tearstained face to meet his gaze. "Is that how you are able to deal with this? You feel nothing?"

"No, I feel too much." He sat back on his heels. "Why do you think I wish to see you laugh? I can sense the pain you are hiding within you."

His gentle words undid her completely. She pressed her hand to her face and sobbed. All the fear, all the disbelief, all the battered dreams burst forth in a torrent of anguish.

"Do not grieve," he whispered. He brushed his fingers tentatively on her shoulder.

With a gasp, she jerked away. She put her hand onto her shoulder and cried, "What did you do?"

"I touched you. Did I hurt you?" He asked the words as if he could not believe them himself.

Slowly she drew her hand back. Beneath it, her skin was scored as if with fire.

"I burned you?" he gasped.

"With cold," she whispered. "As cold as the grave."

Five

The low sky threatened rain as Ellen walked down the front steps of Wolfe Abbey toward Marian's carriage. Lord Wulfric was speaking quietly with Marian, so Ellen had the excuse to rush past them to get into the carriage. She looked back at the grand house.

She gently cradled her aching arm, then winced as she moved her shoulder. Each time she closed her eyes, she could see the horror on Corey's face when he realized how his touch had hurt her. She had not stayed to soothe him last night. Racing out of the room, she had not returned. Marian had graciously let her share her room, and Ellen had allowed her bosom-bow to think she was distressed solely because of the funeral.

And Corey had vanished as completely as if he had never existed.

Lord Wulfric handed Marian into the carriage. "I hope you will call in a few days, Marian," he said. "I recall how empty this house seemed when I was alone before. When mine is the only voice save the servants', it becomes dreary."

"Mayhap you should go to Town."

He shook his head. "Such a stimulating life belonged to Corey or to Nessa, not to me. I prefer this life in grassville, but not always alone." He looked at Ellen and smiled. "Thank you for your compassion during the past few days."

"I fear I have done little."

"That you were so calm in the midst of this, when you were

injured as well, gave me more strength than you can guess. You mourned with such dignity, it inspired all of us."

Ellen longed to tell him the truth. She had not mourned for Corey . . . until now. Only now was she saying good-bye to him. Marian would be a good neighbor and give Lord Wulfric a look-in, but if Ellen had a smidgen of sense about her, she would stay far from Wolfe Abbey and Corey Wolfe.

"Thank you," she said, knowing anything else she might say could betray the secret she must bury as deeply in her heart as Corey's corpse was beneath the earth. "I appreciate your kindness, my lord."

He nodded, looking oddly uncomfortable. She wondered which of her words had so unsettled him, then realized it was the title. Brashly she put her hand over his on the side of the door. His wish that his cousin might come again from the dead to claim the title was futile, but the truth might ease his pain.

"Ellen, recall yourself!" hissed Marian. Shock emblazoned her face.

"Marian," returned Lord Wulfric in the same tone, "do not chide Miss Dunbar when she is only continuing to be generous with her sympathy."

Ellen gulped back her gasp. For a moment, she had seen a resemblance to Corey in the twinkle in Lord Wulfric's eyes. She had dismissed Lord Wulfric as insignificant. Clearly there was more to him than she had guessed. Again she was tempted to tell him the truth. Mayhap she did not need to worry. Corey would not be a quiet ghost, content to wander the corridors of the Abbey in silence. Sooner or later, Lord Wulfric was sure to encounter him.

After a few more words of consolation, Marian signaled for the coachman to drive them along the sea road toward Herrold Hall. Ellen took a single glance back at the huge house.

So lowly not even Marian would hear, she whispered, "Good-bye, Corey."

* * *

Rain struck the windows in a futile attempt to find a way into Herrold Hall. The mighty expanse of glass cast doubts on Marian's assertion that her husband's family had held this land for dozens of generations. Unlike Wolfe Abbey, which had been built to repel any invasion, this house was designed with leisurely living in mind.

Ellen stood by the largest window in the library and stared out at the pond past the gardens at the base of the hill. The day was fading into dusk, and she could barely see the water swirling amid the cattails on the shore.

No day had ever been as long as this one. Marian's prattling had rung through Ellen's head until Ellen had sought any excuse to seek her room. When she had arrived there, she found Sullivan unpacking her things. The abigail had told her, with a smile, that Lord Wulfric wished her to continue to serve Miss Dunbar while she was visiting Herrold Hall.

"Not as if his lordship needs a lady's maid in the Abbey," Sullivan had said with a grin.

Ellen suspected Marian's hand in this arrangement, because Marian had been vexed at sharing her abigail Holmes. Other times, she might have been thrilled to see a friendly face, but all Ellen could think of was finding some place to be alone with her thoughts.

The book room at the back of the house on the second floor had offered that solitude. As a fire snapped on the stone hearth, she had watched the storm sweep up out of the sea to crash around the house.

"Here you are!"

At Marian's merry voice, Ellen sighed. Marian was so resolved that Ellen not lose herself in melancholy she was haunting Ellen here as surely as Corey had at Wolfe Abbey.

No, she would not think of him now. Nor would she think of how she had left the Abbey without seeking Corey out. What could she have said to him? None of the usual platitudes would serve.

"Look!" Marian crowed. "Your arm must be better."

Ellen smiled. She had dispensed with the bandages. Although her arm remained tender around the lacerations and her skin was a peculiar collection of colors, she was delighted to be free of the constraining bandages. "Mr. Bridges told me this afternoon he was pleased with my recovery."

"As I am." Marian settled herself in a chair by the window and shivered. "I do despise rainy days."

"I find them cozy."

"That is because you were raised in that dreary country to the north. I daresay, you seldom enjoyed a sunny day."

Ellen did not want to discuss Scottish weather. Not when it was clear something was bothering Marian. Sitting next to her friend, she asked, "What is amiss?"

Marian's deep sigh filled the room, but she managed a smile. "I had thought to put the tragedy behind us when we left Wolfe Abbey, but I find myself thinking of Corey Wolfe too often."

"You knew him for many years."

"Tolerated him would be closer to the truth." She smiled sadly. "I vow I never met a more vexing man. Even when we were young, he could not resist jesting on every occasion. When he defied his father and went to buy a commission, no one was more startled than I, for I had been certain his claims of doing just that were nothing but another joke."

The door opened, and a maid came in with a tea tray. Marian motioned for it to be set on a table near her. Marian poured tea for Ellen and held out the cup.

Stirring sugar into it, Ellen said, "Then Corey—"

Marian glanced at her sharply. "I did not realize you were such good friends that you were using first names."

"It comes of hearing you speak of him with such affection, I suspect." Hurrying on before Marian could ask another question, she said, "You shall miss his laughter."

"I never thought I would say yes, but you are right." Leaning back in her chair, Marian gazed up at the plaster flowers looping across the ceiling. "I recall a time when I would have been glad to be rid of him. It was the night of my first real party. I had been brought out in Town a few weeks before, but my parents wished me to marry Reginald. The party was to give him a chance to court me."

Ellen took a sip of her tea, so Marian might not see her expression. She had never met Marian's parents, for they had died before she came to England. What she had heard made her grateful their paths had never crossed. Marian's country squire father had been determined to advance their family's status by marrying their only child to the local baron. If Corey had been a few years older, he would have been the target of their matchmaking.

"Corey somehow managed to sneak into the house before the party," Marian continued. "I suspect he was thirteen or fourteen at the time, but he always was able to slip in and out of places without anyone seeing him. Like some kind of phantom, causing trouble when no one was looking."

Ellen choked on her tea. She waved aside Marian's concern. "I am fine. Swallowed wrong," she whispered. If Marian probed further, she would have to devise another lie. She could not own that Marian's words were too close to the truth. "So what did he do?"

"He put some sort of chemical on the cloths in the room where the gentlemen might check their appearance before returning to the ballroom. It was invisible beneath the lights, but when one of them went out into the garden, their hands and faces—and anything they had touched—glowed like Japanese lanterns."

"That must have been most embarrassing!"

"Yes." Marian chuckled. " 'Twas especially embarrassing for Lord Patterson."

"Was he covered with the chemical?"

"The man never touched any of the cloths, but apparently his wife was aglow after her *rendezvous* in the garden with Mr. Winston."

"How do you know the perpetrator?" Ellen gasped.

"Corey owned to the deed. He always did. That was half the fun for him." She balanced her cup on the arm of the chair. "I recall his father was in quite a pelter over the whole, but the old lord loved a joke as much as Corey did. Thank goodness

Lorenzo has more sense than the two of them put together."
Her eyes narrowed in a predatory expression Ellen had come
to recognize. "You seemed very friendly with Lorenzo on our
parting this morning."

"I wished only to comfort him."

"Out of comfort comes other emotions."

"Marian, please do not make something out of nothing."

"Lorenzo is not an impossible match for you, although you
could do better. He may have the title, but the Abbey is not his.
I think we can find a finer match for you."

Ellen stood and put her cup on the tray. "I do not wish to
speak of finding a husband now."

"Oh, dear." Marian rose, clasping her hands in front of her.
"You think you're in love with Corey, don't you?"

"Nonsense!"

"I know you, Ellen! I know how impossibly fast you give
away your heart."

Going back to the window, she looked out. "And you know
how impossibly fast I take it back." She sank to the window
bench. "Yes, Marian, I did enjoy the short time I had with him
in the garden, but that is over."

"Marian, where are you?" came a shout before Marian could
answer.

Ellen tensed as the door crashed open, and a man strode in. Lord
Reginald Herrold was the complete opposite of his wife. A hulk of
a man, he walked with hunched shoulders as if he feared they would
brush against the walls of the wide passages. He seldom was seen
in the company of the *ton*. His life was focused on tending to the
strain of hunting dogs he was breeding at Herrold Hall, and he was
seldom seen without one following on his heels.

Today was no exception. The brindled hound bounded into
the room. One glance in Marian's direction and her disgusted
mutter must have given it fair warning. It turned toward Ellen.

She bent and held out her hand. The dog wagged all over as
it sniffed her fingers. Petting its silken head, she smiled. "Aren't
you a fine one?"

The dog licked her palm as Lord Herrold said in his surprisingly mellow tenor, "Bonnie *is* the best of the latest litter. You have an excellent eye, Miss Dunbar."

"I have always been fond of dogs."

"Reginald," Marian said, "you know these beasts are not trained to be in the house." Turning to Ellen, she lamented, "One of them chewed a large hole in my favorite gown, and another . . ." She flushed. "My rug shall never be the same."

"I shall keep an eye on Bonnie's behavior," he replied before turning back to Ellen. "By the end of the week, I hope to have Bonnie begin her training for the hunt. Mayhap you would enjoy watching, Miss Dunbar."

"I would be delighted, my lord." *Anything,* she thought, *to keep from thinking of Corey.*

Marian sniffed. "You need not be polite, Ellen. Reginald will understand you do not wish to rise before dawn and tramp through wet grass."

"That sounds wonderful," she replied.

Lord Herrold smiled. "I forget. You are a real lass of daisyville, not like Marian here, who enjoys the country only when it is as tame as her garden."

"Now, Reginald," his wife said with a pout, "you know that is not true. I relish a good ride through the leas."

He put his arm around her. "True."

Neither of them noticed when Ellen slipped out of the room.

With a smile, she climbed the curving stairs. Although Marian's parents had thought only of advancing themselves with this marriage, it had brought their daughter much happiness. They shared a kind of love she never had experienced—a love that lasted beyond the first meeting of eyes amidst a crowd, a love that needed no pretense, a love that grew stronger as lief diminishing in the light of reality.

Ellen opened the door to her bedchamber. When she saw it was empty, she sighed with relief. Mayhap she had found a haven at last. She liked this room, for it overlooked the sea.

Marian had tried to persuade her to take a room in another wing, but Ellen had been insistent.

Throwing open the window near the door to the dressing room, she took a deep breath of the fresh air. The rain had slowed to a drizzle and would not come in on the dark green and purple Persian rug. She smiled, suspecting Marian would be even less unforgiving of Ellen's thoughtlessly ruining a rug than she had been of her husband's dogs.

The room was not large. With the tester bed and an armoire filling most of the floor, there was little room for the dressing table and a chair. The small chest at the foot of the bed was covered with a paisley shawl, its fringe dripping on the carpet.

Sullivan had unpacked for her. Ellen was grateful for the considerate woman's assistance, because she guessed Mr. Bridges was right when he said it would be at least a fortnight before she had full use of her arm again.

Sitting on the wide bench at the dressing table, Ellen touched the silver brushes. They had been a gift on her last birthday from her dear friend Romayne. Each time she used them, she thought of her last visit with her friend. They had ridden wildly across the moors and talked late into the night. Now Romayne was a wife and a mother, and Ellen was as confused as she had been when Romayne took her to her first *soirée* in London.

Her hand tightened on the brush. What would Romayne, who was so prosaic and so romantic at the same time, think of this muddle? Ellen wished Romayne were here to advise her.

"But how would I tell you?" she asked aloud.

"Tell me what?"

Ellen peered into the glass. She saw only her own reflection. Glancing over her shoulder, she discovered Corey sitting, cross-legged, on the windowsill. He grinned.

"You look surprised," he said as he jumped down. His boots made no sound on the floor. "Did you think I would fail to see how you were doing?"

She stared. If she did not know better, she would swear he was a living man. The warm bronze of his face suggested he had been spending hours along the strand or riding through the hills. While he walked toward her, the easy motion of his muscles spoke of the hard life he had known during his years with the army. He was as commanding as a phantom as he had been as a man.

"How is your shoulder?" he asked. "Much better, I hope."

Somehow she found her voice. "How can you be here?"

He raised his hands. "Never underestimate the wiles of a ghost, Edie."

"That nickname is growing tiresome."

"I would suggest you acclimate yourself to it. I like how it feels when I say it, and I like how it makes your eyes snap."

She put her hairbrush back onto the dressing table and stood. "You aren't answering my question. How can you be here? I thought a ghost was shackled to the place of his death."

"So that is why you hied out of Wolfe Abbey without saying good-bye. You wanted to rid yourself of me."

"Do you blame me?"

He grinned. "Not in the least. I shall be a most irritating apparition." He sat on the high bed and arched his brows as if daring her to scold him for being so bold. "You need not frown at me. I am not avoiding an answer to annoy you. I simply do not have an answer. I was wondering how you fared, and here I am. Mayhap I am shackled to you as lief Wolfe Abbey."

With a groan, she said, "I hope not!"

"Such a complimentary answer."

"Would you want someone else invading your life?"

"No."

Ellen was taken aback by his quiet answer. Gathering her scattered wits, she fired back, "Then you can see why I wish you to begone."

"How can I when I have a pledge to fulfill?"

She groaned and sat at the dressing table. "What did I do to deserve this?"

Rising, he dropped next to her on the bench. She noted he was careful to keep his coat from touching her. "Look," he said softly.

"At what?"

"At the glass."

She frowned at her reflection. Mayhap she was supposed to discern a clue to explain this madness. "I see only me."

"Only you?" He laughed lowly. "My dear Edie, look deeper. Look at what I see when I look into your enticing blue eyes. See the gentleness within."

"I am not gentle. I have a temper as fiery as the sun."

"That only proves how gentle you are, for you have not lost your temper in my presence, save for when you threw that book at me."

Ellen laughed. It was impossible to remain somber when Corey was determined to tease her. "That should serve as a warning to you."

"It did." He gave an exaggerated shiver, then stood. "So you have not answered me. How is your shoulder?"

Gingerly she touched the spot that remained tender. "It is better." When his face lengthened with despair, she leapt to her feet. "Corey, do not blame yourself. How were you to know?"

"I could have tested my touch on someone else . . . like Marian, for example. I have tested her patience for more years than she would wish to own."

"So I understand."

"What tales has she told you?"

Ellen shook her head. "There are some things you should not know, Corey."

"I know Marian continues with her plan to find you a husband."

"You do?"

He chuckled. "One of the advantages—one of the rare advantages—to being a ghost is that I can eavesdrop on conversations whenever I wish. She is in her chambers right this moment—"

"You are wrong. She is with Lord Herrold in the library."

"No, for Reggie—now there is a lifeless chap if ever there was one—is out in the rain with his dogs."

"Corey, I left them—" Barking from beyond her window

silenced her. When he gave her a superior smile, she said, "I thought they would linger longer in the library."

"Did you think Marian would let one of Reggie's dogs run tame through her house while she enjoyed a few kisses? I have long suspected her rugs are more important to her than her husband's desires."

"You are unbelievable!"

He laughed. "Just realistic. As Marian is, for she is writing invitations to an outing on the morrow. She and Reggie are inviting a collection of eligible lads for you to peruse."

"Tomorrow? Why, your funeral was only yesterday!"

"Life, as they say, continues on, even without Corey Wolfe."

"But Marian would not plan a gathering so close to the funeral."

"She wouldn't? Check for yourself." He motioned toward the door. It swung open.

Ellen looked from the door to him. "How did you do that?"

"I am not quite sure, but it is a handy power to have." He wiggled his fingers. "I wonder what other bits of magic I can conjure up."

"Please spare me an exhibition. This is unsettling enough."

"As unsettling as Marian's plans?"

"How could she? She is your friend."

"And she is extraordinarily practical. I am dead. You need a husband. She can do nothing about the former, but she feels she can do much about the latter." He rubbed his hands together. "This shall be most entertaining. Never have Marian and I combined our efforts toward one common goal. You might as well accustom yourself to the inevitable, Edie. Before the summer is over, you shall be betrothed."

Six

Marian tapped her chin as she looked at the list in front of her. So many details to consider for this gathering. Everything must be perfect. No need to send Lorenzo an invitation, for he would have to refuse. 'Twas a shame. After what she had witnessed upon their departure from Wolfe Abbey, it was possible Lorenzo might wish to be counted among those vying for Ellen's hand.

She smiled. That was what it must be. A contest which the finest suitor would win was certain to appeal to Ellen. How could any young woman turn away from a man who had bested all others to win her attention?

Lorenzo Wolfe would not be Marian's first choice for Ellen. Not even her second or third. Although he possessed that respected title and clearly viewed Ellen with fondness, the Wolfe Abbey lands now belonged to Corey's sister, Vanessa. Marian had heard enough hints of Ellen's past to guess it had been one without many luxuries. If Ellen had not been brought to London and sponsored by the Duke of Westhampton's granddaughter, she might still be living in that dank country to the north. Marian was determined Ellen would have every comfort she wished, for she could imagine wanting nothing less for her bosom-bow.

But which man would be the best choice for Ellen? She had turned down the proposal of a viscount and dismissed an earl's flirting as tiresome. She had been infatuated—at least temporarily—with a man who disdained playing cards and then another who seldom left the board of green cloth. One gentleman who had called was so handsome he could have graced a statue, and another had been as obese as Prinny himself. She had treated each with kindness. Over and over, Ellen had been teased by love, but every time she had ended up unbetrothed.

Marian frowned and tapped her chin. With the end of each flirtation, Ellen's comment had been nearly the same. She wanted a man who was undeniably honest with her, a man she could be honest with in return. No pretense, no court-promises, nothing but honesty. And a man who stirred her heart, bringing to life the aura of romance lying quiescent within her. A man who would not fill her with *ennui* before a fortnight passed.

Did such a man exist for her? Marian dared not cede herself to despair at the thought that no living man could live up to such impossible standards.

When the door opened, she turned on her chair. She nodded to the maid who was bringing in fresh soaps, then turned back to her task. Mayhap she should send for Ellen. The bride-to-be should take part in the choices for the prospective groom.

Marian whirled at a shriek and a crash. The maid was staring at the bed while the soaps were broken in pieces on the gold rug.

"Why are you making all that noise?" Marian demanded.

"My lady," the girl said with a half-curtsy, "forgive me. I thought I saw . . ."

She waited for the girl to continue, then asked, "What?"

"I am not sure. Something moved over here."

Marian set herself on her feet and crossed the room. "What did you think you saw?"

Her quivering finger pointed at the table. "I would swear, madam, that bottle moved from one side to the other."

"Nonsense!"

"But I saw—"

"You saw nothing. Now clean up this mess, and continue your chores. I shall have no foolishness in this house."

Corey hastily stepped aside as Marian went back to her writing table. Although she could not see him and probably could have walked right through him, that was not a sensation he anticipated with pleasure. How many times had he chided her for walking over people? She was a determined woman, and woe be to the man—be he alive or dead—who got in her way.

He went to the writing table and peered over her shoulder. When she shivered, he took a half-step back. Blast this aura of deathly cold surrounding him! How was he to fulfill his pledge if he distressed anyone he came close to?

He never had suspected he and Marian would ever work toward the same end. As he read the notes Marian had made, he guessed he would have to do little, save watch. She had listed all the eligible bachelors of gentle birth in the shire. The stack of notes at one side of the desk showed he had not been mistaken when he guessed Marian was not going to be deterred from her quest for a husband for Ellen by something as inconvenient as her husband's kisses.

He sat on the chair by her bed and shook his head. "I thought you would mourn me a while longer than you shall the chicken for tonight's dinner, Marian."

She looked up at a knock on the door. Corey stood and edged into the shadows as the door opened. Just now, he did not want Edie to see him spying on her hostess. He had guessed Edie would waste no time coming to confirm his assertion.

"Do come in," Marian said with a smile as she stood. "I thought you were resting, Ellen."

"My mind is filled with so many things that rest is impossible."

"Oh, my poor dear." She put her hand on Edie's arm and steered her to the padded bench by the window. "I wish we had not gone to Wolfe Abbey for the fireworks. Then you would not be suffering so."

"But you wished me to meet Lord Wulfric."

Marian sighed. "He might have been a suitable suitor for you."

Corey frowned. *Might have been suitable?* Marian's demure hits had been amusing when he was alive and could counter them with his own, but he had thought she had a sisterly affection for him. It was unsettling to discover how little she thought of him now that he was dead.

"I am sure Lord Wulfric would have been suitable," Edie said.

Now that was more like it. His grin returned.

"However," she continued, "it is senseless to talk about this when . . ."

"Yes, the dear lad is gone."

"So it would seem."

Corey tried to swallow his chuckle, but it burst from him.

Ellen whirled, straining to see into every corner of the room.

"What is it?" asked Marian with sudden alarm. "Is something wrong?"

"I thought I heard—"

"Not you, too!"

Ellen frowned. "What do you mean? Have you seen—I mean, have you heard—?"

Marian interrupted sharply, "*I* have seen and heard nothing. That empty-headed maid who was in here earlier was going on and on about a bottle being moved on the table. Now you are prattling about sounds in the shadows."

Ellen looked around the room again, even though she would not see Corey if he did not wish to be seen. This was beneath reproach. If he was going to hover, being bothersome to an extreme, he should have the common courtesy of being visible whenever he was about.

"Forgive me, Marian," she said quietly. " 'Tis as I told you. I am too much distressed. Even the breath of the wind against the panes makes me uneasy."

"I have just the antidote for your low spirits."

"The most vile spirits may be exactly what I have." She frowned in the direction the sound had come from—a muffled laugh, if she were not mistaken.

"Then I suggest an outing with some of my dearest friends."

"Is it not too soon after Lord Wulfric's death for such a gathering?"

"He would have been invited." Marian's pink wrapper swept

out behind her like a train as she said, "I had concocted the idea
for this gathering before his unfortunate demise. 'Tis a shame.
Corey would have enjoyed what I have planned for the morrow,
if the sun does us a favor and shines warmly. 'Twill be nothing
formal, simply a gathering of old friends—and new—by the
shore."

Ellen smiled. She hoped Corey *was* in the room. It would
serve him right to hear Marian's practical suggestions. A motion
in a shadowed corner caught her eye. Corey? Mayhap, but she
could not be certain.

Her smile widened as she said, "An outing sounds wonderful,
Marian. I would be delighted to meet your friends."

The day was made to order for a sojourn to the beach. Sunshine bleached the sky to the palest blue, and the sea brushed
the shore as gently as a mother caressing her babe. Overhead,
birds circled, their songs blending with the sound of the waves.

Ellen was glad a gentle path led to the sand, for she would
not have been willing to risk clambering up and down the cliffs.
Her white cambric gown was edged with flounces matching the
lace dripping from her parasol. The pebbles in the path pricked
through her thin slippers, and she wished she had dared to wear
her boots. Marian would have been put to the blush by such an
ensemble, for she had insisted Ellen wear her best while meeting
several of the eligibles in the shire.

Solely to herself could Ellen own that she had hoped for rain
today. The whole of her life was a shocking mull with both
Marian and Corey anxious to find her a match. At the very
least, she should be grateful Corey had not joined the caravan
leaving for the beach.

She looked back when she heard a frightened screech. Dear
Marian! Only her determination to find Ellen a match would
have convinced her to come to the beach. Marian had disclosed
on the way to the path that this was the one where she had taken

a header, and since then, she had avoided the cliffs whenever possible.

"Then why are we having an outing on the beach?" Ellen had asked.

"Because 'tis such a perfect site for a gathering of friends."

Unable to argue with Marian's answer, although she questioned her friend's logic, Ellen had asked nothing else. Instead, she had adjusted the light gray ribbons on her tall straw bonnet. She did not want it flying off in the sea breeze.

Dirt sifted into Ellen's slippers as she stepped onto the pebbled beach. In the curve of the cove, she could see a sandy stretch. A troop of servants were setting out blankets and baskets on the sand. Ellen sighed. It would be much more sensible to sit here where the stones would keep away the sand, but Marian wanted a gathering by the sea, and she would have exactly that.

"Do you need some help across this uneven ground?" asked a warm, tenor voice behind Ellen.

She smiled at the towheaded man. His tall hat would not protect him from the sun as her bonnet and parasol did, and already his ears were becoming red. "That is kind of you to offer, sir."

He took her hand and bowed over it. The sun glittered off the gold buttons and watch chain on his waistcoat as he straightened. "Your servant Josiah Adams, Miss Dunbar."

"You're American!"

He smiled as he offered his arm. When she put her hand on his navy wool sleeve, he said, "Not by birth, although my father's work took us to the United States shortly after I was born. I had thought I had rid myself in the past six months of the frightful accent I learned in Philadelphia."

"Only a hint remains." She smiled as he led her around a tidal pool. "Mayhap my ear is more attuned than others, for my own accent announces my birthland as clearly as if it were printed on my forehead."

"Now that is a grim thought. To think of your lovely face marred by such a mark."

Once Ellen would have been taken aback by the compliment,

but during three Seasons in Town, she had learned the art of words that meant nothing. She simply smiled as they reached the blankets and the servant who held a tray with cooled wine.

Mr. Adams handed her a glass before selecting one for himself. "This was an excellent idea, Miss Dunbar. Yours?"

"Marian should receive all the credit for this." Turning, she watched as the litter chair brought Marian across the beach.

It stopped near the blankets, and Marian pushed aside the brocade curtains to peer out. Ellen put her hand out to her friend, whose face was a rather bilious shade of gray. Marian grasped it with her trembling fingers.

"Mayhap this was not the best idea I have ever had," Marian whispered as she eased out of the chair.

Ellen tried not to smile as she assisted Marian out onto the sand. She had sympathy for her friend's queasy expression, but without question, Marian had brought this upon herself. They could have had their outing many other places. They need not have come down these cliffs which clearly distressed Marian beyond words. Yet, Marian had insisted they come here. Mayhap she was trying to overcome the fears that haunted her. If only it were that easy to get rid of a haunting . . .

"Dear Marian, you must sit immediately. The fresh air off the sea and the sun's warmth will surely ease your discomfort at having to come down that steep path. You do like the sea when you are on its level."

"Yes."

"Good. We shall enjoy ourselves here, then find another way we can go to get back to Herrold Hall."

"There is none, so I shall have no choice but to climb that path once more," Marian whispered. She glanced toward the cliffs and placed the back of her hand to her forehead. "Dear me, they look even more precipitous from this angle."

"Mayhap you should sit," Ellen suggested again, although Marian's emoting was raising her suspicions that her friend might not be as distressed as she must want everyone to think. What was Marian about now? Mayhap she was judging her friend unfairly. Marian's face was a peculiar shade of gray. "Is there anything that will help soothe your battered nerves?"

"Wine," Marian ordered.

Ellen pressed her glass into her friend's trembling hand. Marian swayed. Three women and two gentlemen reached out to catch her if she swooned. Ellen took Marian's elbow and guided her to the blanket.

"This is want-witted," Ellen whispered. "You are ill. We must return to Herrold Hall posthaste."

"Give me some time to fortify myself before I go up those blasted cliffs again." Marian winked at Ellen before raising her voice, "You are such a dear friend, always thinking of someone else before yourself. Isn't she a dear?"

As a wave of assent washed through the gathering, Ellen stood. How perfectly Marian gauged the feelings of those around her! She continued to gush about Ellen while their meal was served by the silent servant. Wishing she could find a way to tell Marian to stop without drawing everyone's attention, Ellen picked at her food.

"So you are Marian's latest *protégé*," Mr. Adams said with a chuckle as he sat next to her.

"I would use a different term."

He laughed again, and she knew her answer had been too dreary.

With a smile, she said, "Marian is a dear soul."

"But she will never be happy until you are settled in married bliss."

Ellen set her plate on the blanket and folded her hands in her lap. "Has she been that obvious?"

"I have seen her like before. The British *ton* does not have a monopoly on friends who wish to see other friends enjoying marriage as they do."

Ellen was glad that someone called a question to Mr. Adams. To let her face reveal her true feelings about Marian's marriage would mark her as an ungrateful wretch. Still, the truth was that what Marian considered a happy marriage was exactly what

Ellen wished to avoid. She yearned for a match that was not just advantageous for the families involved, but would be a melding of two hearts and souls into one.

"So what do you think of Mr. Adams?" Marian whispered when the man rose to assist one of his friends in choosing the next bottle of wine.

"I have not had time to think of him," Ellen returned, swallowing her irritation along with a piece of cheese, "for I have spent most of my time talking with him."

"His family is well placed in cloth manufacturing." A hint of excitement entered her voice. "I have heard he was recalled to England to be granted a title by the Regent. All in all, he would be a fine husband."

Shaking her head, Ellen said, "I have not known him more than an hour. I trust it takes longer than that to know if one wishes to marry."

"I knew from the moment I met Reginald."

Not wanting to reply with the obvious that the marriage had been arranged when Marian and Lord Herrold were no more than children, Ellen picked another piece of the pungent cheese off her plate. She did hope Marian would be less candid in her comments to the gentlemen of the gathering.

Mr. Adams returned, smiling. "I would enjoy a stroll along the strand, especially if you would accompany me, Miss Dunbar."

Marian jabbed Ellen in the ribs with an eager elbow. Resisting the urge to decline just to vex her friend who was being undeniably vexing, Ellen put her hand in Mr. Adams's and allowed him to bring her to her feet. She withdrew her hand as they walked away from the others. When he did not press for her to hold on to his arm, she was pleased.

"You looked as if you were in need of respite from Marian's matchmaking," he said.

"As I said, she is a dear friend."

Looking up at the squawking birds wheeling overhead, he chuckled. "And you have more patience than I would have."

"You are very plain-speaking, Mr. Adams."

"An American habit I have grown fond of." He bent and picked up something from the sand. He handed her a perfectly formed shell. "This type of shell is seldom found on these beaches, Miss Dunbar. The waves offer little compassion for anything caught in their strength."

"I shall take that as a warning." She turned the shell over in her hands and admired its pale shades blending together in a lovely pattern.

"Have you ever been a-sea?"

She shook her head. "My nautical adventures have been only upon a pond or a burn along a Scottish brae."

"Mayhap you would enjoy a ride on the waves one day."

"That would be exciting." Gazing at the waves, she smiled. "Although I must own I might change my mind when the last hints of land vanish beneath the horizon."

He tapped the shell. "Hold it to your ear."

"Why?"

"Just do so."

Her eyes widened as she heard the hushed whisper that matched the whisper of the waves when she had stood in Corey's rooms in Wolfe Abbey. Hastily she lowered the shell. Why did he plague her thoughts even when he was not about to tease her?

"Very interesting," she said when she realized Mr. Adams expected a reaction. "I have never heard its like."

"Sounds like the sea, doesn't it?"

"As if the shell had gathered the song during its time out in the water and wanted to share it with us."

"How insightful of you, Miss Dunbar! You have a gift for poetry."

"Only for prattle, I fear." She put her hand on the arm he offered her and settled her parasol over her still tender shoulder. "It is the curse of the Scots—although others have called it a blessing—to be able to talk endlessly about things of the most insignificance."

He laughed as they walked into the curve of the cove. Rocks had been piled by the ocean like a child's forgotten toys. The waves slapped against them as if urging them to fall back into the sea. Gulls gathered upon them, surveying their domain with all the regal disdain of a potentate.

"Would you like to sit and watch the waves?" Mr. Adams asked.

The rocks were covered with plants and debris washed up by the tides. "Mayhap some other time when I am dressed more appropriately."

"That is a lovely gown."

"Thank you."

"I can understand why you would not wish to ruin it." He shrugged off his coat and spread it across the closest boulder. "Allow me to play Sir Walter Raleigh to you."

"Your coat! It will never come clean."

"Think nothing of it."

"I—" She gulped the rest of her words as she stared across the beach.

In the shadows of the cliff, where his steps would not disturb the sand, Corey strode toward them. He had his coat off, slung over his shoulder, as if he had just come in from a long ride. The sunshine glinted off his ebony hair, casting a bluish tint to the glow around him. As he came closer, his smile was as bright.

Her heart thumped with happiness . . . and dread. Each time Corey had appeared when someone else was with her, he complicated the occasion with his comments and his gaze which suggested he could guess what she was thinking. Worst of all, he took no pains to hide what *he* thought.

And his thoughts lured her to fall prey to the fantasies of what could never be. She found herself staring at his lips and thinking of them on hers, of his arms around her as he held her against his firm chest, of his fingers combing through her hair, leaving quivers of yearning in their wake.

Her hands clenched at her sides. Just once, if she could give life to that fantasy just once . . .

"Pardon me," Mr. Adams said.

Ellen hastily looked back at him. She smiled, hoping the expression looked more sincere than it felt. "I am sorry. I was caught up in the beauty of the sea."

"As it should be caught up in your beauty." He gave her no time to answer as he motioned toward his coat. "Do me the favor of sitting and talking with me. As my coat is now ruined beyond repair, it would seem a waste not to use it."

Although she wanted to flee at top speed along the sand, she smiled and sat on the coat. Mr. Adams perched on the rock beside her. Why had she failed to take note this boulder had room enough for two? He had maneuvered her with rare skill into this position. She kept her hands folded in her lap, vowing to take the first opportunity to rise and continue the tour of the beach.

When Corey climbed onto a rock to her right, Ellen fired him a scowl. He cocked his head at her, looking as much like a naughty boy as any man wearing a black eye patch could. With his elbow on his knee, he smiled a challenge she must not accept. To speak of a ghost following her would persuade Mr. Adams to believe she was deranged.

She gasped when Mr. Adams lifted her hand off her lap and clasped it between his. Mayhap he was mad if he thought she would allow such forwardness when they had just met.

Corey chuckled. "This should be good."

She resisted glancing at him. As lief, she said, "Mr. Adams, if I gave you any idea I would welcome such familiarity, I apologize."

"Your manners have been without blemish." Mr. Adams's smile widened his cheeks. " 'Tis I, for I cannot resist the delight of being so close to you, who should apologize."

"Here it comes," Corey said. Putting his mouth close to Ellen's ear, although nobody but she could hear his whisper, he went on, "Miss Dunbar, you are an extraordinary woman."

As if he were taking his cue from Corey, Mr. Adams said, "Miss Dunbar, you are an extraordinary woman."

Corey murmured, "And I can tell you possess a rare intelligence."

"And I can tell you possess a rare intelligence," Mr. Adams continued.

Ellen glanced from him to Corey. How was he doing this? If he could read minds . . . She shuddered. That was too appalling to consider. "You are too kind, Mr. Adams."

"How can I be otherwise to such a lovely lady?" Corey asked, grinning.

"How can I be otherwise to such a lovely lady?" Mr. Adams echoed.

"I think we should join the others," Ellen said sharply.

"Why?"

"Marian was still unsteady when we left them. I am worried about her."

Corey said, "Best idea I have heard all day."

Sliding down off the rock, Ellen looked back and saw no sign of Corey. Regret pricked her. Even though he exasperated her beyond common decency, she appreciated Corey's company while she spoke with the too amorous Mr. Adams.

She picked up his coat and dropped it into his arms. She set her parasol on her shoulder and asked, "Shall we go?"

Mr. Adams put his hands on her shoulders and turned her to face him. When she gasped at his brazen motion, he pulled her closer.

"Mr. Adams, what are you doing?"

He chuckled. "Are you so innocent that you do not know?"

"I know," she said, twisting away, "what the canons of propriety are."

His arm swept around her waist as he tugged her back to him. Tipping back the wide brim of her bonnet, he cupped her chin. She gasped when he drew her mouth toward his.

Shaking her head, she cried, "Let me go!"

"Hush, my dear. We have talked too much. 'Tis time to use our lips for other pursuits."

She shoved against his chest with both hands. He rocked back a pair of steps. Her eyes widened as a log slid across the sand behind him. He tripped over it and sprawled on the ground. Trying to rise, he dropped heavily, face-first, into the sand.

Ellen stared in disbelief as Corey appeared, shaking his hand. He looked down at the man on the beach and smiled before turning to Ellen. "Thanks, Edie, for the opportunity I have been waiting for since he came back to England."

"You hit him?" she whispered.

"Didn't he deserve it?"

Instead of answering Corey, she bent over the man on the sand. "Mr. Adams! Are you hurt?"

He mumbled something, then spit out a mouthful of sand. "Damn gritty. Forgive me my language, Miss Dunbar."

"No need for you to apologize about your language." She scowled at Corey, who folded his arms over his chest and grinned. She stared at the scarlet mark on Mr. Adams's cheek. It matched the fiery mark on her shoulder when Corey had touched her.

"I believe I am fine." Mr. Adams took her hand and slowly stood, drawing her to her feet. Folding her hands between his, he pressed them to his chest and smiled weakly. "My dear Miss Dunbar, your concern for my well-being is the very best medicine I can envision."

She pulled her hands out of his. "If you are fine, then I see no need to continue this conversation."

He caught her by the shoulders again. "You must allow me to apologize."

Corey stepped toward him. Flexing his fingers, he smiled. "Say the word, Edie, and I shall gladly give him another facer. The cad has been in need of lessons in manners for longer than you can imagine."

She bit her lip. Mr. Adams would not be able to see or hear Corey. She was certain of that. Yet she could not keep from tensing. This was all so incredibly absurd. Whoever had heard of an invisible chaperon?

"Your apology is accepted, Mr. Adams," she said in her coldest voice. "Mayhap the ways that are customary in America are different from ours in Britain." She eased out of his grip. "Good day, sir."

"Miss Dunbar, it would be tragic to let our friendship come to such an end."

"I suspect friendship is not what you have in mind."

Again he put his hand on her arm. "You are intuitive, but why do you run away when I only wish to show you how much I admire you?"

"Sir, I have asked you to desist already." From the corner of her eye, Ellen saw Corey edge toward Mr. Adams.

She shrieked when Mr. Adams brought her into his arms. The sound vanished beneath her hand striking his cheek. He released her and scowled.

"Damn, Edie," grumbled Corey as he came to stand beside her. "I wanted to do that."

She ignored him as Mr. Adams said, "If you think this game is amusing, I can tell you that I tire of it."

"As I do." She settled her bonnet back on her hair. "I bid you good day *again,* sir."

"Don't understand it," Mr. Adams mumbled under his breath as he turned to walk away. "Heard she was desperate for a husband. No wonder."

Ellen gasped in horror. What gabble-monger had started that rumor? Marian? She could not accuse her bosom-bow of that. It was too awful.

Mr. Adams took two steps and sprawled across the sand again.

Ellen turned her back on him before he could see her smile. When Corey appeared on the rock in front of her, she asked, "How can you move from one place to another with such speed?"

" 'Tis mostly an illusion." He gave her a wry grin. "I learned quickly during my time in France that speed is as much an asset to a galoot as a good gun and an accurate eye."

Mr. Adams jumped to his feet, brushed sand off his clothes, and lurched away at the best speed he could manage. Ellen laughed. She could not help it. The man looked like a frightened snake slithering away into its hole.

"Much better," Corey said.

"I should not laugh at someone else's misfortune."

"His only misfortune was to be on the wrong side of the hedge when brains were given away." He brushed sand from the lace on her parasol. The lace became as rigid as the handle of her parasol, but she ignored it as Corey continued, "You would have bamblusterated him in the wink of an eye if you were not so blasted sympathetic to blind buzzards."

Tipping back her parasol, she looked at Corey. "Do I owe you a thank you?"

"No, but, Edie, you do need someone to keep track of you." He laughed.

"I would have handled him by myself."

"He seemed to be the one doing the handling."

"You are impossible!"

He shrugged on his coat. "And you are too lovely. I shall have to keep a better eye on you. Do you know how many times I have heard Josiah Adams spin those court-promises to any miss who would listen?"

"Obviously a few."

"Obviously quite a few, especially when you realize he has not been back in England for long."

"Be that as it may, I did not ask you to intrude into my life. I would thank you to keep your nose—and your comments—out of my personal affairs."

"And break my vow?"

She sighed. She had no idea how one rid one's life of a ghost who was determined to play matchmaker . . . especially when the vow she wished for him to fulfill was the passion his gaze promised.

Seven

Ellen lowered her book as the familiar sound of a lilting whistle filled her bedchamber. Glancing around the room, she smiled and plumped her pillows behind her. There was no need to concern herself about sleeping now.

"Very well," she said. "I give up. Where are you, Corey?"

His chuckle seemed to float about the room. It was everywhere at once. Not for the first time, she wondered where he was when he was not visible. So many questions filled her head, but he never gave her a chance to ask a single one.

A glint by the window caught her eye. Was it just moonlight? She shifted on the bed. When a twinge raced up her arm, she winced.

Corey immediately appeared by the chair. "Does your arm still hurt?"

"Not as badly as Mr. Adams hurts after your antics," she replied. She rubbed her arm gently as she added, "And mine."

He smiled. "I thought you were fond of him when you walked away from the others with him, but I hear scanty sympathy in your voice."

"What gave you that idea?"

"You were so solicitous of him, even after he tried to kiss you."

Ellen relaxed into the pillows. "Of course I was. How could I *not* have pity for the poor man when you were plaguing him incessantly?"

"No more than he deserved."

"Deserved? Even if he has the manners of a boor, you were a bit unrelenting on him. There was no need to trip him."

"Come now." He sat on the foot of the bed. "Do you wish me to believe you found his company refreshing?"

"I had not heard his nothing-sayings before."

He laughed. "Save when I spoke them first."

"Yet you guessed I would find a *tendre* in my heart for him? Did you think he would make the perfect husband for me? I thought you knew me better than that."

"Did you?"

"I thought we had become friends."

"Really?"

Ellen was about to retort in the same light tone, then saw his smile had vanished. As before, she was amazed by the drastic change in his visage. A fervor burned in his gaze, and the stern planes of his face hinted at his uncompromising determination to do what he believed was right, no matter what others might think. Abruptly she could see the determined man who had turned his back on his family and gone to serve his country on the far side of the Channel.

"Corey," she said quietly, "although I never imagined anything like this could happen, I am becoming accustomed to the peculiarity of our friendship. I can think of no reason why we should not continue to be friends."

"Under the circumstances, I would say friendship may be the limit of what we can enjoy."

She looked away, but not before she again saw the truth she fought to ignore. The attraction they had relished the night of the fireworks had not died along with him. If he were alive, he would not be satisfied with only friendship.

Nor would she.

Slowly she raised her eyes to meet his gaze. No longer did it seem odd to see the dark patch covering one eye. The incandescence around him had become a part of him. Rising to her knees, she put out her hand.

"Edie, be careful," he whispered. "I do not wish to see you hurt again."

She dropped to sit heavily on the mattress. "This is unsettling to have you separated from me by this cold fire."

"A small price to pay when you can enjoy my company." He gave her one of those irrepressible grins that demanded she smile back. "And I can enjoy a delightful intimacy you would not offer me otherwise."

When his gaze dropped, Ellen tugged the front of her wrapper closed. She adopted a tone of icy hauteur to say, "You are no gentleman, my lord, to take note of my *déshabillé*."

"Even a ghost cannot overlook such a pleasing sight." He tapped his chin as he frowned as severely as a schoolmaster. "I would suggest fewer buttons on that nightdress, however, on the first night you spend with your husband. The man could die of old age before undoing them all."

"Corey!"

"Edie!" he retorted in the same shocked tone. "Do not play the shrinking maiden with me. I have overheard enough conversations among the misses to know they are as curious about their wedding nights as the lads they wed."

"Eavesdropping is—"

"Deplorable. Is that the word you used last time?" He arched his brows. "I have to own it is much easier now, such as when I listened to your explanation to Marian of what happened to Josiah Adams. I am in awe of your Scottish gift for falsehoods."

Ellen stared at him, unable to speak. Finding her voice, she cried, "Jings—"

"Jings? A new name for me?"

She would not let him tease her out of her exasperation. " 'Tis nothing but a Scottish saying for those times when you know that words are useless."

"What words are useless?"

"The ones I speak over and over about you and me and this peculiar circumstance we find ourselves in. If you are going to haunt me, Corey Wolfe, I think it is time for some rules."

"I think not." Standing, he walked around the foot of the bed. "Why should I have to obey your rules when I am trying to help you?"

"I have no interest in your help."

" 'Tis unfortunate for you, because, after what I saw this afternoon, you need it." He gripped the upright on the bed and smiled. "How did you rid yourself of your other suitors, Edie? Did you kiss each of them before sending them on their way?"

With an oath, she fired a pillow at him. He laughed as it sailed through him, then bent to retrieve it. He threw it at her. She gasped when it struck her.

"That is not fair!" she gasped.

"All is fair in love and war, Edie." His smile faded as he sat again on the bed. "Trust me. That I know firsthand."

"Then tell me about the war."

Shock was emblazoned on his face. "Why do you want to hear of that?"

She laughed. "Now you can see how it feels when someone else meddles in your life."

"That part of my life was over before we met, Edie."

"It *haunts* you."

"True."

She was amazed when he did not fire back a teasing answer. This was the first thing he had not found humor in. She put her hand out to his, but he drew back.

"No, Edie, I warned you already. Don't risk hurting yourself."

"It hurt me when you touched me. If I touch you . . ."

His lips straightened into a taut line. "Do not tempt me with the fantasies that already fill my head. I think of your touch far too often."

"I am sorry."

"I'm not." His bright grin returned. " 'Tis one of the few pleasures left to a ghost. I can speak my thoughts of how I would like to hold you, and you cannot slap my face for my bold comments as you did to Adams."

"He deserved it."

"Without question. And so would I, if you could be privy to my thoughts now."

"I shall not allow you to change the subject." She drew her knees up to her chest and wrapped her arms around them, not wanting him to guess how much she wanted to turn the course of the conversation before he discovered how his words unsettled her. If his thoughts matched hers, it would be wiser to speak of something else . . . anything else. "Tell me about the war, Corey. From what little I have heard whispered about here and at Wolfe Abbey, it is rumored that you were captured. Is that true?"

"Yes."

"And you were a hero?"

"A reluctant one. If I had had half the sense God gave a goose, I would have been able to get my men out of that ambush and myself as well."

As never before, she longed to put her hand on his to ease the pain on his face. "It must have been horrible."

"Horrible? Yes, but I never once wished I was dead. Mayhap that is why I survived then." He went to stand before the glass. "Mayhap that is why I still cannot surrender to the inevitable. Then I should have died, but I did not. Every morn, I woke with the determination that I would not give in to my captors. Every night, I went to sleep repeating that vow."

"And you survived."

"With luck."

"And returned to England."

"With the help of those who believed I was not dead." He chuckled. "Unlike most men, my dear cousin Lorenzo was delighted when he received the tidings of my resurrection. He wants the title no more than I do, although his reasons are different from mine."

"What are they?"

"Mine? They are simple. I would prefer to spend my time in London sitting in the Commons and debating the great problems of these days instead of being surrounded by the stuffiness of the Lords."

"And Lord Wulfric's?"

"I—oh, you mean Lorenzo." He laughed ironically. "Odd that I thought often of ridding myself of that title, but yet it clings to me. This all is something I still must adjust to. As for Lorenzo, he wishes to bury himself in his quiet life of reading and writing letters to his comrades around the island. Making decisions and overseeing the lands belonging to the Abbey interfere with that."

"Then I am sorry for both of you."

"Don't be." He grinned. "At least, don't be sorry for me. My life has taken an enchanting turn."

"That is unquestionably true."

"And I have a goal."

She sat straighter. "Corey, after what happened today, you must own that you need to rethink that jobbernowl idea. I shall find my own husband on my own."

"Of course."

"When I wish."

"Of course."

"So you have changed your mind about that absurd vow then?"

He shook his head. "A Wolfe's vow lasts a lifetime."

She raised a single brow.

With another laugh, he said, "Point well taken. Let me rephrase that. A Wolfe's vow lasts forever."

"That is ludicrous."

"I agree."

"Do you?" Ellen leaned forward, folding her arms on her knees.

"But it is a vow I have made, and I shall not break it."

"Even if I ask you to?"

"Even if you ask me to."

Yawning as she gazed across the rose garden of Herrold Hall, Ellen stood and stretched, being careful of her arm, which still ached on each thoughtless motion. Although almost a week had passed since the accident, every thought drew her back to that moment, for every thought was filled with Corey. He was the most bothersome man she had ever met—and she had no escape from his whetted wit and knowing smile.

Nor did she wish one.

She tensed at that thought and was rewarded by another twinge along her arm. Blast Corey Wolfe! Even when he was not with her, he complicated her life. Yet she could not fault him when *she* constantly delighted in thinking of him and the few moments they had stood together by the seawall. Then she had thrilled at the first uncertain steps in a courtship. Now he was becoming as familiar as her favorite wrapper, but he was growing no less enticing and intriguing.

She never had met a man quite like him, and she guessed she never would. She *hoped* she never would, because she had no need for another ghost to be keeping her awake half the night with invigorating conversation.

With another yawn, she closed the book she had been trying with little success to read. Marian would be looking for her by this hour. Her friend could not understand Ellen's need for a few moments of quiet time alone. Thank goodness Corey seemed to sense that Ellen needed this respite from the insanity surrounding her.

"Miss Dunbar!"

Ellen glanced to her left and saw Sullivan rushing toward her with unexpected speed. "What is wrong?"

The abigail slowed and shook her head. "Nothing wrong, Miss Dunbar. Lady Herrold sent me to tell you there is a caller for you."

"A caller? Who?"

"She did not say."

Ellen sighed. Marian was dauntless in her determination to find Ellen a husband. The fiasco at the strand had not lessened her resolve. In fact, it seemed to have strengthened it.

Not wanting to keep the caller—and Marian—waiting, Ellen

hurried to the parlor where Marian received her guests. She faltered as she was reaching to open the door. An unmistakable glow took shape to her right.

Glancing in both directions along the corridor, she saw no one else. Even so, she dared not lift her voice above a whisper. "Corey! Why are you here? Who is in there with Marian?"

"Major Jerome Poindexter. Major Poindexter, retired, if there is any fairness in this world."

"Who—?"

"My one time commander." Distaste dripped from every word. "The very epitome of a carpet knight, if you wish the truth."

The door opened before Ellen could reply. Marian smiled and ushered her into the room. Although she wanted to look back to see if Corey was following, she knew it was unnecessary. He could not be shut out of any room.

A squat man peered at Ellen through a gold-rimmed quizzing glass. His hair was streaked with gray, and she guessed him old enough to be her grandfather. Pinched features did not match his round belly. She was certain his thin lips rarely turned up in a smile.

"Miss Ellen Dunbar," Marian said with all the pomp she enjoyed, "this is Major Jerome Poindexter."

"Retired?" prompted Corey.

"Retired," Major Poindexter said as he took Ellen's hand in his pudgy fingers and bowed over it. "My pleasure, Miss Dunbar."

Marian smiled as she motioned for them to sit. "Major Poindexter called at Wolfe Abbey to give Corey a look-in. He is understandably upset by the events that he had not heard of before this afternoon."

"Do not be so sure," Corey warned. He went to stand behind Major Poindexter, who was picking up the glass of wine on the table by his chair and taking a generous drink. "Jerome never bestirs himself without reason."

"Miss Dunbar," the major said, "I understand you were with Lord Wulfric at his final moments."

"Lord Wulfric?" Corey mumbled something else under his breath before adding, "Now that I am put to bed with a shovel, you have forgotten how it made your nose swell that my title was more prestigious than yours, Sir Jerome."

"Yes," Ellen said, trying to listen to both conversations at the same time. She was becoming no more adept at this than she had been when Corey first appeared in her room at Wolfe Abbey.

"Did he mention anything of me or the unit?"

"A narcissist to the end?" Corey folded his arms on the back of the major's chair.

When Major Poindexter shifted and frowned, Ellen guessed he was sensing the chill that surrounded Corey. She said quietly, "No, he was bereft of his senses."

"That is a shame."

"Yes," she said, although she was uncertain what the major specifically meant.

"Has this so-called accident been investigated?" he fired back.

Marian gasped, "Major, are you suggesting it wasn't an accident?"

"An officer gains many enemies when he has to give orders that can send men to their deaths."

Corey's laugh startled Ellen. When she flinched, Marian put her hand on Ellen's arm.

"I am fine," Ellen whispered. She looked past the frowning major to Corey's grin. A dozen questions filled her head, but she could not ask a single one.

He soothed her curiosity when he said, "Do not judge others by your own standards, Jerome. I did not send my men off to die without going with them. Tell him, Edie, the constable checked the rest of the fireworks and deemed it nothing but an unfortunate accident."

"He did?" She put her fingers to her lips when Marian and the major regarded her with astonishment. Corey chuckled, but she said over the sound the others could not hear, "You may rest assured, Major Poindexter, that a complete investigation was done by the local authorities. It was nothing but an accident."

Marian's eyes were wide. "Who told you that, Ellen?"

"Someone," she answered before turning back to the major. "You can be satisfied nobody wished Corey Wolfe harm that night."

"Save you, Jerome," Corey muttered. "Are you happy now? A quirk of fate succeeded where you did not in getting rid of me."

Ellen choked back her gasp. She waved aside Marian's concern, then rose. "Forgive me," she whispered, "but please excuse me. Thinking of the accident again is more unnerving than I had guessed."

Rushing out of the room, she paused and looked up the stairs. To return to her room meant another conversation with Corey. Just now, she wanted to put as much distance between her and every aspect of this shocking mull as she could. She hurried down the stairs and out to the stable. She did not have her riding habit, but she wanted to race across the hills and try to escape from her thoughts . . . even though she knew it would be impossible.

Searing pain swept up Ellen's arm. She moaned. Why did no one come to ease this agony? She could hear voices. Anxious voices, shouts that ached within her skull, whispers of dismay.

"Send for a doctor!" she cried.

Or did she? She heard only another moan. From her or from another?

Lord Wulfric!

Lord Wulfric or Corey? Her mind seemed lost in time. She could not guess where she was or when. No matter what she called the man who had been the Marquess of Wulfric, he had been with her when the fireworks exploded. He had pushed her aside, protecting her with his own body.

"Ellen! Ellen, can you hear me?"

The disembodied voice struck her like a blow. Marian! She could recognize that demanding tone even in the depth of this horror.

Why did she hurt so badly? Was she dying? Was she dying . . . too?

"Corey!" She willed the last of her strength into that single word.

"Open your eyes," came back the soft command. Corey's voice!

Darkness stabbed her eyes as she obeyed. Gray specters drifted around her. She recoiled. Their faces were nearly as familiar as her own. Lorenzo Wolfe, Marian, Mr. Bridges, Fenton . . . all of them wafted toward her.

"No!" she gasped.

Strong arms turned her against a firm chest. She gripped the front of a satiny waistcoat and sobbed. Fingers stroked her tangled hair with the tenderness of a father. Or of a lover.

She tilted back her head to look up at the sorrow on Corey's face. His palm cupped her chin, his fingers splaying across her face as he brought her mouth toward his. The beguiling warmth of his touch surged through her, freeing her from the bonds of anguish. Slowly her fingers rose. She ached to touch him, to feel his lips over hers, to lose herself in unexplored pleasures.

"Corey," she whispered.

"Edie . . ." His voice vanished into the wave of cold that washed over her.

In horror, she pulled away and stared at the luminescence surrounding him. He was dead. He would never hold her. He would never kiss her. She hid her face in the pillows and surrendered to the grief, her sobs ringing through the room like the bells ringing the passing of the Marquess of Wulfric.

At a soft sound, Corey set aside the book he had been paging through in the small parlor at the back of Herrold Hall. He had hoped to find something here to help him pass the time during the night. Sleep seemed to be something he no longer needed. He had made that blasted vow to respect Edie's privacy the morning after he had first visited her in this ghostly form, so he could not wake her and engage her in conversation. *She* still needed to sleep. He wondered what other spirits did during the darkness.

Mayhap he was supposed to make things go bump in the night, but such pranks grew monotonous.

Reading was a pastime he never had had enough time for before going off from this earth. Now he had all the time he wished and so very much more. A novel or some political satire would make the hours fly by more swiftly until he could pay Edie a call.

He selected another from the shelf. Like everything in this house, the book had to do with Reggie Herrold's dogs. He had seen no books that might have been Marian's, confirming his long-held suspicions that she strained her mind with nothing more strenuous than the gossip of the *ton*.

He heard the sound again. Someone was weeping.

"Edie!" He swore and dropped the book on a table. It clattered against a lamp, setting it to swaying, but he was in Edie's bedchamber before he had the thought to steady it.

He put the blasted lamp from his head and rushed to where she was thrashing on the bed. The bedclothes were tangled around her, and her hair was lathered against her forehead with sweat. She murmured something. The only word he understood was his name.

Sitting on the edge of the bed, he whispered, "Edie, wake up. 'Tis nothing but a nightmare."

Her lashes fluttered against her ivory cheeks, which were streaked with tears, and she stared up at him. "Corey, you—I dreamed—no, 'tis impossible."

"What is impossible, sweetheart?"

A pair of tears inched along her face, and he had to fight his urge to brush them away. If he touched her, she would be left with scorch marks in her skin. But to see her weep, to feel her heartbreak within his heart, he could not let her suffer like this without trying to help.

Gripping a handful of the counterpane, he wiped her cheek. Her eyes widened at his touch, which was insulated by the thick layers of cotton and lace.

"I am here," he whispered. "Do not fear the darkness, for it is when I can be with you most easily."

"I have no fear of the dark," she answered as softly, "but of waking one night and being alone."

"You shall never be alone, sweetheart." He swept her hair back from her face with the blanket. "I promise you that."

"Will you stay with me, Corey?"

A most unghostly tremor raced through him as he imagined lying beside her, drawing her into his arms and tasting the sweet wine of her lips. With every breath he had ever taken, he wanted this woman. It was impossible, but that did not lessen the ache of the yearning to hold her and spend the rest of his life with her.

Rest of his life! That was past. All he had left was this desire and a vow to help her find a living man to be her husband.

Softly he said, "Of course I will stay with you, sweetheart. For as long as I can." He put his finger to his lips as she started to speak. "Sleep now."

She put her hand over his beneath the thick quilts.

When she closed her eyes, he leaned against the headboard to watch each breath she took as she drifted into sleep. He never had been so happy as he was when he had this chance to be with her. Nor had he ever been so utterly miserable.

Eight

"Ah, here you are!" Marian bustled into Ellen's bedchamber, the fringe on her blue wrapper fluttering like feathers.

Although Ellen was tempted to ask where else she might be at this hour of the morning, she simply smiled. She was glad she could when the shadow of last night's half-remembered nightmare adhered to her like the rain to the window. Rising from where she had been finishing her breakfast, she said, "You look agitated, Marian. Is something wrong?"

"Better you should ask if something *important* is wrong," Corey interjected. His chuckle warmed her, and she included him in her smile. When she had opened her eyes this morning, she had discovered him sitting in the chair by the hearth, reading one of the newspapers Lord Herrold had sent out from Town. Remnants of memory teased her, but she was certain she could not have savored his caresses during the night. It could have been only a dream, a dream she cherished, knowing it would never come true.

Marian flung out her hands. "Lorenzo—Lord Wulfric is here, and I thought you would wish to see him."

Ellen looked at Corey, who grinned at Marian's grand announcement and, with a broad gesture, stood and bowed to her.

"Do not let me keep you from being entertained by Lorenzo," he said.

"Ellen?"

She pulled her gaze from Corey to meet Marian's baffled eyes. "Of course I would be delighted to see him."

"Are you well?" Marian put the back of her hand against Ellen's forehead. "My dear, you seem as distracted as if you are suffering from a fever." Her eyes brightened. "Have you changed your mind about Josiah? Can it be that you are in love?"

"I do not believe love causes one to appear ill."

"You are such an innocent. I was ill to my stomach before every outing I had with Reginald." She tapped her chin and frowned in concentration. "Odd, I still suffer that on occasion."

Ellen bit her lip to keep from smiling. If she were wed to that boring man, she would be ill, too.

Corey laughed, loud and hard.

Unable to halt herself, Ellen surrendered to laughter. She put her hand to her lips and glared at him, but he continued to laugh.

"That's much better," Marian said with the familiar expression of puzzlement. "Laughter will heal whatever is bothering you in no time."

"I would like to think so."

"Lorenzo is in the gold parlor. I have sent for tea and some sweetmeats for us."

"At this hour?" She looked at her breakfast tray.

"He rode over in the rain. I thought he would wish something bracing to ease any chill he might have picked up along the sea road."

Corey muttered, "Tea bracing? A good cheerer of flip would better serve the purpose."

Ellen thanked Marian, who scurried out of the room after telling Ellen she would meet her in the parlor and "please do not keep Lorenzo waiting. It would not look good." Ellen took a single glance in the glass, ignored Corey's grin, and followed Marian. Before the door closed, she peeked back into the room.

"I would," she said, "prefer to speak with your cousin without your interference."

He held up his hands in mock astonishment. "I would not think of intruding on Lorenzo's call on you. However, if you do find yourself suffering *ennui,* just say, 'Corey, I miss you more than words can express,' and I shall be by your side."

"You flatter yourself."

"I must when you fail to do so."

Ellen laughed and closed the door. She turned to go to the stairs. With a gasp, she froze as she stared at Corey. "How—? No, do not bother to explain. Just stop popping in and out and startling me."

No amusement lightened his face. "Call me if you need an excuse to escape Lorenzo, Edie. I know how tiresome he can be when he waxes poetic about his poetry."

"I shall be fine."

"True. Mayhap I should worry about Lorenzo. He will have to struggle to devise any interesting conversation to share with you. His words are few and far between."

"Yet he speaks to me with sincerity. That can compensate for many other faults, Corey."

Ellen rushed down the stairs before he drew her into another brangle. Why did they pull caps every time she dared to believe they might be able to enjoy their curious friendship? During breakfast, Corey had acted solicitous of her and had been charming company. Now—as soon as his cousin's name was spoken—the acidic edge returned to his voice.

The gold sitting room was set in a front corner of the first floor. Through the branches of the trees closest to the house, views of the garden offered an ever-changing vista. Shadows chased the dim sunlight across the wood floor and up onto the gathering of chairs and settees that were the same vibrant shades as the silk on the walls.

Lord Wulfric stood when Ellen came into the room. His dark green coat was cut to add breadth to his shoulders, and the nankeen pantaloons flattered his long legs, which appeared as thin as cat-sticks in riding boots. Nothing could detract from his impressive height or from the thoughtfulness in his eyes.

"You choose a poor day to pay a call, my lord," Ellen said as she held out her hand to him. His clothes were dry, save for the glitter of water on his boots, so she guessed he had left his great-coat with the footman. She was surprised Marian was not in the room, then guessed Marian was tending to the refreshments.

He bowed over it. "I wished to assure myself you have recovered as completely as Marian has told me. You look rested."

"I feel much better." She chose a seat on the settee and was surprised when he sat beside her. "You are kind to give me a look-in, my lord."

"Lorenzo, please."

"Lorenzo." She smiled. "And you must call me Ellen."

"If you wish."

"I do."

Silence hung between them, broken only by the sound of the rain striking the windows. Ellen tried to think of something to say, but her mind was as empty as the cheval glass when Corey passed it.

Finally, desperate, she dared to say, "Corey told me that you enjoy reading."

"He spoke of me during your brief conversation under the fireworks?"

"Yes," she said, glad he had phrased his question so she might speak the truth. She was certain Corey must have mentioned his cousin while they walked out to the seawall and back to disaster.

" 'Tis true," he answered with a smile. "I enjoy an interesting book, especially on a cloudy day like today when the wind blows off the sea."

"I would think such a day, if there were no rain, would lure you outside to enjoy the freshness."

His smile became sad. "If I did not know better, I would think I was speaking with Corey. He was always half-mad with anxiety to experience every aroma from the sea."

"Mayhap because he spent so much time far from it in that prison."

"You have become well acquainted with my cousin's life."

"Marian speaks often of both of you." That was no thumper

either. She wondered how far she could stretch the truth before it snapped back to strike her.

Clasping his hands on his knee, he smiled. "That is no surprise. Marian never avoids the chance for a bit of scan-mag."

"She speaks of you in friendship."

"I know what she says." He faced her. "And you are clearly Marian's friend to describe her so generously. Marian, who is happy only when surrounded by a crowd, cannot understand a man who can amuse himself in the serenity of his home. Corey found that difficult to understand as well."

No, he understands very well, she wanted to tell him, but she could devise no excuse to explain how she would know that. Tears suddenly filled her eyes. How sad that these two men, who cared so deeply for each other, never had been able to bridge their differences to enjoy the friendship they could have shared. Mayhap this was another part of the tragedy, as regrettable as the chance she had lost to be enfolded in Corey's arms.

She lowered her eyes as an unfettered yearning possessed her. What an air-dreamer she was!

"Ellen, if I have disturbed you with my comments about my late cousin, forgive me. Our manners tend to become rough here in grassville."

"You did not disturb me." She looked at him and smiled. "I appreciate your honesty."

"Such a pretty picture!" Marian announced as she came into the room. She was followed by a maid carrying a tray. "You look well, Lorenzo. I hope you will excuse my delay in greeting you. I am certain Ellen played hostess well in my absence."

Lorenzo frowned. "Marian, you shall put Ellen to the blush."

"She is accustomed to me." She sat across from them. She prepared to pour the tea. "Aren't you, my dear?"

"I believe I am," Ellen said with a smile. Offering Lorenzo the plate of sweetmeats, she went on as if they had not been interrupted, "So, you amuse yourself on such days as these with reading?"

"Reading and . . ." He gulped, glanced at Marian who was scowling at the tea, then said more softly, "Writing."

"Writing? What do you write?"

"I have tried my hand at a few sonnets."

"Like Shakespeare and Milton?"

"I prefer less sappy work."

She smiled. He was not boring; simply he was as bashful as a lad. There was something utterly captivating about his quiet ways, which contrasted with Corey's brash comments. "You are more daring than I, Lorenzo. I fear I have never mastered the patience needed to write within those strict parameters."

"But that is the challenge."

As he sat straighter, she was astonished to see once more a hint of his cousin in him. Fervor blazed from his eyes, and his hands were clenched as if he were about to come to cuffs with an invisible foe.

Ellen stiffened at the thought. Scanning the room, she saw no sign of Corey. That meant nothing, she feared. If his spirit was attached somehow to her, he might be listening in even now. No, he had agreed to let her speak to Lorenzo alone unless she chanced to call him.

"A challenge that has eluded me," she said when she realized Lorenzo was waiting for an answer. She must keep her mind on the conversation here as lief the one she might have to have with Corey if he eavesdropped on her . . . again.

"Poetry?" Marian sniffed as she held out a cup to Lorenzo, then poured one for Ellen. "Lorenzo, you are wasting your brain on such pursuits."

"How so?"

"You shall use up all your thoughts in pursuit of the perfect rhyme. Then where shall your mind be when you need it for something important?"

"Such as?"

Ellen saw the twinkle in his eyes. He was enjoying jesting with Marian, although Ellen was not sure if Marian realized he was teasing her, for Marian said with rare heat, "Lorenzo Wolfe,

AFFIX
STAMP
HERE

ZEBRA HOME SUBSCRIPTION SERVICE, INC.

120 BRIGHTON ROAD

P.O. BOX 5214

CLIFTON, NEW JERSEY 07015-5214

ll..l..lll....ll.l.l.l.l.l..l.l..ll.l.l.l.l.l..ll...l

you are once again Lord Wulfric. It would behoove you to concentrate on the pursuits of a country gentleman."

As Marian bent to stir more sugar into her tea, Lorenzo said
lowly, "I wonder if she means the pursuits of foxes or lasses."

Marian looked up at Ellen's laugh. "Did I miss something
important?"

"I suspect not," Ellen answered.

Before she could add more, footsteps stormed up the stairs.
Ellen looked out into the corridor, expecting Lord Herrold to
appear. Instead she saw a strikingly handsome man who was as
muscular as a laborer. He tossed his soaked coat at a serving
lass. The girl stared at him, awestruck. Flashing her a scintil-
lating smile, he paused to let the door frame him.

"Kenneth Pratt," Lorenzo said quietly.

Ellen tensed. *This* was the man Marian had been eager for
her meet. It was wrong to take an instant dislike to someone,
but one look at Kenneth Pratt was enough to make her despise
him. He sauntered into the room as if Herrold Hall were his
domain. No, she corrected herself, as she saw him look down
his nose at the room, he acted as if he were the king in the
lowest hovel of his lowest subject.

"Wolfe, good of you to call on Miss Dunbar," he boomed as
he smoothed back his blond hair from his cobalt blue eyes.
"Although I must own that I had hoped to have her company—
and Lady Herrold's—to myself this morning."

Lorenzo gulped. "If you wish to speak with Pratt alone, Ellen, I can take my leave."

"No!" Ellen forced a smile to cover her swift answer. She did
not want to spend the rest of the day explaining her lack of civility
to Marian. "There are plenty of sweetmeats, and another cup can
be brought. Think of what fun we shall have talking together."
She pointed to a chair on the far side of the table where the tea
tray was set. Even there, she suspected, would be too close.
"Please sit with us, Mr. Pratt, and tell us how your mother is
doing."

"You know Mother?" he asked as he flashed that devastating smile at Marian, who giggled like a lass still in the schoolroom.

"I had the opportunity to meet her the night of the fireworks," Ellen said when she realized Marian was too overmastered by Mr. Pratt's good looks to assume her place as hostess. "She seems to be a sensitive woman. She must have been much distressed by the evening."

When she heard an impolite snort, Ellen did not have to look over her shoulder. She had been sure Corey would appear as soon as word spread through the Hall that Kenneth Pratt was calling. In fact, she was surprised it had taken Corey so long to arrive. He had vowed not to intrude on Lorenzo's call, but Mr. Pratt's arrival made it a completely different situation.

Mr. Pratt seized a finely made chair and pulled it within inches of where she sat on the settee. "My mother was not exaggerating when she said you were the prettiest thing to enter this shire in a long time."

"Thank you. You are kind."

"True, but 'tis easy to be kind when I speak the truth."

Corey sat on the arm of the settee, and Ellen pulled back before she could touch him. Seeing Mr. Pratt's eyes narrow at what he saw as an insult, she wished just one other person could see Corey. Then she would not always be caught—sometimes quite literally—in the middle.

"So are you well?" the blond man asked.

"I am better."

"Then you have no excuse not to allow me to escort you to the dance we are hosting Saturday next."

Marian recovered enough to regain her voice. "A dance? What a wonderful surprise!"

"I spoke to you of it," Mr. Pratt said, "only last week."

She waved aside his words as irrelevant. "Then you said only it was a possibility, and now you are asking Ellen to go with you. Isn't that wonderful, Ellen?"

Corey leaned forward as he interjected, "Marian, you always have had a peculiar sense of wonderful."

Ellen began, "I—"

"You need not express your gratitude." Mr. Pratt started to reach for Ellen's hand, but paused, astonishment on his face. Shaking his fingers, he frowned.

No humor lightened Corey's face as he growled, "Pratt, you need not express a word for us to know you are a pompous calf-head. If you will say the word, Edie, I shall give the boor such an embrace that he shall be shivering for days."

"Cold in here, isn't it?" Mr. Pratt asked.

"I hadn't noticed," Ellen said. "I—"

"Blasted draughty house." He turned to Marian. "I have told your husband on more than one occasion he should find a place farther from the sea. We live inland where these cold winds are blocked by the hills." Not giving Marian a chance to answer, he looked at Ellen. "Much wisdom in that, don't you agree?"

"I—"

Ellen gritted her teeth when Mr. Pratt interrupted for a third time. The man was insufferable!

"Of course, I suppose you are accustomed to such draughts. I understand you were raised in that intolerably uncivilized land to the north." He started to move closer to her, then seemed to think better of it. Only Ellen saw Corey's hand waft the air again in front of Mr. Pratt's classically aristocratic nose. "Although I must own, if all the ladies of Scotland are as lovely and demure as you, Miss Dunbar—May I call you Ellen?"

"I would as lief you did not," she replied, amazed at this man. She had never met anyone who was so arrogantly rude. To think she would agree to him using such an intimacy as her given name on their blessedly short acquaintance was absurd.

As if she had not spoken, he continued, "Ellen, you are a tribute to your birthland. If only England had more gracious ladies like you, what a wondrous place this would be. Mayhap we should investigate the idea of sending some of our young beaux to that country and seeking out others like you. Not that any of them could compare to you. How distressed our Englishwomen must have been to meet you and think there were others in that distant land!"

"Scotland is part of Great Britain," Lorenzo said with quiet dignity, "and is not a long ride from where we are sitting right now."

"Wolfe, are you still here?" He started to laugh, then swallowed the sound with a gulp when Ellen frowned. "I mean, you are so quiet one would think you were nothing more than a statue."

"How," Corey asked in that tone which warned her he was contemplating mischief, "can a soul get a word in when you, Pratt, are airing your vocabulary endlessly?"

Ellen was tempted to agree, but Lorenzo spoke before she could.

"Kenneth, your opinions are always a source of amazement to me."

Mr. Pratt preened as if he were surrounded by a score of admirers. "I had no idea you found them so interesting."

"Not so much interesting as amazing."

Ellen stared at Lorenzo in astonishment. Was he insulting Mr. Pratt or lauding him? No hint of the truth was visible on his face.

Corey's laugh drew her eyes to him. "Shame on you, Lorenzo!" he said with another chuckle. "You should know better than to have a battle of wits with a witless man. The victory is too easily won."

She fought not to laugh.

When Mr. Pratt rose, she was able to control her amusement behind a clichéd farewell. She lost her yearning to laugh when he reminded her that she would be his guest at the assembly at the Pratt's country house.

A silent sigh was her only response as Marian escorted him down the stairs, his boot heels battering each riser. Lorenzo was correct. Mr. Pratt was amazing in his arrogance.

"I should take my leave as well," Lorenzo said, setting himself on his feet. "I do not wish to overstrain you."

"I have enjoyed your call. I know Marian did as well. She has been saying she wished you would call more often."

He smiled. "Do you think she would be satisfied if I invited you and Marian and Reggie to an outing at Wolfe Abbey on the morrow?" He clasped his hands behind his back. "Do you think you might wish to join us?"

Corey shook his head as he went to stand next to his cousin. "I know tradition states only a week of mourning for cousins, Lorenzo, but I thought you might wear ashes a while longer than this."

"I would be delighted," Ellen replied.

"*Et tú,* Edie?"

Unable to hear Corey's sarcasm, Lorenzo nodded. "Then I shall look forward to tomorrow." He bowed over her hand before going out into the hall.

Marian rushed into the room. She kissed Ellen on the cheek. "Two conquests with a single smile. My dear, I knew someone would win your heart here."

"I think you may be right." Ellen looked around the room, but save for her and Marian, it was empty. She was astonished Corey had left without trying to have the final word. She wondered what new prank he was devising to spring on them next in his joint effort with Marian to find her a husband. She was sure it would be something beyond anything she could imagine.

Nine

A nicer day could not have been wished for, and Ellen left her dreary spirits at Herrold Hall. Literally, she hoped, for she would enjoy a chance to think without Corey meddling constantly.

She took a deep breath as they paused in front of Wolfe Abbey. The air was flavored with salt. She wished they could ride along the shore, but Marian had insisted on a more traditional journey across the hills to the lake beyond the village.

Marian smiled as she dismounted. "Wait here with the horses. I wish to deliver this basket to the kitchen, so it might be ready for us when we return."

"We could take the basket with us and eat in the hills."

"Nonsense. That would be most uncivilized."

"We ate on the sand earlier in the week."

"That was a gathering. This is just a ride with a few friends."

Ellen could not fathom what difference that made, but she had learned better than to start a brangle when Marian had that stubborn gleam in her eyes. She slid off the horse as Marian went to the house. Looping the horses' reins over a tree, she gathered the heavy bulk of her forest green riding skirt and walked along the path toward where she could look down on the pond in the heart of the garden.

Someone leaped out of the shrubs. She pulled back with a frightened cry. When she heard the raspy laugh over her thumping heart, she frowned. "Fenton!"

"Remember ye. Ye be Miss Dunbar."

"Yes."

He eyed her up and down. "Don't know why he chose ye."

"Who?"

"Lord Wulfric."

"I am afraid I do not understand what you mean."

"Lord Wulfric. Chose ye, he did."

"You must be confused." She forced a smile. The old man was clearly dicked in the nob, so she must be gentle with him. Her last conversation with him had been as puzzling as this one. "I have only met Lorenzo a few—"

"Not him." Fenton spat on the ground. *"Lord Wulfric!"*

"But Lorenzo Wolfe is—"

"Not yet he ain't. Not while his lordship is still about." Standing straighter so his nose was but an inch from hers, he demanded, "Ye know it, too, don't ye?"

She backed away. "I think you are confused."

"Scared ye of old Fenton, they have, but I know what ye know. His lordship still walks the halls of Wolfe Abbey."

"How—?" She gulped, not wanting to reveal the truth. "Why do you say that?"

"Seen him, I have."

"You have? When?"

Fenton chuckled, the sound as strident as an unoiled hinge. "Not as many times as ye have seen him, I guess. Likes the pretty ones, he does."

Ellen turned on her heel and walked away. She had no reply for the old man that was not a lie, and she did not want to resort to dishonesty.

Had Fenton truly seen Corey, or was he just a superstitious old widgeon? She must not allow him to guess how close to the truth his ravings were. Yet, if he had seen Corey, he might speak to others as he had to her. She must warn Corey.

She was tempted to laugh. What could anyone do to a *ghost?*

"There you are!" Marian wore a reproving frown as she strode toward Ellen. "We had wondered where you might be."

Ellen did not ask who "we" were. Marian's tone told her.

Lorenzo must have come out of the Abbey with Marian. All in all, this day was going ingloriously. Mayhap she would be wise to return to Herrold Hall and hide in her room beneath her covers. No, that would be futile. Then Corey would appear to taunt her for being a coward.

She was not afraid of Marian's attempts to find her a husband. She simply needed a chance to be alone to gather her thoughts together. If Marian—and Corey—arranged events to unfold as they wished, she knew it would not be soon.

Lorenzo wore a strained smile as Ellen approached. She understood why when a chorus of yaps, yips, and howls ricocheted along the road. Suddenly, past the top stones of the seawall, a pack of brown and white dogs exploded into sight. Lord Herrold was chasing them, his face as red as his riding coat. His open mouth suggested he was shouting, but the sound was swallowed by the dogs' keening.

Ellen gasped when Lorenzo grasped her by the shoulders and pulled her behind the horses before the dogs could swarm over them. Marian bravely stood her ground. The dogs swirled around her in a muddy river, then raced, barking, over and through the fence past the stables. Lord Herrold followed in close pursuit, paying no attention to the pieces of grass sticking out of his hat and the briars clinging to his breeches.

"Is he breeding persistence into his pups?" Lorenzo asked.

"You would have to ask him." Marian patted her horse on the neck. "I have to own that I do not listen closely when he babbles on and on about his beasts."

"Where is he going?" Ellen asked.

Marian shrugged. "Who can guess?"

Ellen laughed as Marian motioned for Lorenzo to throw her up into the saddle so she could give chase to her husband and his dogs. When Lorenzo turned to help Ellen, she said, "You have much patience with eccentric people."

"A skill I needed when I came to Wolfe Abbey to live." He helped her mount. As she settled in the saddle, he handed her the reins. "If I could learn to deal with the Wolfes, I suspect I can be successful with anyone."

"You miss your cousin deeply." She put her hand on his shoulder.

"Both of them. Vanessa, Corey, and I grew up together. Now she is far from here, and he is gone. Only I remain." He climbed into his saddle with ease. "Odd, but Corey was such a part of the Abbey that, while there is an emptiness, it seems as if a part of him is still about."

The longing to speak the truth burned on her lips. How it would comfort Lorenzo to know that he was right, but if she uttered the truth, Lorenzo would think she was as deranged as Fenton.

"Lorenzo!" Marian was halfway to the stables. "Do hurry! I fear we shall lose Reginald."

"Last time, he raced his dogs to a breast-high scent," Lorenzo said with a laugh, "the good baron got lost in his own greenwood."

"With all that yelping, how could they be lost?" Ellen asked as they rode to meet up with Marian.

"Oh, the dogs found their way back to the Hall. Reggie didn't."

Ellen laughed merrily as they went in pursuit of the score of dogs and Lord Herrold. It might not be such a bad day, after all.

Sitting beneath a tree at the edge of a field, Ellen lowered her book to her lap and watched Lord Herrold as he bent over his dogs and spoke to them as earnestly as if they could comprehend every word he spoke. Beside him, Marian sat on her horse. Her impatient expression was visible even from the far side of the field.

The green shadows beneath the trees lengthened as the sun dipped toward the sea. Ellen could not recall the last time she had enjoyed such a peaceful day . . . and been so suffused with *ennui*. It was the first day since her arrival at Wolfe Abbey that she had not spoken with Corey. Odd that he should have been absent today when he had followed her on every other outing she had taken.

Lorenzo came to sit beside her. Pulling a handkerchief from a pocket, he wiped his sweating face. "My best riding pantaloons," he said with a grimace.

"What happened?" she asked when she saw the foot-long rip in the left leg.

"I failed to remember the ha-ha at the edge of this lea. With luck, my tumble knocked some sense into my head." He uncapped a canister and held it out. When she hesitated, he said, " 'Tis only water, Ellen. I suspect Reggie will be anxious to renew his acquaintance with the bottles from the Abbey's cellars by the time we return. As he dislikes drinking alone . . ."

"Thank you." She took a deep drink to wash the dust of the lane from her lips. "I think you may be worrying needlessly. I cannot believe he will be willing to pause at the Abbey when he shall be eager to get his pack home."

"He has left them with Fenton before."

"Fenton?" She gasped and stared at him. "Lord Herrold trusts Fenton to watch over his precious collection of dogs?"

" 'Tis a surprise, isn't it? Fenton took a knock in the cradle many years ago. I asked Corey many times to retire him to a cottage near the shore, but he never heeded me. When Vanessa returns from the continent, she may decide to give the old man a reward for his long service to this family. I cannot decide that." His eyes narrowed when she did not answer. "You look distressed. Has Fenton said something to bother you?"

Ellen smiled. "If you say he is harmless, Lorenzo, I am sure you are right."

"I hope I am. He certainly shares Reggie's love of beasts. Both men have an uncanny way with them." Again he looked down at his buckskin pantaloons. "Much better than I do, I suspect. I should ask you to excuse me, Ellen, so I can go back to the Abbey and change."

"Will you be joining us for our *al fresco* nuncheon?"

"Marian would be highly displeased if I did not, and I have found it is wise to keep Marian happy," he said with a smile.

He was more insightful than Corey had led her to believe. "Marian does not like to have her plans countermanded."

"And she wanted us to spend this day together." He tugged at his ripped pantaloons. "I can tell you, Ellen, I would have much preferred talking with you than chasing Reggie's pack across the fields."

She laughed. "Did you gather all of them together?"

"He seems to think one is still missing, but cannot decide which one." He pointed to where Lord Herrold was trying in vain to get his dogs to stand still. "He is uncommonly concerned that the beast will return home with an unwelcome addition to his breeding line."

"You are a good friend to your neighbors."

"I like a quiet life, Ellen. Sometimes it requires a great deal of effort to find it here." He tilted her book so he could read the title on the binding. "I should have guessed you would be enjoying poetry."

"Shakespeare's sappy sonnets, I believe you called them."

Resting back against a tree, he said, "Not all of them are sappy. The man has a good grasp of the use of language and twists words like a master. Mayhap I spoke out of jealousy more than anything else."

"Jealousy?"

"Shakespeare was a master, and I am a mere dabbler."

"You should let someone else judge that." She put her hand on his arm. "If you would like, I offer my eyes."

"You want to read my poetry?"

"If you wish me to."

"I am overwhelmed."

Hastily she said, "If you do not wish to share it, I can understand."

"No, no!" He jumped to his feet and grinned like the lanky scarecrow he resembled. "The whole idea is as fine as a five pence. I shall gather some poems for you to read upon my return." Grasping her hand, he pressed his lips to its back.

Ellen gasped at his unexpected fervor.

Hastily he released her hand. "Ellen, if I have done anything to offend you, I—"

"You have done nothing." She did not look at him. As lief, she stared down at the hand she cradled in her other. How could she explain that his action brought his cousin to her mind? Lorenzo would think her completely insane if she spoke of her heart-deep longing for Corey to kiss her hand and touch her with such yearning. "I look forward to reading your poems, Lorenzo."

The delight returned to his voice as he told her he would return after a flying trip to the Abbey. She heard him rush to his horse, then ride away at top speed. The dust from the road washed over her, but could not conceal the truth.

She was falling in love with a ghost. As absurd as it sounded, that was the truth. Would Corey laugh if she told him that she had found the husband she wanted and that that husband was him? Closing her eyes, she imagined how wondrous it would be if he could draw her into his arms then and whisper of his love for her.

"Don't be silly." Ellen closed her book sharply. "This is nothing but a joke to him. If . . ."

Hoofbeats sounded along the road. She looked past the tree. A blond man slowed his gray mount and tipped his hat to her. "Good day, miss. Can you tell me which road to take to Herrold Hall?"

She smiled. "You are upon it, sir. It is no more than a fifteen minute ride in that direction."

Swinging down from the horse, he said, "You have chosen a lovely spot to enjoy your book, miss, and I apologize for interrupting your tranquillity."

"It is a lovely spot, but hardly tranquil." She glanced out to where Lord Herrold was still trying to gather his dogs about him.

"Do you, perchance, know if Lord Herrold is in residence at the Hall?"

"Yes, but if you wish to speak to him, you need look no farther than this field."

The man, who was not much taller than Fenton, grinned. "This is a piece of good luck. Thank you, miss." He hesitated as he was about to turn. "Do I have the honor of being in the company of Lady Herrold?"

With another smile, she shook her head. "Lady Herrold is my hostess. I am Ellen Dunbar."

"Thomas Hudson, Miss Dunbar." He tipped his hat to her. "Thank you."

Ellen bent back over her book as he rode to meet Lord Herrold. She chuckled softly when the sound of barking warned that Mr. Hudson's arrival had sent the dogs into a new flurry of excitement. She ignored the sound as she listened only to the melody of the poetry's words swirling like a symphony through her mind.

"Ellen, what were you doing talking to *him?*"

In amazement, she looked up to discover Marian's face was as gray as the sky at dawn. She had been so immersed in her book, she had not heard Marian's steps. "Him?"

"Thomas Hudson."

"He stopped to ask directions. He seems a pleasant gentleman."

She sniffed her disagreement as she sat beside Ellen. "Gentleman? Not likely, Ellen. He has been disowned by both family and friends, save for Reginald. The two share a revolting obsession for their dogs."

"I had no idea."

"How can it be that you have spent three Seasons in London, and you are still as *naïve* as when you first arrived from Scotland?" Marian fanned her face with her hand and glowered at the two men in the field. "You cannot judge a man to be a gentleman simply because his manners seem polished." Her terse laugh struck Ellen like a switch. "If that were true, then you could not have called Corey Wolfe a gentleman. He spoke his mind far too often and often chose companions who were not fit for a marquess."

"Companions?"

Marian patted Ellen's hand. "I do not mean to disparage a dead man's name unjustly. His companions were not light-skirts, or not that I am privy to. As lief, he often entertained men who had served with him in France, men who were entering the Polite World for the first time. Soldiers learn few manners, I fear."

Ellen clenched her hands on her book. This was no time to give free rein to her temper, which could flash as red hot as her hair. Marian spoke out of ignorance. If she ever had had the opportunity to meet Ellen's stepfather, Marian would have learned that a military man was accustomed to a life of the highest decorum. Her voice was taut as she answered, "My stepfather spent many years in the military before his recent retirement, if you will recall."

"I did not mean to insult your family." She waved her hands about as if she were batting at gnats. "You know the type I mean, Ellen. Uncouth and without the refinement of decent manners."

"I think it would be best, Marian," she said, "if we discontinue this conversation. You have been a good friend to me, and I do not wish to end that friendship over this matter which hurts me deeply."

"Over what matter?"

"You are speaking thoughtlessly about two men I love with all my heart."

"Love? Who?"

"My stepfather and . . ." Ellen bit back her answer. What kind of widgeon was she to let her vexation loosen her tongue like this?

"And?"

She set herself on her feet. "And I find I do not wish to speak of this any longer."

Marian called to her, but Ellen did not slow as she strode away. If she paused, she might have to explain to Marian that her frustration was not totally with Marian's parochial thinking.

But how could she speak the truth of her grief at what could never be? She loved two men who had defended their country through rough years with the army. She loved her dear stepfather, who was the only father she had ever known, and she loved Corey Wolfe . . . hopelessly.

Ten

"Corey?"

At the soft call of his name, Corey sat straighter in the chair near the hearth in Reggie's book room. He swore vividly when his feet floated up off the floor. Grasping the arms of the chair, he set himself on his feet. How long would it take him to accustom himself to the peculiar events in his life as a phantom?

"Corey?"

He frowned. He recognized that voice. Edie! Was she in the house?

Odd, but he thought she had gone with the Herrolds and his cousin for a ride across the hills. She had told him of her plans last night while he had sat by the hearth and watched while she checked the simple coat of her riding habit.

His smile returned to tilt his lips. He had to be thankful that Edie remained, at heart, a Scot, who had been raised to believe that ghosts shared the world with the living. Even now, the thought of presenting himself to Lorenzo sent him into whoops. His cousin, for all his imagination when it came to writing his poetry, would have considered himself bereft of his senses and sent for the doctor.

The wisest thing Corey had ever done was to appear to Edie. Her trust in him warmed him when the cold light threatened to swallow him in despair. As easily as if they had known each other for years instead of days, they would talk. The subject was never important, only that they were together and could share an ease they never would have known otherwise.

He had learned so much about her from her comments and unique insight into what he considered commonplace. She did not consider her beginnings, far from the Polite World, something to hide, for she appreciated the simple ways of the country as much as the spectacular entertainments of Town. With ease, she had bridged two worlds. Mayhap, he thought with a widening grin, that was why she alone could reach past her living world to see him. An interesting supposition, one he would have to discuss with her that evening when the rest of the house had retired and she could speak to him without the fear of being overheard.

But why was she calling to him now?

Corey followed the sound of her voice. He was shocked to find himself in the gardens of Wolfe Abbey. Even though he had not quite determined how or why he could manage this feat, he gave it no thought. As lief, he scanned the perfectly arranged trees and beds of flowers. The shadows could hide nothing from him now, and he saw a slender form striding with unladylike fervor through a copse near the pond.

"Edie?"

She flinched when he stood in front of her. He stared at her in astonishment as he noted how her fingers trembled. Tears glittered in her eyes, and her lips were tight with the effort to keep them from falling.

"Go away!" she said in lieu of a greeting.

"How charming."

Ellen took a deep breath and squared her shoulders. She did not wish to suffer Corey's teasing now. Not when she was so furious! How could Marian be so intolerant? Ellen's family might not have been part of the elegant society for generations, but that did not mean they were no better than the scum clinging to the cattails at the edge of the pond.

"What do you want?" Corey continued when she did not answer.

"Nothing." She edged around him. "Just leave me to myself now."

"If that is what you wanted, why did you call me?"

"I did not call you."

He smiled coolly and shook his head. "You called to me several times, Edie. I may be out of print with my name on a stone in the churchyard, but my ears still work quite well. You called me."

Ellen stared at him in amazement. The only place she had uttered his name was in her mind. If he could sense her thoughts . . . She did not want to consider what that might mean. Regaining her poise, she said, "You are mistaken."

"Am I?"

"Go away!"

"Edie—"

She started to walk away, then whirled to face him. "Thunder, Corey Wolfe! Begone from my life. You have interfered too often."

"Something *is* wrong!" He scowled. "You never use such cant."

"Everything is wrong." She hated the sharp sound of her voice, but she had endured too much today to suffer through his not-so-gentle interrogation. "What is most wrong is that you will not leave me alone."

His brows lowered to brush his eye patch. "Edie, the last thing you need when you are this distraught is to be by yourself. What is wrong? Mayhap I can help."

"I do not want your help."

For a moment, she thought he would continue the argie-bargie, but he said only, "All right. If that is what you want. If you change your mind—"

"I shan't!"

"If you do . . ." His voice grew hard, and she knew she had hurt him. "Just call my name and say, 'I have changed my mind. I need your help, after all.' Even a stubborn Scot can change her mind when she finally sees common sense."

"Seeing common sense would mean I should not be seeing you."

She blinked back the tears that seared her eyes. If she let him woo her out of her outrage, she feared what might happen. This anger could be a barricade between him and the love her heart longed to offer him. *That* was the truth she must never speak; she must not even think it . . . or she could hurt him more than she had ever been hurt.

She did not look back as she strode away.

Ellen opened her eyes when the boat suddenly rocked. She had sought a haven for her thoughts in this rowboat which was in dire need of a fresh coat of paint. Moored by the small boat-house at the edge of the garden pond where swans swam undisturbed, it was shielded from the Abbey by a gazebo shaped like a Chinese pagoda.

Although she had half-expected either Corey or Marian—or both—to come looking for her, no one had disturbed her. She must have fallen asleep. Too many nights of losing sleep while she talked with Corey had caught up with her. No wonder she had been so short-tempered with Marian. She must make her excuses to her bosom-bow and Lorenzo for fleeing to hide here while she gathered her thoughts about her.

The apologies to Marian and Lorenzo would be simple, but how would she apologize to Corey? To let a hint of her honest feelings show was guaranteed to create even more problems. If—

The boat rocked again. Ellen grumbled as she sat and reached for the rope holding it to shore. Pulling the mooring rope into the boat, she saw the loop that had been over the pier had come undone. With a soft cry, she stared around her. The distant shore was shadowed by a wall of black clouds rising out of the sea. She was in the middle of the pond as a storm was about to pounce on the Abbey.

"Blast!" she muttered, not caring who might hear, although

there was no one about. She had gotten herself into this predicament. She would have to depend on herself to get out of it.

Ellen looked under the seat and smiled as she pulled out a pair of oars. The paint was hanging in loose strips from the warped wood, but they would have to do. She put them into the water and froze as lightning brightened the sky. Thunder followed quickly. Another bolt crackled as thunder sounded again. Too close. She slapped the oars against the water and pulled hard.

The boat was sluggish in the water. More thunder cascaded overhead, but the sound of her fearful heart was louder. She had to find shelter from the storm or she could end up as dead as Corey.

Corey! What had he told her to say if she wanted him to come to her? She could not remember!

Thunder cracked like a coachee's whip. She hunched into the boat and fought the waves rocking the boat toward the middle of the pond. Like a bean in a cauldron of soup, she could not fight the froth being stirred up by the storm.

Light flashed in front of her. She screamed.

"Edie, 'tis I."

"Corey," she breathed. "You came."

"You need to get to shore." Humor drifted into his voice. "Me as well. I have no idea how lightning might affect me."

He put his hands on the oar beside hers. He pulled, but it moved only when she tugged on it. He swore and tried again. Nothing happened. Staring down at his hands, he frowned.

Ellen flinched as lightning struck a tree at the edge of the garden. Flames burst through the leaves. Thunder buffeted her ears.

"Move aside!" she gasped.

"Edie—"

"You cannot help, so stay out of my way!"

She bent to her task. The storm was closing in upon them. Splinters caught at her hands, but she did not slow. Lightning glared on the water. She moaned when the thunder followed in the space of a pair of heartbeats.

The boat struck the shore at an odd angle. Corey jumped out and grasped the boat. He held out his hand, then cursed again.

"Edie, you have to do it on your own."

She did not hesitate. Leaping from the boat, she ran up the hill to the gazebo. Rain scored her like a hundred needles. She climbed the steps into the gazebo and collapsed on the uneven floor. She did not look out. She did not want to see the fire consuming the tree. It could have been her.

"Edie?"

Slowly Ellen raised her head to see Corey bending over her. Never had she seen such regret on his face. Wiping rain from her eyes, she whispered, "I am fine."

"I wanted to help you, Edie."

"I know." She trembled as another bolt of lightning scored the pond. Sitting up, she stared out at the rain. She looked up at him. "And I wanted you to help me, Corey."

He struck his fist against his other palm as he sat on the circular bench that followed the wall of the gazebo. "This is so blasted frustrating! So many times I thought only of saving my neck, and I was proclaimed a hero. The one time I wished to be a hero I failed so utterly."

"We are safe." She held out her hand. "Everything will be fine now."

"Will it?" He reached his fingers toward hers. "How can anything be fine when I cannot touch you?"

"You do not know what would happen if—"

"I know too well, Edie. To try again to touch you and hurt you again would destroy the dream that it is possible."

She sighed as driving rain cut through the ornate lattice-work . . . and through Corey. No matter what they might wish, the truth was before them. He was a phantom with no more substance than a dream.

"Will you explain why you took into your head a jobbernowl idea like going out in the boat during a storm?" he asked. "I should have followed my gut instincts and given chase when you flounced away."

"I did not flounce!"

He smiled. "Mayhap, but you did leave me watching you walk away and wondering why. Now I wonder, as well, why you were out in that boat."

Ellen decided it would be simpler to answer his first question. It would be better than speaking of the longings of her heart. Quietly, she said, "It did not look like rain when I got into the boat. Or mayhap it did. I was so furious I did not notice."

"Furious? That *I* noticed, but who infuriated you so much?"

"Marian."

"Are you finally coming to your senses?"

With a smile, she watched the pond's water swallow the rain. "I doubt that."

He edged closer to her. "Then what did you argue about? Not me, I hope."

"Your name *was* mentioned."

"Was it? I was jesting."

"I know." She drew up her feet and wrapped her arms around them as she did when he came to speak to her in her bedchamber. Resting her cheek on her knees, she sighed.

"You are avoiding answering me. What caused you to be at outs with Marian?"

"She insulted my stepfather . . . and you."

"At once?" He laughed. "She is becoming more accomplished in her snobbery, I see. Now how did she manage that?"

"It is not important, Corey."

"It was important enough that you came here to be alone, and it was important enough that you flew out at me." He bent toward her. "What was it?"

When she had explained, Ellen thought he would make a quick retort. Instead he leaned his arm on the seat and looked across the pond where the rain was slowing to a few sprinkles. The storm racing across the hills had passed as swiftly as it had appeared, but she guessed the one raging within him had not lessened with the ending of the war. Suddenly he seemed a lifetime away, in a place she could not envision, recalling a horror beyond any she could imagine. As never before, she wanted to touch him, to offer him the simple warmth of a human touch as he stood at the brink of the dark chasm of his memories.

"So Marian deems me less than a gentleman because I enjoy the company of my fellow red herrings." He shook his head with a wry smile. "Only they understood what I experienced in France."

"I would be glad to try."

He shook his head. "No, Edie, I will not burden you with that. Not even a soldier's daughter should have that horror inflicted upon her." His teasing grin returned. "Shall I teach you the tavern songs we sang while we marched? Marian will be properly outraged if you sang one of them around Herrold Hall."

"If you had asked me a few hours ago, I would have said yes." Too well she knew what that smile meant. He would be as stubborn as her stepfather and say nothing about his soldiering life. To persist in asking questions would gain her nothing but someone else angry at her. "I fear I owe Marian an apology."

"I don't see why. She needs to put aside her prejudices on occasion."

"True."

"And you need to be honest with me."

"More honest than I was earlier?"

"You were honest when you told me to leave you alone, but you failed to say why."

"I wished to revel in my anger for a while."

He chuckled. "A worthwhile endeavor on occasion. Are you done with that fun?"

"Yes." Ellen rose, not willing to add more. "The rain is passing. I should return to the Abbey. Marian will be anxious about me, and I owe Lorenzo an apology for leaving before he returned."

As she climbed down the steps to the wet grass, she held up her long skirts. Corey walked beside her, but no hint of dampness ruined the fashionable perfection of his clothes. It was, she decided, unfair he was not as soaked as she was. Her boots made squishing sounds on every step, and he was in as prime twig as if he were ready to receive callers.

"So how did the ride with my cousin go?" Corey asked.

"Splendidly."

"Because I was not there?"

"In part."

"Could it be that Lorenzo has touched a tender spot within your heart?"

"I believe we can be friends."

"Lorenzo—showing rare good sense—wishes more." He matched her steps as she climbed the stone walk toward the Abbey. "Do not pull caps with me on this, Edie. I saw the expression on his face at Herrold Hall. No doubt he is even now writing sonnets extolling your beauty and kindness."

"He loves his poetry."

"Pap!"

"Mayhap it is nothing but an air-dreamer's doodlings, but he enjoys it."

"Do you really wish to read his poems, or are you being nice?"

"Yes." She laughed.

"You are too kind, Edie." He wrapped one arm around the branch of a tree by the path. "Now Lorenzo shall be drowning you in an ocean of his rhymes."

"Being kind is no sin." She gasped as water pelted her from the branches.

With a laugh, he said, "Of course not, but 'tis damned bothersome. Lorenzo shall spend all night going over his collection of poems to decide which are the very best to share with you. A single word of praise from you will bring more and more to read. A single word of criticism will shatter him, so you, being the considerate soul you are, will speak only of the wonders of his work."

"You are jealous!"

"Jealous?" He laughed and shook his head. "Do not flatter yourself—or Lorenzo—that I am envious of the complications about to bind your lives together."

She tilted her head, smiling. "Yes, you are jealous. Whether they be good or bad, Lorenzo's poems will leave a bit of him here when he dies. You fear there is nothing of you here."

"A dozen men live because of me." His boots made no sound as they walked across the stones of the road by the stables. "If not for me, they would be dead. I believe that is legacy enough for any man."

"I didn't mean to—"

Sharply he interrupted, "I know you didn't. You are incessantly kindhearted. That can be as boring as Lorenzo's poetry, you know."

"You need not linger."

"And leave you to suffer Marian's indignities as a matchmaker alone? I fear you would be wed unwisely before a fortnight passes."

She fisted her hands on her waist. "I have resisted such attempts at leg-shackling me to a husband for the past three years. One thing will never change. I shall wed whom I choose when I choose."

"If—"

"Knew it, I did!"

Ellen whirled around. "Fenton!"

"Damn," Corey muttered under his breath.

Fenton stuck out a spindly finger and jabbed it in Corey's direction. "Knew it. Did I not tell ye, miss? There he be before yer eyes."

"He can truly see you?" Ellen whispered, looking from one man to the other.

Corey folded his arms over his chest. "It would seem so."

Eleven

"Damn, Fenton, must you always be right?"

Ellen was astonished when Corey laughed. From the bent man came a strange sound. She was not sure if the cackle was a rusty laugh or a curse.

"My lord, ye did not heed m'warnin' before, so ye should know that I would be hauntin' ye as ye be hauntin' the Abbey." Fenton's eyes slitted farther until they were but dark creases. "I did not suspect *she* could be seein' ye as well."

" 'Tis a shock to us, too." Corey sat on the low wall at the edge of the walk and rested his shoulder against the thick trunk of a tree. "So what do you know of all of this, Fenton? You have long been a fountain of information on the trivial traditions of Wolfe Abbey. Am I the only one of its past lords wandering about its halls now?"

"Ye be gone before yer time, so the Abbey holds ye here. No lord has left early. Ye be connected to the grounds until yer time comes."

"I don't seem to be connected to the Abbey, but to Miss Dunbar."

Fenton's eyes widened. A toothless grin spread across his face. "That be jiggumbob, my lord. Never heard the like. She don't be family." He reached out and patted Ellen's stomach. "Or is she?"

She pulled back in horror.

Corey's voice darkened. "Fenton, you insult Miss Dunbar."

"But not ye, my lord." He cackled his amusement again and winked bawdily. "So she not be took with yer child. Shame, my lord. 'Twould explain much. No other reason that she should see ye."

"She was with me when I popped off. I made a vow—a death vow, it seems—to her to find her a husband. So here I remain while she seeks one."

When Edie stepped back to stare at both of them, Corey tensed, wondering what she would say. She looked bedraggled in her soaked habit, but he could not ignore how it clung to her body, accenting each enchanting curve. If he had been a little less dead, he suspected such a sight would have pumped life right back into him. Her eyes were wide in her colorless face.

"Why can *he* see you?" she whispered, batting away the water dripping off the brim of her hat. "Neither Marian nor Lorenzo have been able to see you. Mr. Pratt—"

"Couldn't see anything beyond that arrogance of his." Corey jumped down from the wall and walked to her. Raising his hands, he drew her battered hat off her head.

She put up her fingers to touch her hair, which was frosty beneath his touch, then said, "Corey, you aren't answering me."

"Because I have no answer." He glanced over his shoulder at Fenton, who was watching with a triumphant grin. "It would be easier, I own, to believe that he can see me than that you can. Fenton has been seeing things for years."

"And now ye understand, don't ye?" The old man chuckled. "I ain't half-mad."

When Edie shivered at Fenton's words, Corey longed to draw her into his arms and comfort her with his mouth on hers. This was not how he had thought it would be after he died. Mayhap this was his version of the Black Prince's pit. He could look upon Edie's loveliness but never would be able to touch her. If this continued, he was sure to be more than half-mad himself.

"Fenton, Miss Dunbar has taken a chill from the storm," Corey said, glad of the excuse to put an end to this uncomfortable conversation. "I must escort her back to the house. I shall see you later."

"And I shall see *you*." Fenton lurched toward the stables.

Ellen took the hat Corey held out to her, careful not to let her fingers brush his. As they continued along the curving path, she looked back toward the stables. There were not many times in her life she had been shocked speechless, but Corey had been witness to two of them. He seemed as overmastered, because, for once, he was silent.

"Do you believe him?" she asked as they walked past the strawberry beds. "Do you think you will remain connected to me and to this life until the proper hour comes for your death? I thought you could be freed from your ghostly state once you did as you had vowed."

"I have no idea what to believe any longer." His grin returned as he knelt and plucked some berries from beneath the leaves. "I think it would be best if no one else knew I was about."

"Who else might see you?"

He dropped the berries into her hand and smiled when she yelped with the cold. "No one should be able to see me now. I suspect you and Fenton are the only ones lucky enough."

Ellen popped the icy berries into her mouth and smiled at their sweetness. To own the truth, such a simple, commonplace treat was the perfect antidote for her disquiet. "I know the dangers of telling anyone else what I have seen. No one would believe me, not even Marian."

"Especially you should not tell Marian."

"Why?"

"She is so easily obsessed. She would rip apart the Abbey in an attempt to discover where I might be." He grinned as they crossed the lawn to the steps by the side door. "She still is rankled that she never managed to repay me for my last prank."

"Which one was that?"

"No doubt you have heard her lambasting poor Reggie for his pup that ruined her best rug."

"You arranged that?" she asked, climbing the steps.

He smiled. "It was never my intention to inflict such damage on her house. I had thought to tease her stiff-necked husband. However, before Reggie even missed the beast, the pup had left her mark on Herrold Hall."

"You should be ashamed of yourself."

"Should I?" He stepped closer, and she leaned against the door, staring up at him. "Should I be more ashamed of such an accident than of the thoughts filling my head when I see you?"

Even though she knew she was inviting danger and despair, she whispered, "What thoughts are filling your head now?"

"Of how soft your skin would be beneath my fingers." His hand curved along her face, leaving a finger's breadth between it and her cheek.

She held her breath, ignoring the chill as warmth swelled through her. Softly she said, "Corey, you should not torment yourself like this."

"And you?"

Looking up at the intensity glowing in his gaze, she nodded.

"You have never wondered what it would be like if I were to kiss you?"

"I wonder far too often. I—"

Ellen heard Corey's sudden laugh as the door opened and she dropped, ignobly, onto the foyer floor. As Lorenzo's footman hurried to apologize, she stared out the door. Corey gave her a wave and vanished.

"What is this?" Marian called from the stairs. She rushed down as Ellen rose. "Oh, thank heavens! Here you are! Where have you been? Lorenzo and I have been beside ourselves having the house searched for you. It was not very gracious of you to send Lorenzo back to the house and not wait for him to come back."

"Marian, I am fine."

Grasping Ellen's hands, she said, "My dear, I am so sorry if I said something to hurt you. You know you are as dear to me as anyone, and I would never wish to bring you pain." She hugged Ellen, then pulled back. Her forehead threaded with a frown. "Your habit is cold!"

"Isn't that peculiar?" she asked, and turned away before Marian could see her expression.

"How can the fabric be cold when the weather has been so warm?"

"Marian, I think I should return to Herrold Hall posthaste and change into something dry."

"Nonsense," came a deeper voice from the shadows.

Ellen smiled as Lorenzo walked across the dusky foyer to them. "I owe you an apology," she said.

"We can speak after you get yourself more comfortable." His voice was as stiff as if they were strangers.

"I shall order a bath for her," Marian said. "Then once she is cozy, we shall have a nice cup of tea and a pleasant talk. Doesn't that sound fine?"

"Fine," he replied.

"Come along, Ellen. You are dripping on the floor, you know."

Ellen drew her arm out of Marian's grasp. "I shall be right with you. I have something I need to tell Lorenzo first."

"There is no need—" he began.

"Ellen, you shall sicken," interrupted Marian. "If—"

"Marian!" Clenching her hands, she heard the brim of her hat crack. She was tired and cold and hot and wet and miserable for more reasons than she wanted to think about, but she would be doomed to perdition before she was silenced again.

"Really," murmured Marian, her hands fluttering about her.

"Marian," Ellen said in a calmer voice, "forgive me. I should not have taken that tone with you. You are my friend."

"I have wondered about that of late. You have been so distant from me, and you fly up to the boughs each time I speak to you. I wish I knew what was wrong." Tears filled her wide eyes. "I wish . . ." Then Marian rushed up the stairs.

Ellen sighed. "Now she shall be in a pelter at me, too."

"Too?" asked Lorenzo.

"You are angry with me, aren't you?"

"I own that I was until Marian told me how she had upset you."

"She did?"

He smiled, and the sternness drained from his face. "Marian owns up to her mistakes . . . on occasion."

"But I thought you were distressed that I had left when I told you I would wait."

Drawing her hand within his arm, he led her up the stairs. "It is just as well you showed the wisdom to find another place to enjoy the day. I was coerced into helping Reggie search for his missing pup. He did not wish to halt even when the storm came."

"Did you find it?"

He chuckled. "After another count, lo and behold! The pup had been there all along." At the top of the stairs, he stepped back. "I hope you still wish to read some of my efforts at writing."

"Certainly."

He reached under his coat and pulled out a sheaf of papers. "Will you let me know your honest opinion at the church fair at the end of the week?"

"A church fair?"

"Marian assured me that you were attending with her." He smiled. "It is nothing fancy, you should know."

By now, Ellen was accustomed to Marian's machinations and knew how useless it was to argue. "I have not been to a church fair since I left Scotland."

"This fair has been held every summer for as long as the church has kept records and before that. We thought it might amuse you and get your mind off . . ."

She hurried to say, "It sounds wonderful, Lorenzo." No doubt he needed to find a rest for his thoughts as much as she did.

Putting her hand on his arm, she said nothing. Words could not express his grief, which she understood too well. Awkwardly, he patted her hand, then drew away. She feared she had embarrassed him when he urged her, rather gruffly, to take all the time she wished before she came down to join them for some wine before dinner.

As Lorenzo turned to go back down the stairs, Ellen's eyes were caught by a glimmer at the bottom. Her heart did a flip-flop, but the glow slowly faded. It must have been no more than a trick of the day's last light.

Her steps were heavy as she turned toward the room where her bath would be waiting. She had learned to accept Marian's matchmaking, but she doubted she ever would be able to keep her heart from breaking each time she realized her love for Corey was hopeless.

"Delicious!" Ellen laughed as she licked her sticky fingers and looked at the woman serving ice cream at the table in the shadow of the village church's square steeple. Beside her, Marian was trying to eat her ice cream without making a mess. The warm day was conspiring against them, melting the generous portions of chocolate ice cream over the edges of the dishes.

Lorenzo offered his handkerchief. "Will this help?"

"Not much." Ellen set her empty dish on the table by the huge elm that shadowed the churchyard. "I fear I would need a dozen handkerchiefs to repair this mess."

"I look a complete rump," Marian moaned as the ice cream dripped onto her light green dress. "Fudge!"

Her husband glanced up from the book he was reading to regard her somberly. "Not fudge, my sweet, but ice cream, I believe."

Ellen choked back a laugh and was grateful when Lorenzo pointed toward a trough by the road. Going to it, she plunged her hands into the cool water, being cautious that her reticule did not get wet. She rubbed the stickiness from them and said, "Thank you."

"The water was here without any effort by me."

"Not for this." She shook her hands, then grimaced as water spotted her white silk dress. She and Marian would make quite the pair during the fair day that had only begun. "Thank you for giving me an excuse to scurry away before I laughed at Lord Herrold."

"He would not mind."

"No?"

Lorenzo smiled and held out his arm. "I collect he would

not even notice. I have met only one other man in my life who was so single-minded."

"Corey?"

Nodding, he walked with her across the lush grass to where a group of children were excitedly trying to hit a target that would send an empty barrel into a large tub of water. He paused by a table where two young women were selling lemonade. Paying the two pennies for two glasses, he handed one to Ellen.

"You have," he said, after taking a sip, "a clear insight into a man you met so briefly."

"It is not just that. You get this expression of sadness when you think of him."

"I had no idea." He linked his arm through hers as they continued to stroll around the church grounds. "I must own the truth, though. Corey was even more ill-suited than I for this life as the Marquess of Wulfric. He was always looking for adventure. Even as a lad, he would flee out of the nursery and spend the night on the shore." He nodded a greeting to a man who was rushing past with a bucket of biscuits. "He should have been a second son who could have made a career in the military."

"He hated the army."

"He did?" He paused. "How do you know?"

Ellen knew she must not hesitate. "Just from what I have heard."

"I do own that the Abbey is incredibly empty with just me knocking around in it."

She smiled. "Be careful. If you say something like that in Marian's hearing, she will have you airing out the ballroom so quickly your head will spin."

"True. She, too, is single-minded, surpassing even her husband and Corey."

"Unquestionably."

Ellen listened to Lorenzo describe the history of the simple church as they wandered around the grounds and past the table where baskets were set, waiting for gentlemen to bid on a chance to win the contents and the company of the young woman who had prepared the meal. She had noticed the village lasses watching the lads try to peek at the names pinned to the cloths atop the baskets. She looked forward to the chance to watch the auction while she relished the meal Marian's cook had prepared for them.

When Lorenzo was called away by a group of stern-faced gentlemen who used his title in every other sentence, Ellen felt sorry for him. Even if Corey had not told her how much Lorenzo despised these obligations of his title, she would have guessed that from the way his thin shoulders hunched and his voice softened to little more than a whisper.

She decided to look about and come back to his rescue in a few minutes. Not even the town's council should demand all of the marquess's time on a feast day.

"Miss Dunbar!"

Ellen closed her eyes and wondered if there was any way to wish away Kenneth Pratt. When he shouted her name a second time, she turned to face him. Smiling was almost impossible, but she managed it when Mr. Pratt swaggered toward her. Did he have no idea how ludicrous he looked as he paraded about like a bull in a meadow of uninterested cows? No, some of the lasses were eyeing him eagerly. Inspiration struck her when she saw that a pretty blond lass was one of his most candid admirers.

Mr. Pratt was dressed to catch a young woman's eye, for his navy coat was the perfect match for his buckskin pantaloons. Gold sparkled on his fingers and from the chain connected to his garret where his watch fob waited for him to draw it forth to show his importance. The shine on his boots bespoke much attention by his valet.

If he were not so impossibly vain . . .

"Ah, Miss Dunbar," he crowed as if he thought everyone in earshot were interested, "how delighted I am to see you!"

She suffered him to kiss her hand lustily, but pulled it back before he could do more. "This is a wonderful day for the fair, isn't it?"

"I had hoped you would seek me out upon your arrival."

"Me? Seek you out?" She clamped her lips closed. This man was incredible! If he were not so annoying, his self-satisfied affectations would be entertaining.

"Of course." He drew her hand within his arm. "Did you think I missed the eager glances you gave me during my call at Herrold Hall?"

Mayhap, like Marian, he equated queasiness with falling in love, for she had been eager only to rid herself of his company. Stepping away from him, Ellen smiled. "Mr. Pratt, you should know that Lord Wulfric escorted me and the Herrolds to the fair today."

"Good of him."

"Yes."

He had not been so pleasant about Lorenzo before. She wondered why he was today.

"Lorenzo and Marian have been friends for many, many years," he said. "What a shame she married Herrold! Lorenzo would have made her a better match."

Ellen stared at him in disbelief. "Mr. Pratt, you are quite mistaken."

"I do not make mistakes as a custom."

She doubted that, even though she was sure he seldom owned to any error. "Mayhap not, but Lorenzo and Marian would have driven each other mad if they were wed."

His booming laugh made heads swivel in their direction. Seeing the wide eyes and imagining what was being whispered, Ellen wished Mr. Pratt were as invisible as Corey . . . and haunting someone else.

"You are so amusing," he crowed. "As if they were not already crazy as it is."

As I must be to allow this conversation to continue, she thought. Pasting her most innocuous smile on her lips, she said, "Mr. Pratt, I may be mistaken—"

"How wise of you to own to that. Mayhap you will see that you need a more astute head to guide you."

Not yours, for only the greatest stretch of the imagination would label you anything but a widgeon. "I may be mistaken," she began again, "but I think that young woman over there is eager to speak with you."

"Really?" His eyes widened as he straightened his lapels. "Which one?"

"That fetching blonde."

"Really?" he repeated. He took one step away from Ellen, hesitated, then turned back to her. "I cannot leave you here alone, Miss Dunbar."

"I am not alone. Marian will be looking for me, I am sure. She wished me to speak with your mother."

"About my call?"

Her stomach twisted at the thought, but she forced her smile to remain in place. "I suspect so." She looked past him. "Mr. Pratt, that young lady seems very, very impatient to speak with you. I think you would be most gentlemanly to go to her side immediately and ease her anxiety."

She could guess what he was thinking as easily as if his thoughts were her own. He did not want to risk insulting her, but he was intrigued with the pretty lass.

He cleared his throat and said, "Miss Dunbar, I . . ."

Ellen had to be pleased he did not trouble himself—and her—with some banger before he strode toward the simpering baggage who must be as want-witted as he to flap her thick lashes at him. She chuckled to herself as she heard his loud voice proclaiming his delight to speak with the girl . . . repeating the same greeting he had given Ellen. The man was a complete dolt!

Hurrying away before Mr. Pratt took the idea in his head to return to her company, Ellen discovered that Lorenzo was now speaking with the minister. He seemed very intent on what Reverend Stapleton had to say. Intruding would be rude. She glanced across the lawn. Marian and Lord Herrold were debating something with broad gestures before he put his arm around her shoulders and leaned her head against his chest. They would not wish to be interrupted either.

Her reticule struck her leg as she took a step in the opposite direction. Smiling, she clasped the silk bag in her hands. She had promised Lorenzo to read his poems before the fair day. Marian had kept her so busy with plans for a new gown for the assembly at the Pratts' house that she had not had a moment to herself to read them. What better time than now when everyone else was otherwise occupied?

She found a shady spot beneath a tree near the churchyard cemetery's stone wall. Rose vines contorted over the stones and stretched out into the grass, carrying their heady perfume with the blossoms. With her parasol propped behind her, she leaned back to enjoy the poetry.

And enjoy Lorenzo's poems was what she did. No matter how Corey might scoff at his cousin's attempts at writing, Lorenzo had a gift for entwining words to make simple rhymes. These were no grand epics of unrequited love and consummated passions. As lief, Lorenzo penned tales of the changing seasons along the shore and the glories of the gardens coming to life with the first touch of spring.

"Are you having fun?"

Ellen looked up. "Corey! I didn't know you could come here."

"I didn't either, but I thought it worth a try. I have not been beyond the Abbey or Herrold Hall since I dropped perch. It was time for me to wander farther afield."

"If you came for the ice cream, I suggest you eat it quickly."

"My misfortune, but food is not a necessity for me any longer. I never realized how much pomp we put into that simple function and how much time we waste." He sat beside her. "However, ice cream is one pleasure I miss dearly."

She lowered the pages to her lap. "I am so glad you tried to come to the fair. You haven't been about much lately."

"You have been so busy getting that gown made for Pratt's party." He leaned toward her. "You are a charming sight in your shift with strips of fabric hanging along you."

"You watched!"

He chuckled. "Edie, don't act so shocked. After all, I have had *carte blanche* to your bedchamber for at least a fortnight now."

"But this is different."

"How?" Resting his chin on his fist, he reclined on the grass and gazed up at her. "I have sat in your bed with you, Edie."

"You make it sound so illicit."

"Isn't it?" He picked up a corner of the hem of her gown and stroked it slowly. "With your hair soft around your shoulders and your eyes weighted with sleep, you bring the most deliciously illicit thoughts into my head."

"Please don't say such things."

"Why? Because they embarrass you?"

"No." She watched his fingers' gentle caress along her dress. To have him touch her as sweetly, to be surrounded by the warmth of his flesh as his mouth found hers . . . She shook her head. "Please don't, Corey."

"But why?"

She pulled her gown away from him. "You know very well why."

"Do I?"

Taking a deep breath, she counted to ten, then said, "All right, I shall tell you, my late Lord Wulfric. When you say things like that, I wonder how much frostbite I can risk to satisfy my curiosity about how splendid it would feel if you kissed me."

He stared at her.

Ellen folded her arms over her chest and smiled, astounded that the truth had silenced him. "You wanted to know."

"Calf-head that I was, I did," he rumbled as he sat up. "Dash it! Edie, you were supposed to blush and change the subject." Kneeling, he put his hands out to her. As hers started to rise toward them, he whispered, "You were supposed to tell me you regard me with the same tepid affection as you would a bothersome brother."

"I don't have a brother." She gasped as the cold seared her fingertips. Pulling back, she murmured, "That was not a wise thing to do."

He smiled sadly. "Sometimes wishes take precedence over common sense."

"You'd think I would learn that, wouldn't you?"

"And that I would." He cleared his throat and grinned. "If

you will not change the subject, I must. What are you doing here by yourself?"

"Reading."

"What?" He tilted one of the pages and groaned. "You poor thing! Lorenzo's scribblings."

She folded the pages and put them in her bag. "He is quite good, you know."

"No, I don't know."

"You have never done him the courtesy of perusing a single one of his poems?"

He flung out his arms. "By all that's blue, Edie, when do you think I might have found time to exult in such a pastime? While I lay in the French mud, dodging the Frogs' balls as they tried to put an end to us all? Or mayhap, I might have enjoyed one while I was riding about the shire tending to the unending tasks to be done by Lord Wulfric."

"There is no need for sarcasm."

"Then be honest."

"I was. I think he is quite good."

He set himself on his feet. "This is a fair day, Edie. You shouldn't be sitting here alone. You should be singing and dancing and trying to decide which young buck you wish to have bidding on your basket."

"I did not bring a basket."

"You didn't? That is a shame. 'Tis a tradition in the village, you know." He tapped his chin. "You should not break traditions when you are a guest."

She stared at him in horror. He could not have—he would not have—he must have, if his grin were any clue. "Blast it, Corey Wolfe!"

Gathering her skirts, she raced toward the table where the baskets were displayed. Corey's laughter followed her, not growing fainter, so she knew he was close on her heels. She saw Mr. Pratt talking with the blonde, and she sped on the other side of a booth where a barrel waited for someone to hit the target set above it and dunk it into the water.

"Ellen, what is wrong?"

She wanted to run past Marian, but that would cause only more trouble. Pausing, she said, "I want to look at the nuncheon baskets."

"But why in such a hurry?"

"I—" A ball careened toward her.

She gasped when it abruptly dropped to the ground inches from her head. It bounced off the ground and into her hands, which automatically reached for it. The hard rubber was colder than the ice cream had been. Although she could not see him, she knew Corey had halted the ball.

The children shouted for her to toss it back. She threw it. The ball swerved and hit the target. The cask fell into the tank, water splashing upward. The wave crashed down over Mr. Pratt. He shrieked and leaped back into the blonde. The young woman toppled into a gentleman's arms and promptly swooned.

Ellen laughed as Corey appeared. He bowed to her, then toward Mr. Pratt. The children roared their approval.

Marian gasped, "How did that happen?"

"Tell her," Corey said, "that you are tired of Pratt showering you with insincerity, so you sincerely showered him."

" 'Twas nothing but an ill-tossed ball," Ellen said, although she was tempted to repeat Corey's words. "I should apologize to Mr. Pratt."

"Why?" asked Corey. "He deserved the dousing."

Marian said, "I think you should give him some time to cool his temper."

"And his ardor."

Ellen glared at Corey. She had enough problems without him being jealous of a boor. After all, she wanted as little to do with Mr. Pratt as possible.

She went to the table and looked at the baskets. Marian glanced over her shoulder as Ellen read the tags. When she turned over one with her name on it, Marian chuckled.

"Ellen, you have been listening to me! What better way to attract a potential husband than to entice him to join you for a pleasant meal? Why didn't you tell me you were preparing a basket for the auction?"

"I really had not thought about it until a short while ago." She picked up the basket. "Mayhap it would be better if we just made a donation to the church and ate this ourselves."

"Nonsense." Marian took the basket and put it down among the others. "It was a brilliant idea."

"Thank you," Corey said with a chuckle.

Ellen scowled at him, but he only grinned more broadly.

"I told you I was going to find you a husband," he said as Marian turned to speak with a friend.

Motioning toward the area where the carriages were parked, Ellen said, "I need to speak with you."

"You can thank me right here."

"Thanking you was not what I had in mind."

"Then you shall have to wait until another time."

"Why?"

He stepped back and bowed as Marian grasped Ellen's arm.

"My dear," Marian cooed, "I want you to meet Miss Appleton. Her brother is visiting at the end of next week."

"And is unquestionably eligible," Corey interjected. "If you find Kenneth Pratt unbearable, you will learn he is not the worst of the lot this shire has sired. Eugene Appleton, however, is."

"How do you do, Miss Appleton?" Ellen asked, trying to smile at the pleasant-looking brunette.

"Very well, Miss Dunbar. You are right, Lady Herrold. She is perfect for Eugene." She gave a giggle, and Ellen glanced at Corey, who only grinned more broadly. "You must join us for tea next week after Eugene comes home, Miss Dunbar."

"If possible," she answered.

"It *will* be possible," Marian corrected.

Ellen was prevented from adding more when Marian took her arm again and steered her toward a thick-waisted dowager who was holding court on a bench in front of the church. When Corey sat on one edge of the steps, close enough so he could hear everything, Ellen sighed. It was going to be a long day.

Twelve

The crowd gathered for the auction of the luncheon baskets. Marian drew Ellen right to the front of the crowd. Pulling her lace shawl more tightly around her shoulders, Marian mused, "There is a cold breeze today, isn't there? I hope it does not rain."

Ellen ignored Corey's laugh and Marian's comment as he edged closer to them. If Marian took note of her silence, she made no comment. She waved to her husband to join them.

"Do bid on Ellen's basket, Reginald," Marian said, not taking care to lower her voice. "Few of the young men know her. We do not want her to be humiliated, and it is for the church, after all."

Lord Herrold focused his gaze on Ellen. "There appears to be nothing wrong with this young woman. She has nice lines and the suggestion of excellent breeding."

"Reginald!"

"You asked my opinion."

"I did not!"

Ellen did not follow as they strolled away—arm in arm, she noted—but continuing their brangle. What a peculiar marriage they had, albeit not as bizarre as her relationship with Corey. Was it something, mayhap, in the sea air blowing constantly off the water that made everyone here, including her, a bit deranged?

When she saw Lorenzo searching the crowd, Ellen waved to him. He gave her a grateful smile as he walked toward her.

"Forgive me for leaving you like that," he said.

Corey intruded to say, "That was unlike you, Lorenzo. Your manners are usually unblemished. You must watch yourself, or you shall prove that you are, indeed, as much a Wolfe as the rest of us."

"I know there are many with claims on your time," Ellen replied, wishing she could frown at Corey. She did not want to upset Lorenzo. "Especially now when all the people here must be wondering how things will change with a new Lord Wulfric."

He sighed. "I had hoped that they would respect this day of leisure, but I was too optimistic, I fear."

"Did you satisfy them?"

"Hardly." He chuckled, his good spirits returning. "I doubt if they ever could be satisfied."

"You are learning fast," Corey said with candid astonishment.

"They are anxious," Lorenzo continued, "for me to go to Town to represent them during the next gathering of the Lords. I hastened to assure them that they should concentrate instead on the upcoming elections in the borough and send a good man to the Commons on their behalf." He held out his arm. "Forgive me, Ellen. I shall bore you with my talk of political business."

She put her hand on his arm. "I do not find such things boring. On the contrary, I am surprised at your interest in politics."

"Why?"

"Corey said—" She bit her lip to silence the words that would divulge too much.

"You must have had a very interesting conversation with my cousin." His brows dipped into a baffled frown. "Am I mistaken when I thought you and he met for the first time the night of his death?"

Corey moved aside as they walked past him, but matched his steps to theirs. "Do not bamblusterate poor Lorenzo with too much of the truth, Edie. He might swoon right to the ground if he were privy to it. Think how embarrassing it would be to Wolfe Abbey to have its newest marquess senseless in the churchyard."

"You are not mistaken. We—" She did not care what Corey said. She wished she could think of a hint of the truth that she could tell Lorenzo. He deserved the truth, but how could she tell him?

Fenton! She must seek out Fenton and discover if he could help her. That might not do much good, for Lorenzo considered the man daft. Still, it was the only assistance she might have.

Lorenzo politely was waiting for her to continue. She gave him a hesitant smile and struggled to devise something to say. Once again, she was given an excuse not to go on.

"Time to take out your gold, gentlemen!" came a shout from the church's steps. "Buy a basket, and the lady who prepared it will join you for a picnic here in the churchyard."

The auctioneer—Reverend Stapleton, she realized with surprise—was holding up the first basket.

"About time," Corey said as he paused under a tree with a view of the steps.

Ellen's hope that Lorenzo would continue away from the auction died when he stopped right in front of the tree. Could it be possible that he, too, could see Corey's grin? *Don't be jobbernowl,* she chided herself.

The first basket was sold to the only man who bid on it and who eagerly accepted the kiss on the cheek from the young lass standing next to him. The second and third went in much the same manner.

Ellen tensed when the minister held up the one Corey had arranged to be brought here. She wondered how he had managed that, but it was too late to ask now.

"Best of the lot," Corey said as he folded his arms over his chest.

"That is your basket, isn't it, Ellen?" Lorenzo asked.

"Yes, but how did you know?"

He winked. "I was not the only one who perused the baskets before the beginning of the auction. How generous of you to take the time to help raise money for our village church!"

"It was nothing." That much was the truth. She started to add more, then groaned as she saw Mr. Pratt move closer to the auctioneer.

"What is wrong?"

"If Mr. Pratt wins the basket, I swear I shall leave the fair right now."

"Help her out," Corey ordered, although his cousin could not hear him. "Spend a few shillings, Lorenzo, to put Pratt in his place."

Ellen stared at Corey. Was *that* the reason he had brought the basket? To make sure Mr. Pratt was so humbled that he would leave her alone? She was growing more and more baffled by Corey's motivations. When he first had spoken of finding a husband for her, he had listed both Mr. Pratt and Mr. Adams as possible suitors. Now he was going out of his way to show her they were impossible matches.

Lorenzo patted her hand on his arm. "Having Pratt win your basket would be a shame. Let's see what we can do to frustrate his plans."

"Lorenzo, I did not mean—"

"I know you didn't."

Corey chuckled as Lorenzo raised his hand as Reverend Stapleton called for bids. "Lorenzo, you old calf-head! I knew you had some Wolfe chivalry hidden somewhere deep within you."

Mr. Pratt topped Lorenzo's bid before the minister could repeat it. Lorenzo doubled his first bid, which brought gasps of amazement from the crowd and a wide, gratified grin from Marian. Mr. Pratt shouted back another bid, and Lorenzo countered without a pause.

Ellen's smile faltered when she glanced at Corey. He had lost his nonchalance. His brow was furrowed as he stared at his cousin, and she saw his fingers slowly tighten into fists. Although she longed to go to him and ask what was amiss, she could not. How could she explain to anyone that she needed to speak with the ghost of the late Lord Wulfric?

Applause tore her from her thoughts. Ellen turned to see Lorenzo smiling and Mr. Pratt soothing his disappointment with the young blonde who had stayed close to his side.

"Congratulate me, Ellen." Collecting the basket, Lorenzo held out his arm to her. "The best five pounds I ever spent."

"I hope you think so when you see what is in it."

"What is inside?"

"A surprise," she said with a gulp. What *would* Corey put in a nuncheon basket? She dared not think. She looked at Corey, who was edging toward them slowly.

"You need not worry," Corey told her. "I would not put anything in there to poison you."

She frowned at Corey as Lorenzo turned to speak to several gentlemen who came over to him.

"Or Lorenzo," Corey added with reluctance. "That might not have been the truth if Kenneth had proven to be the victor." Corey took a single step into the sunshine, then paused, putting his hand to his head. "I shall speak with you back in your rooms."

"You are leaving?" she whispered, astonished.

"I seem to be most comfortable in the shadows, Edie. This bright sunshine sucks out my energy, making me feel as if I have run from here to London."

"I didn't know."

He smiled sadly. "Nor did I."

"Would you like me to come and sit with you beneath the trees for a while?"

"Enjoy the fair. After all, Lorenzo has paid well for the chance to eat that basket's contents with you. I shall see you this evening."

A tremor of dismay fled through her as she realized the glow around him was weak, so weak it had almost vanished. Was this what happened when a ghost was sickening? Or did ghosts get ill? She could understand none of this.

"Go, if you must," she whispered. "Do not stay if it is dangerous for you."

"Is that concern I hear, Edie, or just elation that I shall not be here for the rest of the day?"

"I own it will not be the same without you being here to comment on everything."

"I thought you would be pleased to be without my voice rumbling in your ears for a few hours."

Ellen stared up at him, wanting to speak the truth. She wanted him with her all the time. Even if he irritated her to the point she had to fight to keep her temper from exploding out, she missed him when he was not about.

Love. She loved this phantom who had no more being than a dream. When had she fallen in love with him? When had she been so want-witted as to let her life get caught up in this absurdity? Certainly it had not been when he had been overbearing or when he had played tricks on her as he had today. Yet when she saw the desire in his eyes, her lips ached for his against them.

"Corey, take care of yourself. I don't want to lose the sound of your voice rumbling in my ears forever."

"You won't." He brushed the brim of her bonnet with the back of his hand. "I promise you that."

He was gone before she could reply.

Lorenzo brought Ellen into the conversation with his friends, whose names Ellen could not remember when she was thinking only of Corey. Pretending to listen, Ellen wondered what would happen when she returned to London at the end of her stay with Marian. Would Corey go with her? If he were attached to her as he had told Fenton, then he must. Or would she be restrained from leaving grassville?

The questions taunted her as she walked with Lorenzo to a sunny knoll overlooking the small stream that twisted between thick clumps of wildflowers. When they were sitting on a smooth stone, Ellen cautiously lifted the cloth on top of the basket. She smiled with relief when she saw meat and bread as well as a canister of wine and two pieces of chocolate cake. Corey had been, as always, honest.

Handing Lorenzo a plate and some of the meat and bread that had been neatly wrapped, she said, "Thank you, Lorenzo. I truly appreciate your bidding on this basket. Mr. Pratt's company is—"

"A fate worse than death?"

"Not quite that bad." Again she lowered her eyes. Death was not the worst fate to be suffered. Losing her heart to a man who was dead was even worse.

"I am glad for your company, Ellen. No one else would wish to speak of the things that you seem to find interesting, although I suspect you are often too polite to tell me to put an end to my babbling."

She unwrapped her food and said, "Then I shall babble about your poetry and tell you how wonderful I think it is."

"You do?"

"I do."

Corey was sure neither Edie nor Lorenzo had heard his silent groan as she innocently uttered those words he had vowed she would speak to another man. The words that would close him out of her life forever. How easy it had been to make that pledge when his mind had been reeling from its passage from life to whatever hell he had been consigned to! He could imagine no torture more horribly exquisite than witnessing this.

From where he stood in the invigorating shadows, he watched Lorenzo's smile broaden as his cousin touched Edie's shoulder lightly. Corey did not move closer, even though he wanted to step between the two. Easily he had thwarted Pratt when the beef-headed block had tried to court Edie. This complication he had not foreseen.

When he heard her soft laugh, something twisted in his gut. Mayhap he was the fool. This should have been the obvious solution from the beginning. Lorenzo was a decent chap, although he had as much imagination as a rock. He would make Edie a faithful husband who would be attentive to her every need.

His fingers curled into fists, his nails digging into his palms. Blast it all to perdition! She had needs he did not want to think of Lorenzo fulfilling. His cousin would have the opportunity to taste her soft mouth and draw her slender form against him.

He slammed his fist against a tree. Damn! Nothing! He could feel nothing when he struck the rough bark. The only thing he could feel was this soul-deep anguish. He wanted Edie for his own. All the other women he had avoided entangling his life with had not prepared him for the sensations swirling through him when he savored her pert smile and sharp wit. When she gazed up at him, the anger, which had driven him to the war and back, vanished into a yearning to make her laugh.

A Wolfe's vow lasts forever.

For the first time, he understood how long eternity could be.

Thirteen

Fenton was perched on a small stool by the door to the stables when Ellen drew in the gig and stepped down onto the crushed stone. Although he looked up, his fingers did not slow as he cleaned the leather harness draped across his lap like a lady's fine wrap.

"I need to speak with you," she said as she pushed back her bonnet so she could see past the brim to be certain they were alone. If someone else chanced upon this conversation, it might cause even more problems.

"Yer welcome to sit and talk." He pointed with a stained finger to another stool. His voice remained calm as he asked, "How be his lordship? Thought to see him again, but he be about with ye."

"I need your advice." She balanced on the uncomfortable stool.

"Ye can tell anyone ye wish about Lord Wulfric."

"How did you know what I wanted to ask?"

He grinned at her, and she wished he had not. Even though there was nothing malicious in the expression, she was unnerved by its suggestion that he knew more about this whole muddle than he would tell her.

"What else would ye be askin'?" He gave a shrug. "Tell anyone ye please. No one'll take heed of ye. Just think ye be crazy like old Fenton."

"Don't you think Lorenzo should know the truth?"

"Do *ye* think he should know?"

She rose, unable to sit as she tried to unsnarl her thoughts. "The knowledge might assuage his grief, if he believed me."

"And that be the rub, missy. Who would be believin' ye?" Again he caught her gaze. "Would ye believe it if ye be told that his lordship be a ghost wanderin' about the countryside?"

"I don't know."

"Ye know." He rubbed the leather more vigorously. "Ye would call anyone with such a tale a moony. Advice ye want? Advice I give ye. Be careful, missy. I would not like to see ye locked away in an asylum. 'Tis no place for his lordship."

Ellen had been about to thank him for his concern, then spun on her heel and stamped back to the gig. His only thoughts were for Corey . . . as hers were, she must own. There must be some way to extricate all of them from this. If only she had some idea how.

Ellen set her embroidery down onto her lap and stared through the windows making up one wall of the solar. Rain slid along the panes, twisting in contorted paths along the uneven glass. For the first time in days, she was alone with her thoughts, and she did not like a single one.

Her life was becoming too complicated. The questions that had taunted her at the fair still had no answers. By the end of the next week, she should be leaving for Westhampton Hall to join Romayne for the duke's birthday party. If she went, Corey might be forced to go with her. She knew how it would hurt him to leave and mayhap never see Wolfe Abbey again, because she was skeptical about the wisdom of ever returning to this place. He might not have wished for the obligations of his title, but she could not mistake his love for his family's home.

He belonged here as surely as he had while alive. To take him into exile across England would be wrong. Yet, she could not stay here forever.

Could she?

If she had not seen the truth on his face the afternoon of the fair, she might have been able to leave without worry. He cared about her too much. Mayhap he even loved her as she loved him. She could imagine no more poignant irony. He had stayed earthbound in order to find her a man who touched her heart. The only one who had was Corey Wolfe . . . the late Corey Wolfe.

A commotion sounded from the garden. Rising, Ellen went to the window. In spite of her grim mood, she could not help smiling as she saw Lord Herrold rush by at the best speed he could. A dozen pups swarmed in a dozen directions, each of them staying just beyond his fingers and yelping loudly.

"Oh, here you are!" Marian came into the room, looked out the window, and shook her head. "I do hope Reginald will think to wipe his feet before he tracks all that mud across my rugs."

"You love him, don't you?" Ellen asked.

Marian stared at her in astonishment. "He is my husband. What a silly thing to ask."

"But do you love him?"

Sitting on the chair in front of an ancient tapestry of a knight fighting a dragon in vain, she said, "I suppose I must."

"How do you know?"

"Ellen, these are the queerest questions." Her eyes brightened. "Does this mean you are in love?"

She shrugged as she went back to gather up her embroidery. "How would I know?"

"You would know." She nodded her head sagely. "He will be constantly in your mind. Even in your dreams. When you dance with him, you tingle as if you stood too close to a pond in a thunderstorm."

"Dance . . ." she whispered.

"Aha!" Marian wore her broadest smile when Ellen looked at her.

"Aha what?"

"Dance! You are thinking of Kenneth Pratt, aren't you?"

She shuddered at the very thought. "Please, Marian, that is not funny, even in jest."

"I did not mean it as a jest."

"Then it is even less funny. The man thinks only of himself and his own pleasures."

"Reginald might be described much the same, and he is a good husband to me."

"Reginald is nothing like Kenneth Pratt!"

"No?" Marian glanced toward the window and smiled gently. "In some ways, they are much alike. There are those who say Reginald thinks only of his dogs. That is true. Reginald concentrates much of his time on his beloved dogs, but he does love me at least as much." Her smile became more genuine. "And that is very, very much, Ellen."

"I am glad."

"But if you have no *tendre* for Kenneth, then who?"

Ellen should have guessed her friend would come back to her question with all due speed. Just as she was about to answer, although she had no idea what she might say, a maid rushed in.

"Milady," the woman cried, "Cook tried to keep him out until he cleaned his boots, but—"

Marian flung her hands into the air as her husband rushed into the room. "Reginald, look at the mess you have made of my rugs!"

"Forgive me. I am all at sixes and sevens." He looked as if he might weep. "One of the pups has vanished."

Marian's anger vanished immediately as she put her hands out to him. "Dear Reginald, surely you miscounted the litter."

"No, one has run away." He dropped onto a brocade-covered chair, ignoring his wife's wince as the dampness on his coat stained the white fabric. "The best of the lot. She's young, but she can already follow a burning scent right to the breeding earth. Dash it!"

"Can we help you look?" Ellen asked.

He shook his head. " 'Twill soon be dark." Putting his hand over Marian's as she knelt beside his chair, he sighed. "All we can do is hope she will return."

When Marian leaned her head on his arm, Ellen went out into the hallway and climbed the stairs to her bedchamber. Once she was certain she was alone in the room and that the door to the dressing room was securely latched, she called out Corey's name.

"Over here," came back the answer.

Ellen whirled to see him sitting on the chair by the hearth. When he cautiously came to his feet, she asked, "Is something wrong? How do you feel?"

"I am dead. How do you think I feel?" he fired back.

"You look . . . different."

"How?"

She shrugged. "I am not sure."

"If I could see my reflection in a glass, I might be able to help you." His jaunty tone sounded coerced. "So what can I do for you today, Edie? Do you need something, or are you simply lonely between calls?"

"Corey, what is wrong?" She took a step toward him, then paused when he turned and walked away to look out the window. "Something is bothering you."

"Nothing important." He clasped his hands behind his back. "Mayhap 'tis nothing more than I grow tired of this folly. You should stop delaying and choose a husband, Edie, so I might rid myself of this baleful existence which is neither life nor death."

"Is it so terrible?"

When he faced her, she saw the truth on his face. She never had viewed such misery. " 'Tis more terrible than you can guess." He shook himself and smiled. "But there is no need to linger on such grim thoughts when you wished to speak with me. What is it?"

"Nothing of import."

"You know how useless it is to try to fill my head with your out-and-outers. The truth, Edie."

"That is the truth." She sat on the bench in front of her dressing table and looked up at him. "Lord Herrold is all upset about his pups, and I wished to speak of something else. That is all."

"Then we shall speak of other things. What—?"

Ellen glanced toward the door when the impatient knock sounded a second time. Rising, she went to open it.

A maid bowed her head toward Ellen. "Lady Herrold wishes to remind you dinner is ready."

"Thank you. I shall be down in the catching up of a garter." The maid nodded and walked away.

Ellen turned, but swallowed the words on her tongue. The room was empty. She went out into the hall and closed the door behind her. Although she waited, no glow filled the long corridor, save for the light from the lamps.

Something was amiss with Corey. That was evident, but she could not guess what the problem might be . . . unless he had been honest. Mayhap he *was* disgusted with being caught in the nether regions between life and death. Mayhap it was time for her to make a decision. She just must make sure it was not one she would regret for the rest of *her* life.

No one spoke in the grand dining room as dinner was served. Ellen worried her linen napkin and stared at her plate. The idea of eating threatened to make her ill. Listening to the patter of rain on the windows that swept from the floor to the friezed ceiling fifteen feet above, she glanced at her hosts. Lord Herrold had eaten no more than she had, and Marian was toying with her roast beef as if she, too, had lost all interest in eating.

"My lord," announced a footman, "Lord Wulfric awaits you in the foyer."

Lord Herrold tossed his napkin on top of his food. "What is Lorenzo doing out on such a dreary night?"

"Mayhap we should go and find out," suggested Marian. She smiled weakly at Ellen. "You may stay and eat if you wish."

"Alone?" She shook her head. "This will give me the chance to thank Lorenzo for his company at the fair."

Marian's smile broadened, and Ellen knew her answer was just what her friend had hoped to hear.

The foyer was bright with the brass chandelier hanging from the rotunda roof two floors above. Lorenzo smiled as they came into the octagonal room. He looked down at the mud dripping onto the marble floor. "Forgive me for making such a mess, but Reggie, I thought you might wish this returned to you without delay."

Lord Herrold rushed forward as Lorenzo swept aside his coat and pulled out a wet, matted ball of fur. "Where did you find her?" He cradled the shivering pup in his arms, climbing the stairs and turning toward the parlor.

"Not my parlor," moaned Marian as she hurried after him. "Reginald, not on my best settee."

Ellen exchanged a smile with Lorenzo. As the footman took his soaked greatcoat, she said, "You are considerate to come out on a night such as this."

"Reginald loves his dogs more than anything in the world, save his wife."

"Mayhap."

He chuckled. "At least as much as he would children of his own. I would not have left a toddler by the side of the road, and to own the truth, I saw her on my way to stop by and bring you this."

He held a book out to her. The leather was spotted with rain, but the pages were dry as she opened it. Her eyes widened as she saw the writing on the page facing the frontispiece.

> *To Ellen,*
> *Friendship is a gift beyond any words I can utter, so I pray these simple poems will speak for me.*
> *With affection,*
> *Lorenzo Wolfe, Lord Wulfric*

Ellen paged through the book and discovered it was a collection of his poems which he had copied onto the blank pages. "Lorenzo," she whispered as she closed the book, "I am overwhelmed. I never have had such a wondrous gift."

"It is not as wondrous as the gift you gave me at the fair."

"I gave you something?"

He smiled and took her hand between his. "You did not chide me for my silly avocation."

"Your poetry is not silly."

"See?" He stroked her fingers gently. "That is what I mean. I can imagine no finer gift to give a man than your faith in what he does."

Ellen stepped back, trying to make the motion seem spontaneous. She recognized that glow in his eyes. It was a tamer version of how Corey looked at her when he spoke of his yearning to hold her. What a muddle this was! If Lorenzo had more affection for her than was appropriate between friends, the situation was guaranteed to become even more addled.

And she had no idea how to undo all the tangles before each of them suffered from a broken heart.

Ellen knocked on the door to Marian's private chambers. When a maid opened the door, Ellen walked into the room, which was flounced with pink and white lace on every surface. The heavy scent of Marian's favorite perfume clogged every breath and rose from the Turkish carpet as Ellen went to where Marian was reclining on a chaise longue. Even Marian's wrapper was white with pink lace edging the modest neckline.

Marian stood and kissed Ellen on the cheek. "My dear, you look positively glowing this morning."

"Do I? I do not feel glowing."

"Can I hope you are in love?"

"Yes."

Marian's eyes widened. "Yes? You are in love? Deeply in love? Forever in love? This is more than just calf-love this time?"

"I fear so."

"With whom? When will the announcement come? Oh, my dear, I must begin planning an assembly to give you a chance to proclaim these wondrous tidings to the shire. I—"

"Marian!"

"—think a light supper will be perfect. The weather has been too warm for more. If—"

"Marian!"

"—we want to do more, we might consider a party with lanterns in the garden. Think of it, Ellen! It would be so lovely if the moon was new and the stars were out. Then—"

"Marian!"

Her exasperation must have reached her friend, for Marian said, "Yes?"

"Please sit, Marian."

"What is wrong?" She pressed her hand to her chest. "Oh dear, are you saying you are not about to announce your betrothal?"

"Please sit, Marian. Let me have a chance to explain."

She obeyed.

Ellen took a deep breath, then released it. Delaying would not make this easier. "I want you to listen and to believe that I am not insane."

"Ellen, what—?"

"Listen please."

"Very well." She smiled. "My dear, you know I wish only to see you happy."

"I know." Ellen did not add that she doubted if that was still possible. "Marian, I know no other way to tell you this than to be blunt. This house is haunted, and the ghost is Corey Wolfe."

"Ellen—"

"You said you would listen! Will you?"

Marian scowled, then nodded.

"I know I sound mad, but Corey first appeared to me as a spirit the night he died."

"And you have seen him since?"

"Often."

Marian looked over her shoulder. "Is he here now?"

"Do you think I would be talking about this if he were?"

"I have no idea." She brushed her hair back nervously from her face. "A ghost? This is most unsettling, Ellen. If you had seen Corey as a ghost only after you were injured, such a vision could be blamed on how hard you had banged your head on the earth. But to see him again and again . . ."

Ellen knelt next to her friend. "Marian, I do not blame you for finding this hard to believe. Even as I speak the words, I wonder how I can give them credence. I know only what I have seen and heard. Corey Wolfe is a ghost within these walls."

"But he should haunt Wolfe Abbey, not Herrold Hall."

"Oh, he is there, too." She sank back onto her heels. "He seems to be about wherever I go."

"Wherever?"

"Here, at Wolfe Abbey, at the fair."

"Where here?"

Ellen swallowed roughly. "You shall not like this answer, Marian. Most often, in my chambers upstairs."

"Oh dear. This is appalling. If it were to be bandied about the shire that you were speaking with a man in your private rooms—"

"A ghost, Marian."

"A male ghost."

"Yes." She could not deny that. Even as a spirit, Corey possessed a raw sensuality that urged her to throw all sense aside and her arms around him. That mischievous twinkle and the smile as he sat next to her while she was nestled among her pillows had suggested what his words had confirmed. If alive, he would have enticed her into discovering something more pleasurable than conversation in her bed.

"Oh, dear."

"Marian, he is a ghost. Nothing untoward has happened."

"This is all so confusing. Mayhap you are mistaken in what you have seen."

"Corey is real." When Marian frowned, she amended, "As real as a ghost can be."

Marian smoothed Ellen's hair back from her face. "My dear Ellen, are you so certain of this? You were distraught in the wake of the accident. Mayhap you have created this fantasy to ease your heart."

"I am not the only one who has seen him."

"Who else?"

"Fenton."

"Fenton?" Marian's face grew as pale as her wrapper.

"Do you know him? He is the old man in the Abbey stables."

With a shudder, Marian rose. "I have known him since I was a child. He is insane, always babbling about some disaster or another."

"He has seen Corey. If you would ask him—"

"I shall not." Again she shivered. "I have avoided him for many years, and I will not seek him out now."

"Why not?"

"He . . ." She shuddered, then said, "Fenton has foretold many disasters at the Abbey. Some have come to pass. Others not. Mayhap others listened better than Corey or I did."

"You?" Ellen stood.

"Fenton told me to stay away from the cliff's paths, that I would take a tumble one day." She touched her left wrist. "And I did. While I waited for my broken arm to heal, I vowed never to speak to that frightening man again."

"Marian, be sensible. That was nothing more than the warning any adult would give to a spirited child. Surely Lord Wulfric or your parents told you the same thing."

"But when Fenton says such things, they happen."

"Marian—"

"And now he has seen this ghost, too." Wringing her hands, she whispered, "So you saw Corey as a phantom the night of his death?"

"Yes."

"And often since?"

"Yes."

"Oh, dear."

Ellen struggled with her frustration. This was nothing like the Marian she knew. That Marian would never act helpless. "Now you know the truth, but I need your help."

"What do you need?"

"You believe me?" she asked, startled by Marian's quick answer.

"Yes." The word left her lips reluctantly.

"Why?"

Marian's smile was strained. "You act as if you wish me to denounce you."

"I fear I would if our situations were reversed."

"Not if you knew old Fenton as I do." She continued to rub her hands together as she crossed the room to pour herself a generous serving of the Madeira waiting on a table by the bow window. "He has been seeing things since before I was born. No matter what anyone says to discredit him, we all know he speaks the truth. Too many things have come about just as he warned."

"Including the accident with the fireworks."

Marian drained the glass in one gulp. "Did he speak of that, too?"

"Only moments before the explosion."

"Oh, dear me. If Corey had listened to him . . ." She refilled her glass, then sat heavily on the closest chair. "This is all too much. A ghost? I find this so hard to believe."

"As I did." Ellen sighed. "I have had time to accustom myself to these peculiar circumstances, but I still find it impossible to accept them."

"So what advice do you need? I know of no way to deal with a ghost."

"But you know about love." She sank to sit on the foot of the chaise.

"Love?" Marian closed her eyes and shook her head. "No, Ellen, tell me it is not so. Tell me you haven't fallen in love with a ghost."

Ellen sighed. "You know how many times I have fallen in love."

"Many."

"And you know how many times I have fallen out of love."

"Just as many."

Leaning forward, she whispered, "But this is different, Marian. I have every reason to fall out of love with Corey, but my heart is filled with longing to be with him all the time, even though I know it is impossible."

Marian took a sip from her glass and swallowed roughly. She looked about the room, her gaze avoiding Ellen's. More than once, she started to speak, then closed her mouth.

"Marian?"

"How does he feel about you? You say you love him, but how can he return that affection? He is a ghost! Surely his emotions are as dead as he is."

Unable to sit still, Ellen set herself on her feet. "I believe he might love me, too, but he made a vow the night of his death which stands between us as much as the fact he is a ghost."

"A vow?"

"He vowed to stay here as a ghost until I found a man to love and buckled myself to him."

Marian rose, drained her glass, and crossed the room. "There is but one solution, Ellen. You know it as well as I do."

"To marry?" She shook her head. "How can I marry when I have given my heart away?"

"Corey cannot claim it."

"But I love him, Marian."

"Then give him the rest he deserves."

Ellen gasped, "You mean marry someone else while I love him?"

"That is the only way he will leave."

"But I do not want him to leave." She pressed her fingers to her lips, but the unthinking words already had escaped.

"You do love him deeply, don't you?" Marian put her arm around Ellen's shoulders. "My dear, if you do love him, you must release him from his connection with life."

"By marrying another man?"

"Yes."

Ellen sank back onto the chair and hid her face in her hands as tears rolled along her cheeks. For so long, she had sought true love. Now she had to push it aside as she settled for something less precious while she lived the rest of her life wishing for what could never have been.

Fourteen

Hearing hoofbeats, Ellen looked up from where she was gathering flowers in the garden of Herrold Hall. Her smile wavered when she recognized the elegantly attired man on the back of the gray.

Kenneth Pratt!

Quickly she ducked her head, hoping the brim of her light blue tulle bonnet would conceal her face. She learned how futile her hopes were when Mr. Pratt drew in his horse and shouted her name.

She stood and draped her basket over her arm. "Good day," she answered.

He swung down from the horse. His brightly polished boots and stylish coat added to his looks that would draw any lass's eye. "Are you gathering flowers to wear tonight?"

"Marian wished—"

"For us to lead the first dance, I am sure." He swaggered toward her and grasped her hand, setting it on his arm. "Fortunately, my plans concur with hers. You and I shall stand up together for that first quadrille. Of course, we shall dance often."

"I am glad you have my evening planned out for me."

As before, sarcasm had no effect on him. "You must, of course, allow me to dance with others. As the host, it is meet that I offer my company to as many of the ladies as possible."

"Of course."

"I hope you will not speak too warmly of me while I am with others. It would create talk."

Ellen stared at the ground, so he would not see her smile. The man was an incredible boor who thought the Polite World revolved around him. Even though he demurred, she knew he would be delighted to have everyone talking about him. In fact, she suspected he would do anything to remain as the center of the *ton*'s attention.

She risked a look around the garden. Where was Corey? She had guessed he would be here by now. It was so unlike him to resist the chance to poke fun at Mr. Pratt. Then, with a shiver, she recalled Corey's unease at the fair. Here, where the sunshine was so bright, he might grow weaker. She could not let him endanger himself—although she wondered anew what could hurt a ghost—simply because she found Kenneth Pratt's company so intolerable.

At the fair, she had rid herself of him by plying him with compliments and suggesting he was irresistible to the blond girl who clearly had been overmastered by him. That had worked once. She could only hope it would today as well.

"I promise you," Ellen said, gazing up at him and fluttering her eyelashes, "I will do nothing to cause talk about you, Mr. Pratt."

"Kenneth," he replied magnanimously. "Do not worry yourself about such matters. I shall handle them for us."

"How kind of you!" She wondered how much air would puff out of this overblown addle cove if a pin pricked him. Enough to float a balloon, she suspected. Slipping her hand out from beneath his, she smiled. "I look forward to this evening. The gathering should be unlike any I have ever attended."

"I shall be there."

"That will make it unique."

"And so very special." He grabbed her hand and pressed his lips to it. "I bid you *adieu.*"

"Au revoir," she answered, wishing she did not have to see him again.

He gave her a baffled look, and she guessed he did not have any idea what she had said. The man was a clod-pate, so much so that she had pity for him.

Leaving him to stare after her, Ellen hurried up the steps and into the Hall. Marian was coming down the stairs as she entered the foyer.

"Oh, flowers!" Marian cried. "What a wondrous idea. We shall select the very best for your hair tonight." Her eyes twinkled. "Did I see Kenneth riding toward the house?"

"He wished to reassure himself that we were attending the gathering tonight."

"That *you* are attending."

Untying the ribbons beneath her chin, Ellen handed her bonnet to a footman. "Why is he so persistent in paying court on me? I have neither title nor wealth."

Marian linked her arm through Ellen's as they climbed the stairs. "My dear, I thought you knew. He needs to be married to obtain the money in the trust his late father arranged for him. The late Mr. Pratt was a frugal man and invested wisely. His son will never be able to spend all that money in a single lifetime."

"Once he marries, it is turned over to him?"

"Exactly."

"No wonder he is so anxious for a bride."

"Yes," Marian said with a sigh as they continued up the next flight of stairs, "for all the young, eligible women around here have rejected him."

"That speaks well for them, although I am baffled why you think I would be interested in him."

"Ellen!" Marian faced her in the upper corridor. "Don't you see? This is the exact solution you have been seeking. You can marry Kenneth and get what you wish."

"What I wish? To be that boor's wife?" She opened the door to her room. "You are mistaken."

Marian gently took Ellen's hands in her own. "My dear, you need to marry if you wish to free Corey from being shackled to this mortal earth. Kenneth is desperate for a wife to get his father's trust. An arrangement, which includes marriage, could be worked out to the satisfaction of both of you."

"But being his wife would mean . . ." She shuddered at the idea of him touching her.

"He surely would wish his own home so that he might live the life he enjoys here."

Marian's careful tone told Ellen much. Even though Ellen doubted Kenneth Pratt would ever be faithful to one woman, she had not paused to think of what being married to such a man would be like. Yes, a marriage of convenience could be arranged, and she would never have to do more than allow him to give her a buss on the cheek in public. He could have his prime articles.

And everyone would talk about him all the time.

It would be the perfect understanding for him . . . but not for her. She did not want to spend the rest of her life yearning for the touch of a man she loved and never knowing it. She knew that loss too intimately now.

"Think on it," Marian whispered. "I know it is not what you wish, but it would free Corey."

"Corey . . ." She drew in a deep breath and nodded. "I will think on it."

"Good." Marian stepped back. "You must realize it shall be for the best."

"Yes, I realize that."

"Then you will accept Mr. Pratt's proposal?"

Ellen laughed suddenly. "Marian, he has said nothing of a proposal."

"He will." Her voice grew darker. "He will. I promise you that."

Ellen peeked into the glass and touched the flowers in her upswept hair. White roses were the consummate complement for her gold silk gown. Adjusting the deep neckline that dropped in a vee across her breasts, she looked down at the row of roses sewn to the hem of her gown. Her white kid slippers matched her white stockings and gloves.

She was dressed perfectly for the dance at Pratt's country house this evening. Everything was in place to snag a *fiancé,* save for her heart which, with every beat, reminded her of her hypocrisy.

"Very nice."

Her heart thudded against her breast. Ellen smiled at Corey, who dropped to sit on the bed. "Thank you."

"So you will be Pratt's guest tonight?"

She sighed. "He is anxious to welcome me to his mother's house."

"Is that what he is anxious for? That is not what I would have guessed."

"I had hoped," she replied, not acknowledging his comment, "in the wake of what happened at the fair, he would be more interested in that young blond woman who caught his eye."

He laughed and stretched out across the bed. Leaning his chin on his folded arms, he said, "You should know Kenneth better than that by now. He wants all the ladies for his own. I have often thought it was a great misfortune he was not born a caliph with a harem to answer his every need. Then he could have you and his pretty blonde and an ebony-haired lass as well."

"Corey!"

"Are you shocked?"

"Only that you think I would consider living such a life."

"But you are, aren't you?" His expression became sober. "You are walking into that house tonight like a lamb being led to slaughter."

"Do not be so melodramatic! I am going to a dance with Marian and her husband."

"Not Lorenzo?"

"No."

He sat up. "Odd, for I thought he would be accompanying you. Has Marian persuaded him to step aside so you might gain yourself a husband with plump pockets?"

"You don't understand!"

"No, I don't."

Ellen wondered if the emptiness within her was the result of her heart shattering. She had dared to believe that, of everyone around her, Corey would understand the truth she could not speak. She knew she should say something to him. Something that would reveal what he needed to know of her ache to be within his embrace as he held her to his heart.

"Ellen?" Marian's voice was distorted as it came down the hall.

"I must go," she whispered, not wanting to pull her gaze from his.

"Be careful, Edie." Standing, he closed the distance between them. "Tonight could change your life forever."

"As your life was changed the night of the fireworks?"

"Mayhap more than that." He held up the French shawl she had left over the chair. Draping it cautiously over her shoulders, so she was touched by nothing but a breath of chill, he said, "Be more careful than you have ever been."

"Do you know—?"

His smile was ironic. "Even ghosts are not privy to the future, Edie." He went to his favorite chair by the hearth and sat. "I shall wait here as patiently as I can to hear how your evening passed."

"Ellen! We shall be too late for the first dance!" Marian's impatience filled her voice.

Looking back at Corey, Ellen said, "I shall be fine."

"I pray so," he answered in such a solemn tone a shiver sliced through her. "If you need me . . ."

"Ellen!"

She nodded and rushed out of the room before she could tell him how much she truly needed him as a part of her life forever.

Ellen whirled to the country dance. Her head was light, for she searched the room as she was spun about by her partners. The grand ballroom of the Pratts' house was alight with candles and lamps, as if the family feared what the darkness might bring. Light glittered on the wood floor and off the gilt on the walls.

Once again, Corey was proving to be as good as his word. She had thought he might appear at the Pratts' house to keep an eye on the assembly, but she had seen no sign of him.

The dance came to an end, and she smiled at her partner. He opened his mouth to speak, but was interrupted by Kenneth's arrival.

"The next dance is mine," he announced loudly enough so no one could miss his words. "A very special dance with a very special lady."

Ellen closed her eyes as she heard the first strains of a waltz. A waltz! Now she would have to endure Kenneth's prattling until the music came to an end. When he held out his hands, she gingerly put hers in his. He tried to draw her closer, but she kept a respectable distance between them.

"Relax," he said beneath the music as he tried to pull her closer. "You should be melting into my arms now."

"Should I?" The man was unbelievable.

"That would show people how much you adore me, so that our marriage will be touted everywhere in the shire."

"Our marriage?" She smiled so coldly he loosened his grip on her. "Mr. Pratt—"

"Kenneth, my dear."

"Mr. Pratt, a woman likes to be asked if she wishes to wed before the rest of her life is planned out for her."

He shrugged. "I saw no reason to ask when I assumed you would say yes. After all, I have been told that you have been waiting for a husband for three years. Now you have the chance to have me as your husband."

"Am I supposed to say you were worth waiting for?"

"There is no need, when we both know the truth."

"Which is?" She knew she should put an end to this idiocy, but she was curious how far his vanity would take this conversation.

"That you are a lucky woman."

Ellen fought back her laugh. Did he think she was so want-witted that she would swallow his tale whole? He needed a wife, but save for helping Corey, she did not need a husband. Certainly she did not need Kenneth Pratt. Not even for Corey could she marry this dolt.

"You have no idea how lucky," she answered. "I am fortunate enough to have savvy."

Puzzlement creased his brow, but she did not bother to enlighten him that the word simply meant common sense. She suspected it would be a worthless effort. The man was as dense as the plaster friezes overhead.

Ellen did not even linger to offer an excuse when the dance ended. She simply thanked him and walked away. When he called after her, she did not turn. Her apprehension that he might follow eased when she heard someone speak to him. She looked back to see him waylaid by a dark-haired gentleman.

With a smile, she took her chance to escape. She rushed through the doors of the ballroom and along the corridor toward the back of the house. She paused only long enough to collect her shawl. Slipping into the first open door she found, she crossed the dusky room and threw open the French doors. A small balcony welcomed her into the solitude of the night. Faint music drifted from the ballroom, but she had found a haven.

She drew off her kid gloves as she walked to the edge of the balcony and leaned on the low, stone wall. Her problem was not solved, but there must be another choice. To spend the rest of her life leg-shackled to Kenneth Pratt was a future she did not want to contemplate. Instead she wished to dream of a life with Corey and to forget it was impossible.

"Alone, Edie?"

She whirled, smiling. Corey! Jings, but she was glad to see him. She wanted . . . She faltered as he perched on the thick stone railing of the balcony. Once she had feared he could read her mind. Thank goodness he could not tonight, for he would know how much she had come to love him.

"Not any longer," she answered, trying to keep her tone light. "I thought you were going to wait at the Hall for me."

"Unless you called me."

"I did not . . ." When he raised his brows, she smiled. "Mayhap I did without realizing it."

He smiled. "I did not expect to find you hiding from the rest of the gathering."

"I wanted to have some time to think."

"About your upcoming betrothal, or can I hope you finally have come to your senses and put an end to Marian's matchmaking by giving Pratt his *congé?*"

"Graciousness only goes so far."

"He would try a saint."

"And I am no saint."

He moved closer to her, his hand resting on the wall so near to hers that she could sense the icy caress sliding across her skin. "You would make a lovely angel, Edie."

"Something you should know better than I."

"I have to own I have not had a chance to meet an angel yet." His smile vanished as he whispered, "Save for you."

When Edie looked away, obviously overmastered by his compliment, Corey clenched his hand on the railing. Deuce take it! With the moonlight glowing on her hair and glittering off the jewels she wore at her throat and wrist, she was surrounded by a warm light. Yet even the warmth of her gentle heart could not melt the cold of the grave that encased him. So close and so impossibly far apart, they stood on either side of a fathomless abyss they could not bridge.

He plucked a blossom off the tree stretching its branches over the balcony. The flower stiffened at his touch, as dead as he was. Holding it out, he said nothing while Edie's slender fingers rose to take it.

"Thank you," she whispered so softly the night breeze nearly drowned out the sound. She raised her eyes to him. "Corey, will you tell me the truth?"

"About what?"

"About what is wrong with you."

Blast it, but she possessed an insight that traversed the chasm between them. He started to tell her of the strange malaise that had begun the day of the fair, then closed his mouth. He was unsure if he could explain what he felt: the weight grinding into him and the thinning of his very soul until it seemed as if he would be compressed into nothingness. He had no word to describe the sensation or his failure to discover a way to halt it.

If she became distressed on his behalf, she would turn her attention from her search for a spouse. Then he would linger here, forced to watch as other men held her as he could not while they delighted in the gentle brush of her fingers which he had savored so briefly.

He smiled and drew his boot up on the railing. When he swayed, she reached out to him. He laughed and motioned her away. "Have no fear, Edie. Even if I fell, what is the worst that could happen?"

"I don't know." Ellen locked her fingers together in front of her before she foolishly threw her arms around him. "Do you?"

"No, but I doubt if it would be anything more horrible than having to pick myself out of the bushes."

"You are not answering me again. You seem . . ." She searched for the right word. "Subdued. If you were . . ."

"Alive?"

"Yes, alive," she said with a short laugh. "If you were alive, I would suspect you were becoming ill."

"Then 'tis fortunate I have already toppled off my heels, isn't it?"

"Corey, why are you evading answering me?"

"Because tonight should not be a night for being down-pinned. It should be a glorious night for you."

"With Mr. Pratt's company?" She rolled her eyes.

"You don't call him Kenneth as he wished?"

"No, and if I have an ounce of luck left, he will not call on me any longer." Ellen turned and smiled as a new melody wafted through the night.

"What is it?"

"That song. I love to dance to it."

He swept out his hand. "Then dance, Edie."

"A waltz is not meant for dancing alone."

"No, on that I would agree completely with you." He held out his hands.

She stared at him. "Corey, we can't. If—"

"Give me your shawl."

"Why?"

He smiled gently. "The music will not last forever."

She drew off the triangle of lace and silk and dropped it into his hands. Twirling it into a silken rope, he swept it around her waist. Gently, he herded her closer.

"Hold here," he whispered as he gazed down at her.

She put her hand on the silk, only inches from his as if she was settling her fingers on his palm to dance. Her other hand gathered up her skirt as he spun her to the tempo of the music. The silk against her back was chilled, but heat glowed in his gaze as they moved as one. She stared up at him, letting him steer her about the narrow space of the balcony and then into the shadowed room.

The music dimmed, but it mattered little. She heard it play as sweetly as if the orchestra were in the room. All of the magic metamorphosed into this moment when the impossible became real.

With a laugh, he released one end of the silk, and she twirled beneath his arm. She caught the shawl and matched his steps as he led her back out onto the balcony again. As the last note from the violins faded, they slowed.

The shawl fell from his fingers back onto her hand. When he bowed deeply to her, she could not mistake the longing in his gaze. The wind pulled at the blossoms in her hair as he drew a single curl toward him. He brushed his lips against it.

"Sweet Edie," he whispered, "you make me believe anything is possible, even falling in love."

"Do not say that."

"Why not?" He smiled, but the mockery was missing from it. "Let me enjoy the advantage of caring little what others think of me." His voice lowered to a murmur as powerful as the wind off the sea. "Save for you, Edie, I care nothing of what anyone thinks. I . . ." He winced and turned away, sitting on the balcony wall again.

"Corey?"

" 'Tis nothing."

Ellen knew that was a lie. She gave him another appraisal. Even here, where shadows reigned, the light surrounding him was growing dimmer. She could ignore it no longer. Just as she could no longer ignore Marian's advice.

She must let Corey fulfill his pledge. She must find a *fiancé*. Not Kenneth Pratt, but someone else. Someone who would not appall her, someone who needed her, too.

Even as the answer burst through her mind, she fought back a sob. Her heart ached to belong to one man. As she met Corey's gaze, she wished she could run her fingers along his strong jaw. Would it be rough with whiskers or smoothly shaven? His lips would hold sweet, dangerous secrets that she would learn when her mouth met his. Everything she wanted could be found in his arms, but it would never be.

Gathering up her gloves, Ellen forced a smile. "A short night would be best for all of us, I believe."

"That shall convince Kenneth of his failure to win your affections."

"Painlessly, I pray," she said, continuing the façade that nothing was wrong. This part of the game they had fallen into hurt her more than anything else. Like him, she cared only what one person thought. She wanted to be honest with him as she told him of the love aching in her heart.

He chuckled. "Don't fret about Pratt, Edie. He shall find a woman—eventually—who hungers for a share of his blunt enough to tolerate buckling herself to him. Are you returning directly to Herrold Hall?"

She hated the bangers falling from her lips. "Yes, Corey, I

am going home. Will you be giving me a look-in this evening before I go to sleep?"

"Have I ever missed any chance to hear how your suitors have lathered you with court-promises?" He jumped down from the stone railing. "I shall wait for you in your rooms."

"Good." As she turned to the door, he whispered her name. "Yes?"

He took a step toward her. She gazed up at him. Even though his ebony hair was lost against the night sky and the eye patch sliced shadows into his face, she could see his longing. The same longing that was consuming her in its merciless maw. He drew a blossom from her hair. She did not shiver as the coolness stroked her.

With the flower that was taut with the cold, he brushed her cheek in a sinuous caress. She closed her eyes to savor each sensation as the flower slipped along her chin and down her neck. Her breath caught as the petals grazed the deep *décolletage* of her gown, sending ripples of pleasure across her breasts.

He murmured her name again, and she opened her eyes. Holding the flower to his lips, he offered it, with a bow, to her. A sob of frustration wrenched her from the splendor as she took the rose.

"Later, Edie," he whispered. "I shall be waiting."

Before she could answer, before she could give voice to her desire to be in his arms, he had vanished, leaving her alone to face the only choice she could make to protect the man she loved from an eternity of grief.

The foyer was dark when Ellen was shown into Wolfe Abbey. She thanked the footman who took her shawl and asked, "Is Lord Wulfric at home?"

"I shall check, Miss Dunbar." He padded away silently, leaving her in the shadows.

She glanced around, trying to imagine this grand house when it was filled with Corey's family instead of as gloomy as a mausoleum. The echo of childish laughter must have rung down the stairs while Corey and his sister played with their cousin on the wide risers. Had Corey's father's voice rumbled after them? And his mother . . . He never mentioned her, so Ellen guessed Lady Wulfric had died while he was young. Scanning the shadows, she wondered if Lady Wulfric still walked the stone hallways.

"Miss Dunbar?"

Ellen turned, expecting to see the footman. "Armstead!" she gasped.

Corey's valet walked across the stone floor to her. He smiled. "You look well, Miss Dunbar."

"As you do." She hesitated, then, knowing Corey would want to know, she said, "I did not expect to see you back at the Abbey so soon."

"I found there was something missing in my life when I was far from here." He appeared embarrassed as he added, "Something called me back here. Something reminded me that my home is here."

"Even without Corey?"

He nodded. "It will not be the same, but my life is here."

A throat cleared, and Ellen looked to her left to see the footman waiting impatiently. She gave Armstead a smile, then climbed the stairs after the footman. He led her to Lorenzo's book room.

Lorenzo was seated at his desk. He leaped to his feet and motioned for her to join him in the cluttered room.

"Forgive me," he said, drawing his open red waistcoat closed. For the first time, she saw him without a cravat and coat. "I had no idea you might be calling this evening, Ellen. I thought you were going to the assembly at Pratt's."

"I should have sent word, but . . ."

"Something cool to drink?" he asked when the silence thickened between them.

"Yes."

"Lemonade?"

"Yes." She wanted to add something more, but she was as tongue-tangled as the first few times they had spoken.

While he went to give the orders to his servants, Ellen slid her shawl from her shoulders and sat on the window bench. She stared out the window. Night sounds slipped through the glass, and she could see bats flitting about, chasing insects. The distant hoot of an owl warned of the end of a field mouse's life.

Tears filled her eyes. A chapter of her own life would soon be closing if all went as Marian suggested. How could doing what was right feel so wrong?

Mayhap because she was unsure if this was right. No, she was certain this was right. Furthermore, it was the sole alternative remaining if she wished to garner even a smidgen of happiness for the rest of her days.

Lorenzo was pulling on a navy velvet coat as he returned. "More appropriate, don't you think?" he asked with a smile.

"You did not need to change when I have intruded without so much as an invitation."

He pointed at the window seat. "May I?"

She nodded, not trusting her voice. Mayhap he would hear her disquiet and ask her to explain. How could she tell him that she was willing to marry him solely because she wished to give his cousin a chance to escape from her life, although not from her heart? How could she hurt Lorenzo, too? He was a friend, and she enjoyed speaking to him of his poetry, but she could never love him as she loved his cousin. This was such a complicated bumble-bath.

"Ellen, I would hope you feel welcome enough at Wolfe Abbey to run tame through it anytime."

"You have always been a good host."

He clasped her hands in his, and she blinked back tears. *This* simple warmth was what she longed to share with Corey. His hands would be much firmer than Lorenzo's long fingers. Easily his hands would swallow hers, surrounding her in his flesh.

Lorenzo said, drawing her eyes back to the ones in his thin

face, "Tell me why you are here tonight when you should be enjoying the music at Pratt's."

"I went there."

"But you left so early."

She smiled. "You are such a good host, Lorenzo, but not all your neighbors are as solicitous of their guests' feelings as you are."

He chuckled. "Was Kenneth that tiresome this evening?"

"He was persistent."

"That you knew before you went there."

"What I did not know was that arrogant block assumed I would be ecstatic at the chance to be his wife."

"So you told him . . ."

"I would not marry him." She drew her hands away when they trembled in his. It was going to be more difficult to speak these goose's gazettes than she had feared. Lorenzo deserved better. Mayhap she should simply tell him the truth and let him decide if he wished to help Corey.

A shiver cut across her shoulders as she recalled Fenton's words. The truth could consign her to an asylum. There would be no escape for her or for Corey until her death. Mayhap not even then.

"You were right to tell him that," Lorenzo said. "He should not have presumed that you would marry him."

"I hope you don't think *me* overly presumptuous to call here unbidden tonight."

Again he took her hands. He folded them together between his and raised them toward his lips. She stiffened as she wondered what his kiss would be like. Instead of pressing them to his lips, he looked over them and said, "I cannot help but believe fate drew us together, Ellen."

"You may be right."

"I know I am not the wisest of men nor the most handsome, but my affection for you is genuine." He knelt beside her. "I ask you to consider sharing my name and my life."

Tears filled her eyes. In her heart, she could hear the echo of a deeper voice. *Corey* should have been speaking those words to her in breathless expectation. *Corey* should have been touching her with eager anticipation. *Corey* should have been gazing at her with unfettered desire. *Corey* should . . .

She swallowed the ball of tears searing her throat. This was all wrong, but what else could she do? Corey needed to be freed from his purgatory. If she loved him, there was only one answer she could give Lorenzo.

"Yes," she whispered, "I will marry you."

Fifteen

The night wind played off the sea, tossing the waves high and scouring the land with salt. It seized the carriage door and pulled it out of Ellen's hands as she stepped down on the driveway before Herrold Hall.

"Be ye all right, miss?"

She flinched at the voice, then smiled. For a moment, the coachee had sounded like Fenton. She was glad she had not encountered the strange man at Wolfe Abbey, but a confrontation waited her within the Hall that she was not ready to face.

How could she tell Corey that he had succeeded in doing as he vowed? If not for him, she would not be marrying his cousin. Guilt stabbed at her. Lorenzo sincerely loved her. He deserved better than a woman who was marrying him simply because the man she loved was dead. As he had given her a chaste kiss on the cheek when she left Wolfe Abbey, she had to acknowledge the cost of granting Corey his freedom from the limbo where he was now.

Ellen hurried into the house, for a soft rain was beginning to fall. As she shrugged off her shawl and was walking toward the stairs, she heard her name called in a furious voice. She took a deep breath, then turned to see Marian striding toward her.

"Where have you been?" demanded Marian. "We have been half-mad with anxiety for you."

"I left a message at the Pratts' that I was leaving."

"But where have you been?"

Ellen hesitated, glancing around the oak walls of the foyer. "I cannot tell you now."

"Why?"

"Corey should hear first."

Marian pressed her hands over her mouth but squeaked, "You have become betrothed!"

"Marian, please. Corey should know first. He—"

Grabbing Ellen's hands, Marian laughed. "How wondrous! Best of all, you shall be only a short drive from me when you wed Kenneth."

"Not Mr. Pratt."

"Not—?" She gulped. "Then who, Ellen?"

"I should tell—"

"Who?"

She closed her eyes and sighed. To own the truth, she did not want to speak the words that would knell the death of her dreams of giving her heart to Corey. Looking at Marian, she said, "Let us talk in your rooms where we can have privacy."

"Not from—"

Ellen gasped, "Marian, don't even say it!"

Marian stared at her a long moment, then nodded. In silence, they went up the stairs. Ellen waited for her friend to say something, but Marian was oddly reticent until they entered her private chambers.

"Who?" asked Marian as soon as she had closed the door.

"Lorenzo Wolfe asked me to be his wife, and I said yes."

"You agreed to marry *him?*"

Ellen frowned. "What is wrong with Lorenzo? He is a nice man. He is—"

"Boring and only the custodian of Wolfe Abbey. He has that grand title, but little else." Marian covered her face with her hands and cried, "How could you agree to marry *him?*"

Down the hall, Corey looked up from the book he was reading as he heard Marian's screech. He smiled and shook his head. Had another hapless mouse entered her bedchamber or mayhap one of Reggie's pups? He could imagine nothing else that would set her to squealing at this hour.

He was about to return to his book, as he waited with what scanty patience he possessed for Edie to return, when he heard her soft voice answering Marian. Putting the book on the table by his chair, he rose. He frowned as he heard the sharp sound of Marian's answer, then Edie trying to soothe her.

Curiosity taunted him. He was about to go to Marian's room to determine what was happening when he heard a door slam. Angry footfalls came toward Edie's room, then stamped past.

The door opened slowly, and he said nothing as Edie entered. She dropped her shawl on the chair closest to the door. When her abigail Sullivan came to help her get ready for bed, Corey hesitated. He wanted to know what had caused Marian's cross words, but he had told Edie he would respect her privacy.

Which proved he was the greatest widgeon of them all.

As he wandered through the gardens later—he was not sure how much later, because time had become unimportant to him—Corey heard her call to him. He willed himself to go to her rooms. In amazement, he realized he remained in the gardens. He tried again, but again he stayed where he was.

Something was wrong . . . very, very wrong. As he saw the lights go out in her room, he sat on a hummock under a tree. He raised his hand to prop his chin on his fist. Astonishment filled him anew. The light that had surrounded him was only a flicker. Could it be like a candle he was burning out? That he had but a short time left before he went on to whatever?

Something *was* wrong, so terribly wrong he could not guess what it might be.

The word of a possible match between Lord Wulfric and Miss Ellen Dunbar raced through the shire as if on a winged mount. Although neither Lorenzo nor Ellen had caught sight of any of his servants listening at latches, someone must have overheard the conversation in the book room. By the time the sun had reached its apex the next day, callers were appearing at the door of Herrold Hall, eager to satisfy their curiosity about the rumors of a most unexpected match.

Corey sat on the sill of the largest window in Marian's parlor and watched as Marian welcomed each guest wearing a triumphant, but slightly baffled smile. He shook his head in amazement. This match must have been the cause of her distress last night, but now she acted as if she should take full credit for arranging it. Marian Herrold would never change.

He could understand everyone's amazement. A match between Edie and Lorenzo? It seemed too ludicrous even to consider. She was a vibrant, beguiling woman, and his cousin was . . . dull. Corey could think of no other, more flattering description. As soon as he had a chance to speak with her, he intended to discover if she had devised this as a ploy to keep Kenneth Pratt away. He could conceive of no other reason why she would wish to pretend to agree to buckle herself to his cousin.

If only he had been able to speak with her last night, then he might be able to enjoy this much more. He had to give Edie credit. This was an inspired idea, and it would tweak Pratt's nose in the grandest style to think he had lost Edie to timorous Lorenzo.

"Yes, I knew it from the moment I first saw them together," Marian said to a dowager who had been driven more than ten miles to bring her felicitations. "I believe it is a match made in heaven."

"Close, but not quite," Corey mumbled.

A low murmur swept through the room, and he looked toward the door. He could not keep from smiling as he feasted on the sight of Edie. In her simple white muslin gown with its short sleeves ruffled to complement the ruching at the modest neckline, she could have been an angel.

She seemed overmastered by the reception of Marian's score of guests. When he saw her glancing about the room, he knew she was searching for him. He was not tempted to materialize enough so she could see him. The questions he needed to ask her were not for now. She could not answer him when she was surrounded by the callers.

It would be better if he took himself off to another place in the house and waited for a chance to speak with her alone. Then he would learn the truth he dreaded hearing.

Ellen flinched when her eyes caught a flash near the huge window at the far side of the room. Her hope that Corey would appear came to naught. His absence unsettled her more than she had guessed, but some sense that had no name told her he was still nearby. For now, that must be enough.

"Thank you, Mrs. Henning," she said to the dowager who was smiling so broadly Ellen would have thought the betrothal was all Mrs. Henning's idea. "I am pleased as well."

"Where is she?"

Ellen spun about at the shout. Her eyes widened when Mr. Pratt stormed across the room like a hurricane, leaving a jumble of shocked women in his wake. He was dressed in riding clothes, which, as always, were cut to flatter his muscular build. His face was creased with a fierce frown.

"Good afternoon, Mr. Pratt," she said, not letting him daunt her.

"What are these loud ones I have been hearing?" he demanded.

Marian inched forward to say, "Kenneth, my dear boy, you should sit and talk more quietly with us. There is no need to shout."

"There isn't?" he bellowed. He jabbed a finger in Ellen's direction. "*My fiancée* is rumored to be marrying another man."

"I am not your *fiancée*," Ellen replied with quiet dignity.

"I asked you to marry me last night."

"You assumed, as you should recall, that I would marry you." She clasped her hands in front of her to keep them still. If she flung them about and released the frustration within her, it would solve nothing. "You never asked me, Mr. Pratt."

"A technicality. You know you would prefer me to Wolfe."

"Then 'tis odd, isn't it, that I agreed to wed him?"

Mr. Pratt sputtered something, too angry to make sense. He slammed his fist into a table, making several of the figurines dance wildly. "Then you leave me no recourse. I shall take up this matter with Wolfe directly."

"How?" she asked, caution warning her not to infuriate him more.

"If he wants you, let him prove it."

"He did," Marian averred stoutly, "by asking Ellen to be his bride."

Mr. Pratt's lip curled. "I was thinking more about a battle of honor."

All the women gasped as if in a chorus. Mrs. Henning put her hand to her forehead and collapsed back against the cushions of the settee.

Ellen glared at Mr. Pratt before rushing to call for *sal volatile* to bring the old woman back to her senses. She ignored Mr. Pratt's continuing petulance as she watched the footman put the horrible salts beneath Mrs. Henning's nose. The old woman awoke with a gurgling gasp.

"Marian," Ellen asked softly, "will you watch over Mrs. Henning while I acquaint Mr. Pratt with the absurdity of his suggestion?"

"Absurd?" Mr. Pratt stared at her in disbelief.

"Go home," she said as she faced him. "I have suffered too many of your childish tantrums. I pity the poor woman who finds herself in such need for money that she will wed you." He started to retort, but she went on, "Go home."

"I shall—"

"Nonsense!" Marian was recovering her composure. "Kenneth, you shall do nothing, save listen to Ellen. Your mother should be calling within the hour. Think how she will feel when she discovers you have been acting like this." A sly edge entered her voice. "You would not want her to suggest to your late father's barristers that you are too childish to handle your father's money, would you?"

"Lady Herrold, I—"

Again she cut him off, wagging her finger at him as if he were no more than a child. "Heed this for your own good. That money will come to you when you are wed . . . and when your mother deems you adult enough to handle it."

Ellen stared at Marian. That small fact Marian had failed to mention previously. She wondered what else Marian had not told her. Not that it mattered now, for she had no intentions of speaking with this lout again.

Mr. Pratt opened his mouth to speak, then closed it. He strode out of the room. A dozen voices spoke at once, but Ellen listened to none of them as she slipped out another door.

She hurried down the dark corridor and out into the summer sunshine. Mayhap its warmth would burn away the ice around her heart. As it scorched her hair, she realized she had neither a parasol nor a bonnet. She did not care if she was seared as red as a soldier's coat. She needed time to gather her thoughts.

Her breath strained against her side when she stopped by a low, undulating stone wall. She sat on the stile steps and stared at her dusty slippers.

"So dreary?"

Ellen looked up in shock and saw Lord Herrold's smile. "Where are the dogs?" she blurted before she could halt herself. She never had seen him without one or more in tow.

He pointed across the field on the far side of the lane. Straining her ears and eyes, she could pick out the distant forms of the pack and heard their yelps.

"I hired a huntsman to complete their training," he said as he sat beside her. Pulling a pipe from beneath his black coat that was sprigged with twigs and leaves, he lit it. Smoke encircled his head before drifting away on the breeze. He balanced his pipe in his hand as he gazed across the rolling hills. "I know many think I am an air-dreamer, concentrating only on developing a fine line of hunting dogs."

"I—"

His chuckle interrupted her. "You do not need to demur, Ellen. We both know the truth of what is said when folks believe

I'm not listening. Mayhap they are right. I spent the first two decades of my life doing exactly as everyone expected, and I was miserable. For the past ten years, I have done as I wished, and I am happy."

"Then you are a lucky man."

"No, I am a fool."

She stared at him in shock. "To do as you wish?"

"No, to have let the canons of society rule me for so long." He smiled. "Fortunately, Marian clings to them fervently, so we are not ostracized. As lief, I am considered an eccentric block. Not a bad arrangement in retrospect." Without a pause, he said, "I hear you have agreed to wed Lorenzo Wolfe."

"He has asked me, and I told him yes."

"Is it what you really want?"

"It is a good match."

His smile returned. "That sounds like Marian and all those purveyors of the canons of propriety. I would like to hear what you think. Is it what *you* really want?"

Ellen faltered on her answer. Lord Herrold was correct. She had dismissed him as a moonling without a thought, save of his dogs, in his head. She would not make that mistake again.

"Lorenzo is a kind man, and we share a love of poetry," she said.

"Marriages have succeeded with less in common." He puffed on his pipe. "I simply wished to be certain you were not looking for a way to heal your heart after the loss of Corey in that horrible accident."

"Lorenzo and Corey are two very different people."

"True." He set himself on his feet. "You seem to have thought this matter through, so I offer you my felicitations. Marian is so pleased you will be remaining here in the shire." He looked across the field. "Blast! Excuse me, Ellen," he threw over his shoulder as he ran across the lane and leaped over the wall as if he were half his age.

Ellen rose to see Lord Herrold working with his huntsman to keep the dogs from jumping over another wall to enter a field where sheep were bleating in terror. With a smile, she strolled back to Herrold Hall. This would be her life for the rest of her days. A quiet, country existence where the crises would be small ones as would the times of happiness. If she could not have a life with Corey, it was an acceptable substitution.

That was a lie.

She blinked back tears as she went into the Hall. When had she started being false with herself? Nothing would replace the life she wished she could have with Corey. Everything else would be a colorless dream.

Ellen went up the stairs and opened the door to her room. Lord Herrold's insight had unsettled her assumptions more than she wanted to own. Everything she had deemed to be true was being undermined.

When a low radiance appeared in the chair by the hearth, she breathed, "Corey! Where have you been?"

He did not rise. "I thought it would be wiser if we were alone when we spoke about your betrothal."

"Then why didn't you come to me while I was outside?"

Slowly he stood. "There is a heaviness about me of late, Edie. I cannot wander about as I once did."

"But you are a ghost! There should be nothing heavy about you."

"No?" He put his hand to his chest. "The heaviness is here. Do you know its cause?"

"I fear 'tis I." Her fingers trembled as she fought to keep tears from filling her eyes.

"How could you do anything to harm me? I do own you have looked at me with such fury I knew, had I been alive, you would have wished me dead." He chuckled, but it was a weak shadow of his usually booming laugh. He grew somber again as he said, "Sit down so we might talk."

Ellen glanced at the pillows piled at the top of her bed. How she longed to lean back on them while they laughed together as they talked about anything that might come into their heads!

That camaraderie was gone, banished at the very moment she told Lorenzo she would be his wife.

She sat on the window bench where he often had appeared. When he lowered himself slowly to the chair she had come to think of as his, she bit her lip to keep in her moan of despair. He moved as slowly and stiffly as an old man. Something was drawing the last bits of life from him so swiftly he was fading before her eyes.

"Corey, I wished to tell you last night," she whispered.

"About you and my cousin."

"Yes, but you were not here."

He smiled sadly. "Edie, do not look like the wandering wife who has been caught cuckholding her husband. You have done nothing wrong by considering Lorenzo's suit."

"It is more than considering."

Pain flashed across his face. "I feared that was so when Marian welcomed all of her cronies for a celebration." He took a deep breath, then released it. "So you will wed Lorenzo?"

"He cares deeply for me, Corey."

"And do you love him?"

"I care deeply for him." She hoped he would forgive her for embellishing the truth. She did care for Lorenzo, but love? No, she could not give Lorenzo her love, for her heart did not have a yearning to belong to him.

"I see."

She waited for him to say more, to say anything, although she doubted if there was anything he could say.

When he smiled, it was with irony. "Who would have guessed that my attempt to play the matchmaker would end with you becoming Lorenzo's wife? Mayhap it was, as Fenton would say, your fate to become Lady Wulfric. As Lorenzo presently holds that title, you must be his wife."

"I thought this was what you wished."

"Aye, so did I." He stood. His smile was as forced as the lightness of his voice. "See? I have done as I pledged. I found you a husband, a task that others have despaired of accomplishing. What would Marian say if she ever learned that I have bested her yet again?"

"She was not pleased by the match."

"No?" He lifted a single brow. "I had not thought Marian and I would ever agree on such a thing. Lorenzo is the wrong man for you, Edie."

"Who would you have me marry?" She jumped to her feet. "Would you have me marry Mr. Adams or Mr. Pratt?"

"There are others."

"How many," she asked, her voice rising, "must I parade myself before like a horse being sold at a fair? Lorenzo is a kind man. He does not want to marry me so he can get his father's money."

"Edie—"

"No! You will listen to *me* for once!"

"Lower your voice. Everyone in Herrold Hall is listening to you at the moment."

Fury gripped her. How dare he admonish her when he could shout as loudly as he wished and the only one to hear him was her! "Why can't you understand? I have good reasons to marry him."

"What reasons?"

"I should not need to tell you such things. Why can't you understand? Marian understood when I told her I needed to find a husband before you—Oh, no!" Ellen put her hand over her lips.

His brows dropped into a fearsome scowl. "You told her about me? I thought we agreed no one but you and Fenton would know of this."

"I had to talk to someone I trusted about . . ."

"About what?" he asked.

She put out her hands, then pulled them back. How could she tell him the truth which would break his heart if he still had one within him? Yes, he had a heart, for on his face, she could see the pain of it rending. "Corey, I needed to speak to a friend. Fenton may see you as readily as he does the other ghosts in Wolfe Abbey, but he would not heed the disquiet within me."

"At the thought of marrying my cousin?"

"No."

"Then what unsettles you so much that you needed to reveal the truth?"

"Corey, I . . ."

The door came open, and Marian bustled about the room. What once had been amusing and frustrating was only painful. Waiting for Corey to make some teasing comment, Ellen wrung her hands in her muslin gown. He said nothing.

"I thought you might be here," Marian said, "after that barbaric Kenneth Pratt upset you so."

"What did *he* do?" asked Corey.

"It was nothing," Ellen replied to both of them. "He will not be calling here again."

"And he will not dare to ask Lorenzo to name his friends." Marian smiled. "His mother will be much distressed when she hears of her darling son risking himself so needlessly."

"A duel?" Corey shook his head. "I should have stayed and seen the entertainment, Edie."

Marian gave Ellen a kiss on the cheek. "What a lovely bride you shall be! Think of all the excitement ahead of us. When shall you wed?"

"As soon as the banns can be read."

"So soon?" asked Marian and Corey at the same time.

He strode toward Ellen. She wanted to back away, but then she would have to explain to Marian that Corey was in the room.

"We thought it best," Ellen answered. "A quiet wedding in the chapel at Wolfe Abbey with the least fuss."

"Best to air it out first," Corey said. "The incense from the funeral—from *my* funeral—may still be lingering."

She looked at him with pleading. This was not how it should be. She had thought he would be pleased that she had helped him accomplish his vow. When his frown etched lines in his brow, she longed to smooth them away.

Marian's voice yanked her back to that conversation. "I think that is an excellent idea, even though I must own I had hoped for something grander for you."

"It is what I want."

"Do you?" Corey's question lashed her.

"Yes," Ellen repeated, "it is what I want."

Marian's smile wavered. "I believe you, my dear. Why are you acting so uneasy?"

"It is a new life I am facing," she said tritely. "I am over-mastered by what lies before me."

"You have done the best you could under the circumstances." Marian hugged her. "Think of it! We shall be neighbors and will be able to exchange visits for years to come."

"Just what you deserve, Edie," Corey said grimly. "If you wish to marry my boring cousin and live a boring life here with calls on Marian being the grandest excitement of your day, then I wish you all the best."

Ellen shook her head. Why couldn't he comprehend the truth which she must not speak? She had made this decision for him.

"Ellen?"

She paid no attention to Marian as she walked to where Corey was standing by the bed. Looking up at him, she whispered, "Please be happy for me."

"Happy for you?" he asked over Marian's gasp. Going to the chair by the hearth, he sat and glowered at her. "How can I be happy for you when I know you shall be miserable?"

"Ellen?" Marian's voice trembled.

"You may think," Corey continued, "that Lorenzo can touch your heart with his silly poetry, but he is much like Reggie Herrold. He thinks only of what brings him pleasure. What of your pleasures, Edie? Will his touch fire your soul and awaken the promise of passion I see in your eyes?"

"Ellen?"

She ignored the panic in Marian's whisper. "Would you have me choose another?"

Marian seized Ellen's arm and cried, "Who are you talking

to?" All color fled from her face. "Corey! Are you speaking with Corey? Is he here? Now?" She spun about as if she expected to see him materialize at any moment.

Ellen nodded, not trusting her voice.

"Where?"

She pointed toward the chair where Corey was scowling at her. "Right there."

"I see nothing." Marian brought her quizzing glass to her eye and squinted through it. "Nothing at all." Raising her voice, she called, "Corey Wolfe, you were the most stubborn man I ever knew. Are you going to continue to be so stubborn all through eternity and berate Ellen when she is doing only as you wished?"

Ellen clasped her hands over her ears. "Marian, there is no need to shout. He can hear you."

"Is he talking to me?" Again she peered through the glass. "Is he still there?"

Corey slowly set himself on his feet. "Edie, a bit of honesty is sometimes a fearsome thing, especially when you are speaking to someone who has no more imagination than Marian Herrold. However, I would appreciate you being honest with me."

Again Ellen nodded. To Marian, she said, "If you will excuse us, we need to talk."

"Us?" She shivered. "Are you certain you wish to be alone?"

"I am not alone."

"I mean with . . ."

Corey chuckled tersely. "Has she forgotten my name so soon?"

Ellen reassured Marian, but said nothing until her friend had left, looking back on every step. She half-expected the door to reopen. When it remained closed, she looked at Corey. "Say what you wish."

"I wish you to be honest. You do not love Lorenzo, do you?"

"I have already told you I care deeply for him."

He stared at her as if he expected her to continue. When she did not, he sighed. "Then I guess there is nothing else to say, is there?"

"One thing." Taking a deep breath, she whispered, "I love you."

Instead of answering, he walked toward the window.

"Corey . . ."

He turned, and she saw her pain mirrored in his eyes. Rushing to him, she flung her arms around . . . nothing. A sob burst from her as she saw he had stepped aside.

"Do not be jobbernowl," he warned in a whisper. "To touch me will injure you."

"Corey, there must be some way—"

"There is no way!" His voice grew as cold as his touch. "Do not torment both of us with what can never be, Edie!"

"How can you know that? *You* should not be, but here you are before my eyes."

A cool breath brushed her, and she lifted her eyes to his. How she longed to feel his fingertip beneath her chin as he tilted her mouth to his!

Slowly she raised her hands to the luminescence enveloping him. Her fingers curved along his face, although she might as well have been cupping a shadow.

"Kiss me good-bye," she whispered.

"You know I cannot."

"Please."

"I would do anything to please you, but this I cannot do." His hand moved over her shoulder. When she shivered at the cold, he murmured, "My dearest Edie, I cannot."

Corey stepped away from her and the sorrow sending tears along her cheeks. He clenched his teeth as he fought the fury building within him. This was not the way it should have been. For so long, he had been seeking adventure, fighting his battles, winning each one—even when it appeared he had lost. This battle, this most important battle, he could not win.

"Forgive me, Edie," he said as he turned away. "I never should have embarked on this silly attempt to find you a husband."

"But you did, and you succeeded."

He smiled. Even now, she thought foremost of bolstering

him. Looking over his shoulder, he wondered if anyone had ever been so precious to him. Her lips parted with a sweet invitation to taste them. Damn! He wanted her more than he had ever wanted anything. More than he had longed for glory in the war, more than he had wished to be rid of the burdens of overseeing Wolfe Abbey.

"Marry Lorenzo," he whispered, "and be happy, my love."

Her breath caught on a sob, and he was sure someone was twisting a knife in his gut.

"Corey . . ." She wiped tears from her cheeks. "Thank you."

"For helping persuade you to leg-shackle yourself to my cousin? You owe me no thanks. As lief you should curse me."

"Thank you for letting me fall in love."

"With Lorenzo?"

"With you." Taking a step toward him, she raised her hand as if to run it against his cheek. She did not touch the icy fire surrounding him. She did not need to, for through it, she could sense his longing which matched her own. "You have given me a most precious gift. The chance to discover that I could truly fall in love . . . forever."

"As I will love you forever, my love." He took a step toward the hearth, then paused. "You will be happy with him, won't you?"

"Lorenzo is a fine man. He will be a good husband."

"If you ever need anything, call for me. Mayhap I can return."

"Mayhap?" She clenched her hands by her side.

"I said I would stay until you found a husband. You have. Now . . ." He did not finish as his form thinned until she could see the curtains behind him.

"Corey!"

He did not answer, and she did not move as his light faded into nothingness.

Sixteen

All the wedding preparations came together more quickly than Ellen had expected. Nothing elaborate was planned, for the Abbey remained in mourning. In the three weeks while the banns were read, Ellen sent an invitation to her parents to join her. Their eager reply arrived two days before they did on the eve of the ceremony.

After a convivial meal in the grand dining room of Herrold Hall, Ellen walked with Lorenzo out onto the balcony overlooking the rose garden. That they were alone was due mostly to her mother's determination that Marian would not intrude on every aspect of the brief courtship.

Stars pocked the night sky. Among the trees, night birds cavorted. The enthusiastic croaking of frogs broke the silence.

Ellen leaned on the balcony and stared up at the sky. Just a short time ago—although the past three weeks had seemed a lifetime—she had stood on another balcony and freed her heart to go with a man who could not claim it. Never would she forget that dance or the heat in Corey's gaze as she had swayed so close to him.

Fingers brushed her shoulders, and she flinched. When Lorenzo apologized for startling her, she touched the shawl he had draped over her bare shoulders.

"Thank you," she said as he came to stand beside her.

"Your mother does not wish you to take a chill in this autumn air. She fears you will sicken before our wedding on the morrow."

"My mother or Marian?"

He smiled. "I have never seen Marian so happy. Not even when she wed Reggie."

"Marian derives so much delight from helping others."

"That is one way of putting it. I would, as lief, say she enjoys poking her nose into others' lives."

Ellen laughed genuinely, for what she suspected was the first time in three weeks. "True."

"And are you happy, Ellen?"

Her smile faded as she turned to look at him. "That is an odd question tonight."

"I feared you might be having second thoughts." He cleared his throat and tugged at his waistcoat. "I know you were much taken with Corey, and I am not the man he was. He was a brave hero who saved many lives."

"Including mine."

"Yes, and I know how it hurt you when he died." He gazed up at the stars. "I am just a pale shadow of him."

"You are not his shadow. You are simply not like him."

"That also is true."

She put her hand on his arm. "Lorenzo, he did not have your gift for creating poetry."

"But he did create a glow in your eyes, Ellen, which remains even now as you speak of him."

In amazement, she stared at him. She could not deny what he was saying, for she suspected it was the truth. Part of her listened constantly, even in the depths of sleep, for Corey's voice. Each splash of sunlight on the rug caught her eyes, for she hoped Corey was about to reappear.

"If you do not wish to marry me . . ." she whispered.

"Marrying you will make me happy, but will it make you happy?"

She was glad she could be honest when she said, "As happy as I can imagine being at this moment, Lorenzo."

He drew her into his arms and kissed her lightly, then released her as he spoke of the newest rhymes he was devising. Only later, when she was alone in her rooms, did Ellen release the tears that had burned behind her eyes all evening.

She looked around the room and whispered, "Corey, my darling Corey, you promised me I would never be alone. Here I am, and I am so very alone. Where are you, Corey, when I need you so desperately?"

"You are a lovely bride," Ellen's mother said as she stepped back to regard her daughter with a critical eye. Dora was a tall, thin woman with hair only a shade less red than her daughter's. "Lord Wulfric is a lucky man."

"No," Ellen replied, drawing on her gloves. "I am the lucky one that he loves me."

Her mother bent to brush a wisp of lint from Ellen's gown. "And do you love him?"

"I would not marry him if I did not have great affection for him." She frowned, hating to be less than completely honest with her mother. "Why are you asking such a question *now?*"

With a hug, her mother chuckled. "After watching you think so many of the gentlemen might claim your heart and then changing your mind, I wish to be sure that you are certain about Lorenzo. I know you have a Scotswoman's gumption, but sometimes common sense flies out the window when love touches you."

"There will never be another love for me like the one I hold in my heart now." That was the truth, although her mother must not guess that Ellen spoke of Corey.

"That gladdens *my* heart!"

A trill drifted through the open window. Ellen raced to it and looked out. Her heart plummeted when she realized it was only a bird. How silly to believe that she had heard Corey's whistle! He was gone. She must accustom herself to that.

As she walked out of her room with her mother, Ellen ran

her fingers along the molding. She would never come back here to where she had fallen in love so futilely.

On the way to Wolfe Abbey, Marian gave no one a chance to notice that Ellen was as silent as the flowers she cradled in her lap. Marian discussed every aspect of the wedding ceremony and the party to follow as if no one else were familiar with the plans she had prattled about for three weeks.

As soon as they arrived at the grand house, Marian herded Ellen's mother and Lord Herrold toward the chapel. Ellen's step-father offered his arm to her.

"Papa," she said to the short, heavyset man who seemed un-comfortable in his fine clothes, "go with the others. I want a moment to myself."

"Are you sure?"

She hugged him and kissed his pudgy cheek. "Yes. To own the truth, there are some flowers I want to pick to include in my bouquet. I want to gather some from the Abbey's garden."

"Go then, child."

Ellen gathered her silk gown around her as she went along the path to the garden where the fireworks had been set off. A flower from there would be the only part of Corey she could bring with her to this wedding.

As she plucked a golden chrysanthemum from beneath the trees that were donning their autumnal glory, something moved within them. She tensed as a bent man popped out of the bushes, then smiled grimly. She should have guessed Fenton would not miss the wedding.

"Good day, Fenton. I am glad you are joining us for the celebration."

"Shouldn't be no celebration." Fenton frowned. "This be all wrong, Miss Dunbar! All wrong! Ye be marryin' the wrong one."

"I cannot marry Corey."

"Not now."

"Then do you wish me to spend the rest of my life here with only a ghost for company?"

"Is that not what ye wish?"

She almost said yes. Each moment she had had with Corey was doubly precious now that she knew she would never delight in his loving jests again. Brushing her hand against her cheek to wipe away any telltale tearstain, she whispered, "I could not be so selfish to keep him here when he needs to go on to enjoy the wonders of eternity."

"Ye've consigned him to the bleakest pit."

"No!"

"Should be here, he should. This be all wrong. Once gone, he can't return." He gripped her arms. "Ye must stop this."

"But how—?"

"Stop the weddin'. Ye can't marry the wrong one."

"Ellen?" Her mother's voice drifted over the bushes.

" 'Tis too late," she whispered. "He is gone already."

Fenton's shoulders sagged even farther. "Ye must be wrong, Miss Dunbar. He must still be about."

She shook her head. "He vanished before the first banns were read. I have not seen him since . . ." Icy chills sliced through her. "Since I told him I had agreed to marry Lord Wulfric."

"Alack! Alack!" he moaned. " 'Tis too late. He be gone. Oh, this be all wrong."

"I know it is not what we want, but it is what he wanted."

Fenton frowned. "What he wanted? To be gone?"

"He told you of the vow he made, the vow he would see come to fruition before he could go on to . . . wherever."

She was shocked when Fenton's thin hand grasped her arm. His eyes glittered, and she saw the madman Lorenzo had warned Corey of. "The vow! Tell me! What be the vow he made, Miss Dunbar?"

"To find me a husband."

"Is that exactly what he said? Ye must be sure!"

Ellen glanced over her shoulder. No one else was in sight. She fought back the scream for help that battered her lips. Corey had trusted Fenton, so the old man must not be as deranged as he appeared. Or had Corey been mistaken by loyalty to an old retainer?

"Miss Dunbar!" cried the old man. "What be his exact words? Ye must tell me."

"I told you—"

"His exact words. Ye must recall them." His voice cracked, and she heard the pain that echoed within her. "Please, Miss Dunbar. It may be his only hope."

"There is no hope left."

"Are ye so sure? Tell me what he vowed."

She closed her eyes. Again, out of the blur of the confusion surrounding the accident, she could see Corey appearing in the bedchamber in the Abbey as she stared at him in disbelief. His voice had been so rich then, not thinned to oblivion as the last time they spoke. So sure he had been then of being able to do what he pledged.

Opening her eyes, she met Fenton's desperate gaze. Quietly, she said, "He vowed to do as Marian wished and to find me the perfect husband before the chrysanthemums bloomed at the end of the summer."

"That be his vow? Those words? 'To do as the lady wished and find ye the perfect husband 'fore the mums bloom'? Ye're sure?"

"I think so."

He clapped his hands and cackled a laugh. "I hope ye be right, Miss Dunbar. I hope ye be."

Ellen stared after him as he scurried away. The poor sawney had lost all connection with sanity. And so had she, if she had dared to believe he might help her and Corey. It was too late. Why must she keep believing otherwise?

She drew the fine lace of her veil over her face to hide the tears that would remain in her eyes no longer. Nobody must see her weep as she went to marry Lorenzo.

The call of her name added speed to her feet. She must not embarrass Lorenzo by being late to their wedding. As she came out onto the drive, she was surprised to see a wagon slowing near the front steps of the Abbey. Her mother paused by the steps, and Ellen went to meet her.

"Miss?" called a man.

She looked at the wagon. It was filled with men she did not know. "Yes?"

The man who had spoken, a man whose hair was nearly as red as her own, jumped down to the drive. He tipped his dusty cap to her and wiped his hands on his simple, wool breeches. "Is this Wolfe Abbey?"

"Yes. Who are you?"

"We served with Lord Wulfric in France." He shuffled his feet in the dirt. "We heard how he was killed, and we came to pay our respects." He did not meet her eyes as he said, "We didn't mean to intrude when there's a wedding, miss."

"You served with Corey?" The flower stems crushed beneath her fingers as she searched each face among the half-dozen men, although she had no idea what she sought. These must be the men whose lives he had saved nearly at the sacrifice of his own.

"Yes, miss. He always looked after us when the major invented some foolhardy plan, and we . . ." He paused, looking at the ground. "Well, miss, we just want to pay our respects."

"If you will come with us," she said softly, "you can see where he is buried."

The man twisted his hat. "We don't want to interrupt your happy day, miss."

"You haven't. Just looking at you and knowing you are here today because of Corey Wolfe gladdens my heart in a way you may not be able to understand. As long as *you* live, a part of him remains alive."

The man looked at her as if she was daft, but her mother smiled gently. As they walked toward the chapel behind the Abbey, Ellen smiled honestly for the first time since before she had said farewell to Corey. Mayhap he could now rest in peace, along with her heart.

* * *

The chapel was as bare of decoration as it had been during the funeral. The pews were crowded with guests, and Ellen wondered, as she stood by Lorenzo, if they would have been wiser to be married in the village church. Even though the wedding of every Lord Wulfric for nearly three hundred years had been celebrated in this chapel, it was too small today. Many of the villagers had come to see their marquess take a bride.

Lorenzo did look every inch a marquess with his black velvet coat and vest of silver satin that he wore over unblemished white breeches. Gold glittered on his fingers, and she noted one ring bore the crest of the Wolfe family.

As Reverend Stapleton read the marriage rite, Ellen peered through her veil at the corners of the church. She tried to be inconspicuous, which was not easy when every eye in the chapel was on her and Lorenzo.

"Do you, Ellen Dunbar, take this man to . . . ?" She heard no more of the question as she searched the shadows within the choir box.

Nothing. Corey must be truly gone to whatever place his soul sought.

She should not be surprised. He had said he would stay only until she found a man to marry. Even if she put a halt to the ceremony now, it was, as she had told Fenton, too late. All traces of Corey Wolfe were gone. Only the stone in the graveyard beyond the chapel remained as a memory of the man he had been.

"Ellen?"

At Lorenzo's soft voice, she turned to see he was holding a lighted candle. She took it as he took another from the minister. Recalling what Reverend Stapleton had told her, she stretched to put her candle to the wick of the one on the altar. Something bumped her side. She looked down and almost laughed as she realized Lorenzo had a roll of paper in his pocket. He must have been working on a poem when the time came for the ceremony. Corey had been right. Lorenzo thought first of his own work.

"Watch out!"

Ellen stiffened. Who had said that? Corey? Was that Corey? What was——? Flame dripped from her candle into the silver goblet on the altar. The wine flared and exploded. Fire struck her arm. She fell back. Her dress caught beneath her heel, and she collapsed. A moan burst from her when her head hit something—or someone. Arms enveloped her and enfolded her to a firm body in the moment before everything vanished into darkness.

"I thought she blinked."

"Is she awake?"

"Give her some air."

The cacophony of anxious voices resonated through Ellen's head. She was tempted to let them babble on while she floated on this sea of nothingness.

She shifted. Pain seared up her arm. Her arm? She had struck her head when she collapsed. Had she hurt her arm again as well? Everything was a muddle of confusion in her mind. With a moan, she opened her eyes.

Over her head, the familiar boards of the tester bed she had used in Wolfe Abbey were shadowed with dusk. She must have been senseless for a long time if they had brought her here and drawn the drapes to hold out the sunshine. In a burst of painful memory, she recalled strong arms cradling her as she was lifted and placed against a broad chest. The shoulder beneath her cheek had been firm, yet as comfortable as her favorite pillow.

"How do you fare?"

Her eyes widened as she turned her aching head to stare up into Corey's face. *Corey!* He was not gone! Mayhap he had decided to stay and see her marry Lorenzo. Mayhap he had been as unable as she was to face the finality of their farewell. Fenton! She could not forget the smile on the old man's face. Was this his doing? Had he found a way to bring Corey back to them? She was torn between delight and despair, knowing the frustration Corey had suffered in the last few weeks. She let elation win as she stared up at him. No glow surrounded him, save for the light of the room's single candle reflecting off his dark hair.

She tried to speak, but joyous tears filled her throat, choking her.

"Try a sip of this," Marian murmured, bending toward her with a cup. "It might help."

The wine was sweet, and Ellen nearly gagged. She took a second drink, swallowing slowly as she wondered where her mother was. Every time Ellen had been ill as a child, her mother had hovered about, determined to do whatever was necessary to bring her back to health.

"Is that better?" Corey asked.

"Thank you," she whispered.

"How do you feel?" He stepped forward and leaned his hands on the bed. He smiled when she stretched her hand toward his.

"I am . . ." She stared at her hand as Corey's fingers closed around it.

She could feel his touch!

"You are alive!" she cried. She sat, ignoring the dizziness that threatened to undo her, and ran her hand along his chest. It was as firm as she had dared to dream and warm with life.

Corey smiled more broadly even as Marian gasped, "Ellen! Remember yourself!"

Ellen ignored her. "You are alive."

"Barely," grumbled Lorenzo. "Corey, now that you have re-assured yourself that Miss Dunbar is not about to hop off, will you rest?"

Miss Dunbar? Lorenzo had not called her that for—how long?

"I am barely scratched," Corey replied to his cousin.

"More than a bit scratched, I would say."

Lorenzo could hear Corey! What was happening?

She looked down at her grass and bloodstained dress. It was the one she had ruined the night of the fireworks. In disbelief, she stared at each of them. Corey's waistcoat was splattered with blood and a thick bandage crowned his head. And Lorenzo . . . He was wearing a simple evening coat, nothing like the elegant coat covering his silver satin waistcoat she had seen by the altar. Marian's gown was not the grand white silk she had been wearing in the chapel.

Everyone was dressed as they had been the first night she came to Wolfe Abbey. That night . . . or this one?

"Ellen," Marian chided in her most overbearing tone, "you should not be sitting up. My dear, you have given us quite a scare."

"What happened?"

"The fireworks—"

"I know that. They exploded on the ground. The doctor came over to check us. I hurt my arm." She tentatively touched her bandaged arm and winced. "But Corey, you were much more seriously injured. I heard him say so."

Even as Marian grumbled at her informality with the marquess, Ellen saw Corey smile. She had not seen that impertinent expression in more than a fortnight, and she feared her heart was going to burst with joy.

"You were deprived of your senses when I knocked you from your feet," he said as pillows were plumped behind her. Helping her lean back into them, he added, "Forgive me. I am more accustomed to the company of hardened soldiers than a dainty woman."

"He saved your life," Marian interjected.

"As she may have saved mine, by giving me an excuse to be focusing on a single guest. If my attention had been caught up in playing the good host for all of them, I might not have seen the misfired rocket in time," Corey replied, bringing her eyes back to him. "We both are lucky to be alive."

"Alive," Ellen whispered, still too astounded to be able to think clearly. If this was the night of the fireworks, then she must have imagined all the rest. She touched the center of her breast. It might have been a dream brought on by a blow to her skull, but within her heart, the love for Corey pulsed with every beat.

Marian settled the covers around Ellen and said, "You should rest, my dear. Lord Wulfric has been kind enough to welcome us to stay here tonight."

She remembered to look at Corey instead of Lorenzo. "Thank you, my lord."

"I liked the sound of my given name in your soft voice much better." He looked past her as Lorenzo opened the door to the hallway. "Rest easily."

"Wait!"

All of them stared at her, but she did not care. Fighting to control the tremor in her voice, she asked, "Corey, will you stay a moment?"

"You need to rest," Marian said sternly.

"Only a moment." She knew she sounded as petulant as a child, but she needed to ask Corey—what? What could she ask him that would not sound as if she was bereft of sanity?

His gaze swept over her, but he did not meet her eyes as he nodded. "A moment, Marian. It might ease her despair at finding the night ending like this."

"Then I shall stay."

Corey chuckled. "We do not need a watchdog, Marian. Even as unsettled as she is, I cannot believe Miss Dunbar would allow me to be untoward."

Marian refused to be put off completely. "I shall go to have some tea brewed for Ellen."

"The kitchen can manage that," Lorenzo said. "You should rest as well."

"Nonsense!" She linked her arm with his and went out of the room. Her voice drifted back, outlining all the shortcomings of the Abbey kitchen.

Corey closed the door slowly and walked back toward the bed. "Marian never changes."

"I know. You said—" Ellen bit her lip, unwilling to continue. If she told him that he had spoken those exact words to her before, he might demand that she tell him when. Then she would have to explain the unexplainable.

When she did not continue, he set a chair by the bed. He was careful its legs did not strike the floor, and she guessed his head ached as fiercely as hers. Sitting, he said, "I doubt either of us shall forget this celebration."

"From what Marian says, I owe you a debt for my life."

"To quote her as well: 'Nonsense!' "

Ellen smiled.

"Much better," he said. "You were so still for so long that we feared you might never awake."

Touching her scorched sleeve, she sighed. "You will have to forgive me if I say something bizarre. My brain was jostled during the explosion."

"I am sorry to hear that."

The familiar pressure of hot tears filled her eyes. This trite conversation was what two people who were embarking upon a friendship should share, but Corey was more than a friend to her. He had shared an intimacy with her that she had given no other man, for he had found a place in very center of her heart.

"Do you wish to rest, Edie?" he asked. "I can—"

"Edie?" she gasped, staring up at him. "You called me Edie, but—"

He folded her hands between his as he whispered, "I know your name is Ellen, but indulge me by listening to what I have to say."

"But—"

He put his finger to her lips. She nearly was overmastered by the heat of his touch. As she leaned toward him, wanting more than his finger against her mouth, he whispered, "I know you see me as a stranger, but nothing could be stranger than experiences I have had."

"When you were a ghost?" she asked cautiously.

His eyes widened. "You know?"

"I feel as if I know nothing right now. Memories of events that could not have happened resound through my head." She pressed her hand to her chest, then winced as she touched the stickiness of the blood splattering her bodice. "Mayhap this is nothing but a dream. I saw you die. I know I did."

"And I saw you there beside me." His brow furrowed as he took her hand again. Stroking her fingers, he whispered, "I can recall that as clearly as I can recall seeing you lying on the ground in the garden. How could I have carried you here if I was lying in the other room dying?"

The door crashed open. Together they turned. A slight silhouette was outlined by the lamps in the hallway.

"My lord! 'Tis ye, my lord!" came a shout.

"Fenton, you old dog!" Corey exclaimed with a laugh. "I should have guessed you would waste no time in sticking that large nose of yours into this."

The stableman scowled as he strode into the room like a welcome visitor. "Ye be alive, master."

"Aye, I be alive," he answered, copying the old man's accent.

"Somethin' amiss here." Fenton pulled off his felt hat and scratched his balding head. "Thought ye . . . Never mind."

Corey's voice gentled as he squeezed Ellen's hand. "Everything is all right now, Fenton."

"Aye, 'tis." Fenton grinned. "Things have been in a muddle, but all is right as rain now."

As the old man was turning away, Corey said, "Tell us what you know."

"There be those who think old Fenton's short a sheet or two, my lord. If I were sayin' now what I know, even ye might think that."

Corey glanced at Ellen and smiled. "I think we would believe just about anything you tell us right now. You know *things*. Can you explain what happened to us?"

Again he scratched his head, then pointed at Ellen. "She knows."

"I know?" She laughed, but wished she had not when the sound resonated through her head. "What do I know?"

"My lord's exact words."

She looked from Fenton's smile to Corey's face, which was furrowed with bafflement. Of what did the old man speak? *His lord's exact words?* Her hand clutched the covers as she sat straighter and gasped, "Oh, my!"

Fenton nodded.

Corey frowned. "Would one of you enlighten me?"

Taking his hand in hers, Ellen whispered, "Do you remember what you vowed when you came here the first night?"

"To find you a husband."

She glanced at Fenton. "You said you would stay here as a ghost and find me the perfect husband before the blooming chrysanthemums signaled the end of summer."

"The flowers came, and summer ended," crowed Fenton. "Failed, he did. Knew that soon as she told me the vow. Ye couldn't leave, my lord, with yer vow uncompleted. After all, ye couldn't find her the perfect husband when . . ." He winked boldly at Corey. "Said enough I have."

Corey shook his head in amazement. "Do I understand you correctly, Fenton? Are you saying I was not able to find her the perfect husband because, while I remained a ghost, he no longer existed?"

"Couldn't go forward. Couldn't stay where ye were, fer ye were gone 'fore yer time. A Wolfe's vow lasts forever, as ye've said yerself, my lord. So ye came back here, fer 'tis the only way to keep your pledge to find her the *perfect* husband."

"A single word made all the difference?"

Fenton became serious. "A single word often can be makin' the difference in how the future will unfold. If ye say 'Nay,' yer path is in one way. An 'aye' will lead ye elsewhere."

"So you did die, Corey?" Ellen whispered. "It really happened?"

The old man scowled again. "He stands before ye, doesn't he?" He looked at Corey and tapped his temple. "She may be a bit touched, ye know."

"I know." Corey laughed when Ellen glared at him.

Fenton rushed out of the room, shutting the door and leaving them alone once more.

"That was an unkind thing to say," Ellen said.

"But so true." He laced his fingers through hers. "You have been only a bit touched if my memory proves even a hint reliable, for we could not do this when . . . when whatever happened."

"No," she whispered as she leaned back in the pillows, "but you did not sit so far from me then either."

"Marian will be outraged if I take such liberties."

"True."

He laughed. "You are a vixen, Edie."

She held out her other hand, and he took it gently as he sat on the edge of the mattress. When he slipped his arm around her, being cautious not to jostle her injured shoulder, she leaned against his chest. Every dream she had ever had, every longing she had feared would never be fulfilled, was given life as she listened to the steady thud of his heart.

"Out of all this bumble-bath, one thing is clear," she whispered.

"What?" he asked gently, his fingers curving along her face.

"I love you, Corey Wolfe. I loved you enough to marry another man to free you from that place that was neither life nor death."

"You were a fool."

"No, only so in love with you that no sacrifice is too great."

"None?" He tilted her face up toward his. "Even being married to me, Edie? I shall make you a difficult husband."

She stroked his broad chest, delighting in the motion of his breathing. "That I know, but I can think of no other husband I would as lief have."

He laughed. "Marian will be beside herself with delight and bafflement at this abrupt announcement."

"How shall we explain this to everyone?"

"Why not with the truth?"

"I am not sure if I know what it is any longer."

"The truth is I love you, Edie, and I want to spend all of this life"—he laughed softly—"and any others with you."

"Forever."

He brought her lips to his for the kiss she had waited so long to savor. "Forever."

WATCH FOR THESE ZEBRA REGENCIES